THE NATURAL HISTORY of

Uncas Metcalfe

THE NATURAL HISTORY *of*
Uncas Metcalfe

BETSEY OSBORNE

ST. MARTIN'S PRESS ⚞ NEW YORK

Library of Congress Cataloging-in-Publication Data

Osborne, Betsey, 1957–
    The natural history of Uncas Metcalfe : a novel / Betsey Osborne. — 1st ed.
        p.   cm.
    ISBN 0-312-34277-2
    EAN 978-0-312-34277-7
    1. Teacher-student relationships — Fiction. 2. Parent and adult child —
Fiction. 3. Fathers and daughters — Fiction. 4. New York (State) —
Fiction. 5. College teachers — Fiction. 6. Botany teachers — Fiction.
7. Middle-aged men — Fiction. 8. Botanists — Fiction. I. Title.

PS3615.S27N38   2006
813'.6 — dc22

                                                      2005016682

First Edition: May 2006

10   9   8   7   6   5   4   3   2   1

To my father
and
to the memory of my mother

ONE

Uncas Metcalfe's Raleigh had been stolen. There was a time, not so long ago, when he'd ridden his bicycle everywhere, in all but the most inclement weather. Now he rode locally, for errands, and, occasionally, a mile or so for pleasure. No doubt it would turn up. It had disappeared before, and unless the thief were equipped with a wrench to lower the seat, he—or she, his daughter Fauna would probably add, wanting the fairer sex to be equally considered even in matters of thievery—in all likelihood wouldn't be able to reach the pedals. Uncas was six and a half feet tall, tall even for a Metcalfe. He wasn't as put out by the absence of his bicycle as he might have been earlier in the fall; he had promised his wife he would put it away at the first snow, which the chill temperature indicated could be any moment. He could see it as a seasonal shift. Besides, the several-block walk from his house to his office often put him in a contemplative mood.

He turned onto Sparta's main street and looked across at the triangle of land occupied by the Laconia Avenue Shopping Center. Before urban renewal, there had been a Flying A gas station at the tip, with more practicality—Johnson's Office Supply and Wells's Dry Goods—anchoring the two corners. The new indoor mall seemed to specialize in whimsy. It was occupied by stores like Der Klockhaus (filled with cuckoo clocks) and Water Bed Warehouse; no one Uncas knew had either a cuckoo clock or a water bed. As absurd as those shops were, at least they were still downtown and independent. With its big chain stores, the box mall on the outskirts of town had siphoned off much of the commercial vitality. If that continued, Sparta proper would be a ghost town. The sidewalks were virtually empty. No one walked more than half a block anymore; they were all tethered to their cars. Even he and Margaret no longer made do with just one: he had his Jeep; she had her station wagon. He nodded to the pharmacist as he passed Fulmer's Drug, which had been there since his childhood, though the soda fountain had been discontinued. Soon, no doubt, the store would be shuttered completely, unable to compete with the lower prices and vaster array of choices on the outskirts of town. Quality of service and product seemed to be irrelevant. The physical upheaval and near abandonment of the heart of Sparta over the last forty years were in sharp contrast to the occasional hiccup in his own life, which was absorbed with little fuss by the resilient stasis he had achieved.

Farther up the street, outside the old jewelry store, Uncas saw a young woman; with torn camouflage pants and crew cut, she looked ready for the army. Bleached spikes radiated from her head like the filaments from an exotic flower. She was, apparently, engaged in conversation with someone he couldn't see, someone standing in the recess of the doorway. He wanted to hurry by—the girl looked upset, agitated—but instead he found himself slowing down. As he approached, she grew quiet. Without meaning to, he turned to see to whom she'd been talking.

"Hello, Mr. Metcalfe," the girl in the alcove said.

He hadn't anticipated being greeted by name, though in a town this size and given his family's prominence, he was used to it. He nodded; she had on a T-shirt covered only by a white apron with some kind of doughnut stitched on it. Collins's Jewelers was long gone. Was the new shop a bakery? Uncas looked around surreptitiously. The words painted along the bottom of the store window—HOT COFFEE WARM BAGELS COOL CUSTOMERS COLD CASH—provided a clue. He wondered why he hadn't noticed the place before, and was disconcerted to realize he had walked right past his own office building, the Menelaus, without the faintest inclination to turn in, and was now faced with a young woman whose name flickered at the edge of his memory. Uncas looked back at the spiky-haired girl, but she didn't look remotely familiar. She had an earring in her nose. Cool customers, indeed.

"How are you, Mr. Metcalfe? Here for some bagels?" The aproned girl stared at him; not in an unfriendly way—she was smiling—but more as though she'd exhausted conversation of the type reserved for people over the age of twenty-five. She turned to the door. "Come on in," she said. "It's cold out here." Something about the tilt of her head, and her composure, jogged his memory. She was the granddaughter and great-granddaughter of his father's business partners. She was Joe Stephenson's girl; he was surprised he hadn't seen the likeness immediately—above his desk hung an oil painting of old Mr. Stephenson, his son, and Uncas's father in the heyday of Laconia Farm Works. She had come to his father's Christmas parties. He tried to will her name into his memory. Anna, maybe. No, that didn't sound right. Miss Stephenson was going to have to do.

A bell jingled when she pushed open the door. As eager as he was to get to his office, he followed her into the shop, unwilling to reveal that he'd overshot his building. The Stephenson girl turned around and, ducking past Uncas, caught the door before it closed, setting the bell off again. "C'mon back in, Alex," she said. "I'll just be a minute."

Uncas found himself staring again, as the army girl stepped in the door.

"Oh," the Stephenson girl said. "Sorry. Mr. Metcalfe, this is Alex Miller. She's Betty Delafield's stepdaughter."

"Hello," Uncas said. He had forgotten that Betty had married.

"She'll be a sophomore at Mott next year. Like me."

The girl nodded, silent.

Mott College—that explained her outfit. It was an all-girls (women, he could hear his daughter correcting him) college in the next town over from Laconia, where Uncas was a botany professor at Wright University. The local youngsters weren't quite so outlandish. He offered his hand and she shook it. Her solid grip surprised and impressed him. He liked a little oomph in a handshake. Most young people looked puzzled when you offered your hand. She looked him in the eye, too, which was another surprise.

"Pleased to meet you," he said. The room was as humid as the university greenhouses; Uncas's glasses started to fog up. If he took them off, he wouldn't be able to see; removing them also wreaked havoc with his astigmatism. If he left them on, it would take longer for the glass to defog. Both options made for a fuzzy world, which he disliked. Sometimes at night, after he had taken his glasses off, he could still feel their weight on his nose. He would run his hand down his face to see if they were still there, when he knew perfectly well they were folded on the nightstand next to him. Now, he kept them on his nose and squinted, trying to see what was on offer.

"What would you like?" the Stephenson girl asked from behind the counter. "A dozen bagels?"

Uncas frowned. Better than doughnuts, he supposed. Slowly the shop came into focus.

"Why not, Miss Stephenson?" Uncas said.

"Hannah."

"I beg your pardon?"

"Hannah. It's Hannah Stephenson, Mr. Metcalfe. That's my name." She smiled briefly. "Mixed?"

"That would be fine," he said, wondering what on earth he'd do with a dozen bagels. Did Margaret like bagels? He wasn't sure *he* did.

"Would you like me to choose?" she asked, though she was looking over his shoulder as she spoke.

He studied the wire bins. They looked like extra-deep in-baskets, loaded with seeded tufts of bread.

"Why don't you?" Uncas said. He could feel himself get warm. The Stephenson girl was in her T-shirt behind the counter; she'd also donned a paper cap. He was bundled up for the chill outside. A dozen bagels. Margaret would think he was daft. His grandchildren were expected today. The bagels could be for them. He felt his shoulders ease. "Hannah, were you in my daughter Fauna's class?"

"She's older than me. I remember her though. Doesn't she have a kid?"

Than I, Uncas thought. *Older than I.* "She and Doug have three children. Or as I like to think of them, three grandchildren." And a fourth on the way, but he'd save that information.

"Wow. Three. My mother was saying that Doug was coming back. We live across the street. It's been weird having that house empty." Hannah wiped her forehead on the sleeve of her T-shirt.

"That's right. They're scheduled to arrive from Illinois today.

They'll spend a few days with us and then they'll be your responsibility."

Hannah looked puzzled but then smiled. "Oh, because they'll be across the street," she said. "I get it."

Uncas recalled the time he'd seen Delores Fletcher, his son-in-law's mother, in that house. She had had a few too many, as usual. "What's that?" he said, cocking his ear toward Mr. Stephenson's granddaughter.

"Baker's dozen, Mr. Metcalfe. You get one more. Do you want me to choose that too?"

"Make it a cinnamon raisin, please." He himself didn't care for fruit in bread or in chicken or ham or in any dish except dessert or oatmeal, but his grandchildren would like the raisins. That seemed to be the kind of thing they thrived on.

"That'll be six dollars even, Mr. Metcalfe."

Uncas tried to contain his surprise. These were big-city prices for glorified bread. Still he supposed it was too late to refuse to buy. This would teach him not to miss his building. He handed the girl a ten and a one; he would get a five-dollar bill in change; he preferred to limit the number of ones crowding his wallet.

"This is too much, Mr. Metcalfe. It's six dollars. You gave me — oh, I get it."

Uncas relaxed himself into patience. All the time in the world for her to figure out a simple math problem.

"Jeez, sorry, Mr. Metcalfe. No fives today."

Hannah counted out five singles into his hand. As he left the shop Uncas saw Alex sitting at a table in the corner. She looked glum, at odds with her bright spiky hair, which seemed cheery against the gray cold. It was mysterious what governed the temperaments of the young. At so far a remove from mortality, her distress seemed luxurious, an indulgence.

As Uncas retraced his steps to the Menelaus, he tried to remember himself at Hannah and her friend's age. His own dark moods had seemed to increase as he grew older. Otherwise, not much had changed. He still had suits that he had worn just after he'd graduated from Wright. True, he wasn't yet married then, but he had already decided to go into botany and to stay in Sparta. Like his father, grandfather, great-grandfather, and great-great-grandfather, Uncas had been born and raised in Sparta. And like his forebears he was staunchly proud to be a Spartan. But they had all been successful businessmen—first scythes, and then harvesters and balers; Uncas was the first Metcalfe professor. Not to go into the family business ("Four generations and you won't make it a fifth?" his father had said more than once), yet to remain in Sparta, were, he continued to feel, the decisions that had shaped his life. It would have been easy enough to move to Laconia, where the university was. Margaret might have liked it better—the town was more cosmopolitan. But by twenty-three, Uncas Metcalfe had decided to stay in Sparta, come what may. In a way, it hadn't even seemed like a decision. A move to Laconia might have been perceived as turning his back on his family, cowering even; it was enough to roil the seas with a change in profession. At Wright, he was the only member of his department who didn't live within walking distance of the campus, and he found he liked that distinction. In recent years, he made the trip to the university less often, choosing instead to work out of what had been his father's in-town office; he found he preferred the nearness of home and the pokiness of Sparta. In his experience, people, like plants, grew best in their native soil.

He climbed the stairs of the Menelaus and considered that it was one of the few downtown buildings that had escaped the wrecking ball. The bank that had provided ballast for the bottom floor was now a restaurant, but the upstairs offices had remained untouched. Maybe a little too untouched. The elevator was a temperamental old box. Two years ago, half an hour trapped with the third-floor dentist's receptionist had convinced him forever after to take the stairs.

He sat at his rolltop desk. Contemplating nativeness, he slid down into his chair and extended his long legs onto the writing slide, which he sometimes used as a footrest. Would his daughter and her family flourish upon their return? Had uprooting his wife from Boston put her at a disadvantage? His eyes were closed—he had drifted off—when the phone rang.

"Uncas, Floyd Brewster here. Glad to track you down. There's been a little accident. Nothing to worry about, but they took Margaret to the hospital. Elsie tells me a table at the book fair fell and clipped her calf and then she— Well, now, the doctors can tell you."

Uncas took a moment to focus. Margaret was hurt, that much was clear, but he couldn't tell how hurt. "She's in the emergency room?"

"I expect so. Now, Uncas, I can pick you up. You won't want to be riding your bicycle. I'm down here at the shop, but I can find someone to cover."

"No, no, Floyd. The Raleigh's gone missing again. I'll head right there on foot. The walk will do me good."

"Now, Uncas, it's started to snow, and it's probably a lot windier than it was when you sat down at your desk."

Uncas looked out of his window. The snow was swirling about, like some half-crazed nor'easter tumbleweed. But so far nothing was sticking. The hospital was less than half a mile away. He'd be fine walking. "This won't stick. I'll be fine walking. I appreciate your call."

"If you say so. Goodbye, now. Let us know if we can be of help."

Uncas stretched and was alarmed to find that his heart had quickened. His palms were sweating, though the room was drafty and cool. *She's as hardy as pachysandra,* he told himself; *she'll be walking around in days.*

As he was leaving the Menelaus Building, the wind caught the door and slammed it open. Snow blew in, and Uncas instinctively closed his eyes: this was going to be a hell of a walk. He forced the door closed, and bent his bare head resolutely against the wind; his new hat, the one Margaret had knitted him for his birthday, would have come in handy. More than that, he wished he had a companion, a dog to walk with him. It was about four-thirty and the light had begun to fade as Uncas made his way north along Seneca Street.

Hut, two three four, hut, two three four. There it was—left over from his stint in the army (six months in New Jersey just before the war came to a close). It had been a short time, but the twenty-mile marches and the precise execution involved in making one's bed or shining one's shoes had made their impression. More than forty years later, the voice of martial discipline prodded him along.

He slowed as he passed the firehouse, in front of which was a bronze statue of an earlier Uncas Metcalfe, who had died two days after Uncas himself was born. Caught in a web of traffic (the new east-west highways sandwiched the firehouse), the statue of his grandfather, known to his family as U. M. the Fifth, still conveyed enormous dignity. He had been a cabinet member during Teddy Roosevelt's presidency and had introduced conservation measures long before the environment had become the cause of the moment. He'd been a zealous advocate and the force behind many of the state's preserved areas, but he was also a thin-skinned man, who bore grudges, yet held himself above retaliation. He had been respected, but not loved. Uncas hurried along—try as he might to avoid their pull, he was often caught in these eddies of nostalgia.

A nurse directed him to Margaret's room, from which he heard a familiar laugh, not his wife's. It didn't surprise him that she would already have a visitor. Margaret was well liked in Sparta—had been ever since she arrived over thirty years ago. He answered his own earlier question: she was a rare, blossoming transplant. At Sparta Memorial, there were several nurses, doctors, and aides who had attended her nursery school. The parents of her charges had been the doctors once upon a time, but their children were grown and were now the doctors and lawyers and, sad to say, layabouts of Sparta. A visit to the hospital or to the grocery store or dentist's office often led to an encounter with a former graduate of Miss Margaret's and to the claim that the nursery school had been their favorite, most influential schooling. But this laugh was too familiar to be a casual acquaintance. It was doubly confusing because it had the cadence of his wife's. Uncas closed his eyes for a second: it sounded like Margaret when he had first known her. He opened his eyes and saw his grandson Nik poking his head into the hallway. Of course. It was Fauna's laugh he had heard.

"It's Pup-pup, Mommy. Pup-pup had his eyes closed."

Nik, the youngest of his daughter's children (until March, when number four was due), ran toward Uncas and grabbed him around the knees, and then ran off.

Uncas heard Fauna's voice. "Poppy, sweetie. His name is Poppy. You can say that now."

Uncas approached the room with trepidation. Suddenly it seemed thoughtless to have walked instead of taking Floyd up on his offer. He hadn't rushed to the hospital as quickly as he might have. Margaret wouldn't care, he was sure, but he felt a little uneasy around Fauna.

"Dad, glad you could make it. What did you do, crawl? You look like you got lost in a blizzard."

Uncas looked at his wife, whose leg was in traction. Tears, which he tried to blink away, came to his eyes. How helpless she looked.

"Oh, that's all right. There was no rush. Your father would have been sitting around with nothing to do. No sense in both of us being stuck in this dreary place."

This was lovely practical Margaret, Uncas thought. He gingerly kissed her and sat down in the nearby chair. Fauna lifted Nik off her lap and came around the bed to kiss Uncas hello; she looked aggrieved already. Margaret looked off. She was slurring her words as she described the accident. A table had buckled; the legs gave way and one of the ends had caught her calf and then somehow landed on her ankle and then an avalanche of textbooks—algebra of all the rotten things, she said, and Fauna laughed—had pinned her to the ground, facedown.

"And other than that, how did you enjoy the play, Mrs. Lincoln?"

Uncas was surprised there was no laugh from his wife. He looked closer and realized she had gone abruptly to sleep. They must have her on painkillers, he thought.

He turned to Fauna who was saying something in a low voice.

". . . bad, Dad, really bad. I got here and she looked terrified, like they were going to amputate her leg or something. I tried to reassure her, but kept getting funny looks from the doctors. God, they're all about eleven years old, and they have zero bedside manner. I couldn't get any information. They kept saying I had to wait until the chief surgeon got here. Even Charley Bisgrove wouldn't give me a straight answer. Five minutes later she's in traction, and they're telling her it's a precaution and pumping her with painkillers. Now they say she has nothing to worry about, and we didn't even know what she had to worry about to begin with."

Fauna was exhausting, Uncas thought. He longed for coolheaded Marcia, his eldest child. She'd be a little less sensitive, have a little less information, and be a little less aggressive with these poor doctors. Uncas believed in letting the doctors run their own show.

"How did you know your mother was here? When did you arrive?" Uncas asked.

Fauna laughed. "Well, aren't we filled with questions all of a sudden? Mom left a note saying she was down at the book sale, thinking the kids might get a kick out of it—"

"Where are the other children? And Doug?"

"—no way were Janey and Tommy getting back in the car, so Doug stayed with them while Nik and I drove down. We took your car. I couldn't bear getting back into our loaded station wagon. When I got there, they were putting Mom into the ambulance. Talk about scary. I called Doug when I got here and tried to find your office number, but I can never remember what it's listed under. It's some joke, isn't it?"

"It's listed under Tiger Lily."

"Right, that pamphlet."

He had produced a monograph on the flower years ago in Cambridge as part of a fellowship, and, also, the character in Peter Pan had been his father's favorite.

"I finally called the Menelaus Café," Fauna said. "But they said you'd already left the building. How'd you find out?"

"Floyd Brewster called. Mrs. Brewster was running the sale."

"Juicy, juicy, juicy, juicy," Nik said, bumping his head against Fauna's leg.

"That's not how you ask, sweetie."

After Nik said please, Fauna took out a carton of apple juice and tore the straw off the side and poked it in the hole provided. Minutes, it seemed, after Fauna and her family arrived these very cartons littered the refrigerator; half-drunk boxes, precariously balanced on the shelves of the refrigerator, tipped over as soon as you opened the door. Uncas didn't remember them from his own children's growing up; they had used tin mugs and had been taught not to waste food. The bagels. He had forgotten the bagels.

"This is funny, Poppy. Having breakfast for supper."

Uncas looked at Janey, who was smearing butter on her bagel. At Uncas's insistence they had stopped at his office and fetched his baker's dozen. Doug had scrambled several eggs in the large frying pan. Uncas could taste the butter they had sat in, and imagined it clogging his arteries. He wasn't complaining—he was impressed by Doug's efficiency and speed. It had been six o'clock by the time Margaret was settled in her room. They'd left her passed out, a result, the doctor had said, of exhaustion and the painkillers.

"What did the doctors say, Mr. M.?" Doug asked.

"Doug, we're about to be neighbors. Why don't you call me Uncas?"

He hadn't talked to Margaret about this, but it seemed silly for a grown man to call another grown man "Mr. M." It made Uncas feel foolish and always had. When the issue first came up, when Fauna and Doug were married five years ago, he was barely eighteen and Margaret had announced (what a summer!) that she was damned if she were going to let a child call her by her first name. Doug's mother, who had come to the wedding recently divorced, had made things a little awkward by insisting that everyone, including her own son, call her Delores.

"Okay, thanks, Mr. M. I'll call you Uncas." Doug paused. "I mean thanks, Uncas. Fauna and I are looking forward to living here again; I mean in Sparta, not with you and Mrs. M."

There was a long silence while they ate their bagels and eggs—no Margaret around to say, Please call me Margaret. Tommy tugged at his bagel with his teeth, trying to tear off a bite, and suddenly burst into tears.

"Tommy, sweetie, I think you're tired," Fauna said. She turned to Doug. "Would you mind, Mr. F.? I'll bring Nik up in a minute."

The two older children went upstairs without protest. Nik climbed into Fauna's lap. "Pup-pup, where's Granny?"

"It's Poppy," Fauna said.

"The boy can call me Pup-pup."

Uncas saw the surprised look on Fauna's face and realized he'd sounded sharper than he'd meant to. But really, what earthly difference did it make? Pup-pup was no more absurd than Poppy.

"I thought you preferred Poppy."

Uncas realized he shouldn't have said anything in front of the child. Fauna had always been quick to take offense, and now she had people—well, children—to fight for. Children were a different business once they had children of their own.

"Okay, Nikky, my love," Fauna said, "give your grandfather a kiss good night." Her gentle voice, her patience with her children—as if they were customers—held none of the irritability that Uncas thought characteristic of his younger daughter. "I'll come down and help you with the dishes once the kids are squared away," she said.

As Uncas cleared the table, he thought of Margaret. He wondered why she had been looking at textbooks of all things; why she had gone to the sale to begin with. They'd probably donated a hefty percentage of the books, and what they hadn't were probably library discards, and she'd likely read at least every mystery the Muir Library had to offer. Since moving to Sparta she'd borrowed ten books a week and just run through them, turning them in for ten more every Tuesday. But textbooks?

The doctor said she would probably only be at the hospital one night, possibly two if they decided against a cast, but she'd be laid up for at least a couple of weeks at home. He said he didn't want her to put any weight on the leg. In a way it was good timing. Fauna was here. Uncas cut off the chewed ends of the children's bagels and opened the drawer he thought contained the wax paper and such; after two more tries he found the resealable bags and put into one the reclaimed remains of the half-eaten bagels. He was surprised at how much he knew about the kitchen—where things were. He'd always fixed himself and his children breakfast, but he hadn't done much cleaning up. At the end of their meals at home he'd watch Margaret tidy things away while they'd talk about their day. There was a beauty to the economy of her movements. She'd put the leftovers in bags or plastic containers, then carry the dishes to the sink, where they got a quick rinse before they were put in the dishwasher; wooden-handled knives and the like were carefully washed by hand, soaped up first and then rinsed under a thin hot stream. She wasn't a water waster, either.

"Jeez, Dad, you've really made progress. I wasn't positive you knew what room you were in."

"You see, Fauna, you *can* teach an old dog new tricks."

That was it. He and Margaret had been able to adapt before. Her being laid up in bed would be no different. He could certainly fend for himself when it came to lunch. That just left dinner.

"Have you been over to see the progress at Delores's house?" he asked.

"It's Doug's and my house now. And when would I have had time to see it? I barely had time to—"

"Of course. You were at the hospital."

"Sorry if I'm a little testy. It's been a really long day."

Delores Fletcher had died a year ago—she had drunk herself to death—and had left Doug, her only child, everything, including her house. Fauna and Doug made plans almost immediately to move back from Illinois to Sparta, but delayed when Doug's father had contested the will. He and Delores had been divorced for several years, but apparently there had been Fletcher family furniture, furniture that Ray Fletcher felt should go to him. It took everyone by surprise, especially Doug, and most blamed Ray's second wife, but Uncas wasn't so quick to agree. He put the responsibility squarely on Ray's shoulders—the man threatened his own son with a court battle. But Doug wouldn't fight with his father. He gave him the keys to the house and told him to go in and help himself. And Ray had.

How Doug had turned out to be such a solid citizen when his father was such a thin reed, Uncas couldn't understand. He himself felt that whatever backbone he had was handed down through the Metcalfe generations, tempered by those with whom they had chosen to mate, and it was pure arrogance to think otherwise, to think that you were an unblemished ingot and could mold yourself to fit the times. Your stock mattered. Though it might not always be apparent how it would manifest itself. His own son, Hank, while competent and kind enough, was something of a passive fellow. Uncas would never describe him as a thin reed, but he wasn't yet foxhole material, either.

"Dad," Fauna said, "we may have to stay here longer than we thought. When Doug was at the house the boiler kept cutting out. I'm worried about the kids if the weather stays this cold."

"We're glad to have you for as long as you need a place."

Fauna said thanks but didn't meet his gaze.

Uncas felt a pang. It felt strange to have to assure her, to have the conversation at all. It was the kind of thing their children talked to Margaret about, and she reported back. But Margaret was doped up at Sparta Memorial, and he was cleaning up the kitchen, about to spend the night alone. It would be only the second unplanned separation of their marriage. The first still filled him with shame and anger—talk about thin reeds.

To put off the moment when he'd retire to his own room for the night, Uncas had helped Fauna finish up in the kitchen. Then they'd unloaded a few suitcases from her station wagon and brought them upstairs. They'd found Doug asleep—passed out from exhaustion—in the extra bed in Tommy's room. Fauna had roused him and led him to their room. Uncas kept finding ways to avoid his and Margaret's king-size bed. He went back downstairs to lock up; he swept the kitchen and disposed of a bunch of roses whose petals were about to drop. Margaret would have let them go and gathered the petals in a basket, but Uncas had never liked seeing flowers tucked into vases. After sorting through the mail, which included a circular from Bagel Falls (Hannah's place of employ, he realized), he relegated most of it to the wastebasket, then shut off the lights downstairs. In his pocket, he found a card Hannah had given him as he left the store. Apparently, if you bought enough bagels—and remembered to get the card stamped each time—you were rewarded with a free baker's dozen. How did these places make any money? And then he answered his own question: by charging outrageous prices. But he'd had to admit, if grudgingly, the bagels were a nice break from regular toast. As he turned right on the landing, he hadn't anticipated that his room, in addition to being empty, would be dark: Margaret hadn't been there to fall asleep with the lights on.

Once he was settled into his side of the bed, Uncas pulled out his album of plant life. Years ago, when he had first become interested in botany, he'd begun to photograph different species at Poplar Creek, the Metcalfe summer place on Iroquois Lake. He would take several shots of, say, a tiger lily or a mint plant, hoping to get at least one that articulated the identifying marks of a particular specimen—the spots of the tiger lilies or the jagged edges of the mint plant. This would be the photograph of record. The one that would end up in the album. The photographs were all different sizes, and the first were of course in black-and-white; over the years the color got better, more true to life, but he had a fondness for the square, early color shots, with their white borders. His first camera had been a Brownie—chunky and simple. And he had stuck mainly with the simple cameras—these weren't photographs for publication; he was recording the information for himself and for, he hoped, posterity; he imagined a grandchild out at Poplar Creek looking through the album after he was dead, and then maybe continuing the tradition by starting another volume. A new camera given to him by his wife several Christmases ago had been a disaster—very expensive with a light meter and nonsense about f-stops. He found he was better off with Marcia's so-called idiot-proof automatic. It made a lovely whirring sound as the

lens came out for close-ups, and—best of all—you didn't have to focus. To this day, if he came upon an unfamiliar plant or flower—
which was, of course, rare—he would take a picture, research it, and
then paste the photograph in the album. On a card underneath he
would catalogue its genus, its everyday name, where he'd found it,
and when. The data was often followed by commentary ("The tiger
lily is native to Central New York. F.L.R.M. [his mother's initials]
transplanted several from the lakeside to the banks of the creek,
where, she had been often heard to say, 'they rooted and flourished
as though they had returned home'"). He'd also included dried and
flattened specimens, haphazardly, the way a child might collect
sparkly rocks or pretty shells. In more recent years he had begun to
include pictures of striking flowers and plants already represented.
He would often flip through the album before going to sleep (he
viewed it as a diary of sorts) and would remember walks in the woods
(there was a leaf from the black maple with the tire swing that always
reminded him of his wife on the morning of Fauna's wedding) or
picnics near the creek or the bouquet of wildflowers he'd picked for
Margaret the evening of their engagement party. Through the decades the photographs got better and better (until the blurry year of
the too-fancy camera). Some pictures he found he avoided because
they had an agitating effect, a reminder of less pleasant times. (There
was a particular oak leaf and the cap of an acorn that never failed to
conjure up an argument he'd had with his father about the factory; a
little pine sprig that he associated with the last Christmas his mother
was alive; and, appropriately enough, a spotted touch-me-not he
linked, probably inaccurately, with one of Margaret's first chilly
withdrawals.) Mostly he would drift off, relaxed and almost intoxi-
cated with the memories the albums held. Margaret would be long
asleep, a mystery from the library open on her chest, pushing her

breasts to the side. Through one of her thinning nightgowns he would see the dark aureole surrounding her nipple; it always reminded him of a *Rudbeckia*, specifically a black-eyed Susan, which looked as though the color bled from the central disk onto the petals. He'd remove her glasses, find a bookmark to keep her place, and turn off her reading light. She'd rarely wake fully, but instead would pat his hand gently or sometimes his face, in a gestural thank-you.

Uncas arose about an hour later than usual the next morning. Typically, he slept not the sleep of babes (anyone who had raised a child knew that babies were the most erratic sleepers of all), but the sleep of the carefree. His days were filled with interesting work, he'd take a long run or ride his stationary bicycle before dinner, and then Margaret's meals would leave him full, content, and drowsy. Search your conscience, he would tell his children when they complained of insomnia: guilt makes a poor bed companion. Worry was another poor companion: he thought of Margaret unconscious, with her leg in the air and her mouth sagging open. Remorse, another. Fauna's disapproving *Glad you could make it, Dad* and Margaret's sudden conking out had played in his head over and over again. A mostly sleepless start to the night, followed by periodic jerking awake had led finally to a deep, intense, and disturbing sleep for about two hours. He wasn't prone to dreams normally, but he couldn't shake this one. Awful images of a legless Margaret, only she was smiling and waving as she rode his bicycle down the Poplar Creek driveway.

There was a note from Fauna downstairs. She had gone to the hospital. Doug had taken the children over to their new house. They planned to meet for lunch at the house at twelve thirty. Uncas prepared his usual breakfast of oatmeal, toast and jam, a glass of orange juice, and a cup of herbal tea. He had called the hospital as soon as he had gotten up. Yes, the nurse said, Mrs. Metcalfe had slept through the night. No, doctor hadn't been in to see her. No, she said, doctor will tell you if she can go home today. Discharge is in half an hour. Yes, she said, that would be short notice, but doctor will tell you. Uncas found the false efficiency of her speech—as though using the article "the" took too much time out of her busy schedule—irritating. He wanted a simple piece of information: his wife's release date. He would have to be patient.

The snow hadn't stuck; the day was close to balmy, like the sweetest day of an Indian summer. Uncas felt warm in his tweed jacket; his tie—one of old Mr. Stephenson's, given to Uncas by his widow—felt constricting. He was glad he'd left his sweater vest at home. Fauna had taken his car—they'd agreed on that last night—and Uncas would find his wife's car. It wouldn't be far from the book sale, which was set up in the abandoned Modern Store. While he was nearby, he'd buy a couple of dozen mysteries for Margaret to read while she mended; maybe, like Bagel Falls, they'd punch a card and he'd work his way to a free book. A dozen secondhand books were probably cheaper than a dozen bagels, as well as more nutritious. He stopped at his office to retrieve the spare set of car keys and caught a glimpse of himself in the glass of the Menelaus Building's door. He was surprised to see a dapperness, a youthful vigor that he didn't feel; it was as though his bones and muscles made it their business to take over and crowd out a worried, regret-filled, sleepless night. He was glad to have the appearance of fighting form, though the reality was a different story—he felt like a hollow tree in the process of being eaten away from the inside out. Soon he was looking in the window of Bagel Falls, wondering if Margaret might like a bagel to supplement her hospital diet. Probably not. He laughed to himself. She was one of the few people he knew who found something to compliment about hospital food; she often declared, as though looking for someone to contradict her, that she looked forward to flying she so enjoyed airplane meals. He heard the jingle of the bagel-shop bell and had to step closer to the window to avoid knocking into the girl with the bleached hair and work boots; she was coming out of the door toward him, head down. She glanced up at Uncas with that same dark look she'd had on her face the day before. After he said hello, she nodded and then smiled—she remembered him, he thought—and then she walked on. Uncas felt her brief smile suffuse him. The transformation of her face was remarkable, as though he were the agent of change in reversing the sequence of a wilting flower.

He forwent the bagel and found his wife's blue car (she always bought blue) parked in front of the Modern Store, with a ticket slipped under the windshield wiper. Uncas looked at the fine (ten dollars) and tucked the ticket into his inside pocket; he'd pay it this evening. He was about to put a dime in the meter, when he saw that there were forty-five minutes left. Probably someone who recognized his wife's car had fed it recently.

Elsie Brewster, Floyd's wife, was manning the cash box at the book sale. Margaret never had much use for her and spoke of her, Uncas thought, a little harshly ("a spotless house and a spotless mind").

"Oh, hello, Uncas. I'm so glad to see you. We've been so worried about Margaret."

"Hello, Elsie. Please tell Floyd I'm grateful for his call."

"I wish he'd scolded you into letting him give you a lift to the hospital. How's my friend doing today?"

"I'm on my way up there, but I thought I'd stop and pick up some books for her. I think I'll steer clear of the textbook aisle."

Elsie smiled, but looked anxious. "Oh, we're so sorry about Margaret. We can't figure out how it happened. We've taken the table off the floor and we've double-checked all the others. It's in fine condition. I'm worried that the legs weren't locked in place."

"Margaret will get over this. I'm sure it wasn't anyone's fault. These things happen."

Elsie looked relieved. "You say you haven't been up yet to visit?" She said this tentatively. Almost, Uncas thought, in disbelief.

"Fauna's with her now."

"Oh, yes, that's right. Fauna and the Fletcher boy are back. Oh, Uncas, I almost forgot. Here are the books Margaret had set aside to buy when . . . when it happened."

"Splendid. That makes my job easier." He felt behind the parking ticket for his billfold. What business was it of Elsie Brewster's when he went up to see his wife? Margaret was right: she was a busybody. She set the bag of books on the table in front of him.

"Oh, Uncas, please take these up to Margaret for us. There's no need to . . . I mean with what happened and all, please take these."

Uncas thought about protesting—the sale was to benefit the library, after all—but he had to agree it seemed appropriate. If Margaret disagreed, she could tack on a little extra to her next contribution. "That's very nice," he said. "Margaret will appreciate these."

"Oh, I hope so. It's the least we can do. And, Uncas"—Elsie rested her hand on the side of her face—"in all the commotion last night we forgot about Margaret's car. I noticed you picked up the ticket. We feel responsible. I've been feeding dimes in this morning, but I'm afraid it should have been moved off the street last night. It seems only right that the book sale pay."

"That explains why there was time left on the meter." Uncas looked from the car back to Elsie, whose face was tightened by what seemed to be permanent worry. The book sale's responsibility for Margaret's parking ticket was only the most recent concern. Maybe it explained why Floyd was such an easygoing fellow. "The fine's nothing," Uncas said. "Cheap parking when you think about it. It could have been towed."

"Always the gentleman," Elsie said. "Thank you. Tell Margaret from all of us to read the books and get better. And tell her I'll be up this afternoon." She paused. "I understand Leila Benson was checked in a few days ago. For detoxification." Elsie's face pinched with disapproval. She seemed to be waiting for Uncas to say something, but he had no idea to whom she was referring.

"You haven't seen my bicycle around, by any chance?" he asked.

"Oh. No. Did it get stolen again?"

"I like to think of it as borrowed. I missed it yesterday. Had to walk to the office."

"Oh. I haven't seen it, Uncas. I'd recognize it anywhere. Can't be too many bicycles with the seat that high. And I'll ask the other girls. We'll keep an eye out, and I'll ask around."

Uncas was reminded of the old joke, Telegraph, telephone, tell-a-woman. It was a joke Margaret liked, too.

Uncas heard the firehouse siren signal noon as the automatic glass doors swung open and ushered him into Sparta Memorial. The hallway smelled of hospital food, potent and sickly all at once. When he walked into the room, Fauna was lifting the round cover off a thin sandwich, slices of pink cold cuts between white bread. His wife and middle child looked up at the same moment, with the same impassive expression. He knew they expected him, and so his presence seemed to barely register. Fauna continued unloading the tray before greeting him; his wife said hello after taking a bite of her sandwich. In Margaret's case, it didn't mean she wasn't glad he was here, but that she reserved her outward enthusiasm for the unknown commodity. Had Uncas been an orderly or a nurse's aide, someone Margaret had never laid eyes on, he would have been greeted like a valued customer. Fauna had, in her high school days, accused her mother of being warmer to shop clerks than to her own children, but Uncas had experienced Margaret's true frostiness at a much closer range. The chill one morning after he'd drunk too much; her swing in mood from teasing to cold when he wouldn't be jollied out of the blackness that sometimes weighed on him. She had a code of behavior, and if you stumbled, she retreated in cool disappointment. "I'm sorry" would be met with "I should think you would be." What Fauna complained about, and what was on evidence here, could be seen, in comparison, as simply reserve.

"We were just discussing what beds and such Fauna might take from the attic. It seems a lucrative garage sale has stripped them of the basics."

Fauna looked a little embarrassed. "Well, it seemed stupid to cart secondhand, junky stuff back and forth across the country. I mean I knew we'd need some of it, but it didn't seem worth it."

Uncas hoped no family furniture had been sold to strangers. He tried to remember what she'd been given.

Fauna turned back to her mother. "Here's what I think we need— a couple of single beds for Tommy and Janey and some small bureaus, if you have them. We'll get a new couch with a pullout bed for the television slash guest room. And I'll have to look into a crib for

Nik, though I don't know how long he'll stand for that. He's practically ready to drive, never mind a grown-up bed."

"What happened to your father's crib?" Margaret asked.

Fauna's face wrinkled. "I don't know why I even let you talk me into taking that thing to Illinois. It was rickety and seemed designed to sever kids' fingers. We didn't even try to sell it; we left it for the garbagemen."

"Oh, Faun, you didn't," Margaret said.

Uncas inwardly winced as his fear was confirmed. It had been a fine old crib—at each corner there had been hand-carved pinecones, with worn patches where his father and then Uncas's brothers and sister and then Uncas himself, as well as his own children, had, as it were, nursed. He'd expected to see future generations launch from its confines. The lack of respect he sometimes saw in his progeny was a great disappointment.

"Yep. I'm sorry, but I did," Fauna said. "Do safety regulations, even for your own grandchildren, mean nothing to you people?"

"But," Margaret persisted, "it wasn't yours to give away. Much less throw away."

Fauna shrugged. "I thought it was mine. I thought you'd given it to me. It didn't occur to me that you'd want it back. I didn't know you and Dad were considering . . . Do you have some news you'd like to share?" She patted her own extended belly.

Uncas checked his irritation. Fauna's sense of humor escaped him; she must see that Margaret was upset, that the crib meant something to her.

"I wish you hadn't," Margaret said.

"But I did," Fauna replied.

Margaret turned to Uncas. "What news of life in the free world?"

Uncas took his wife's cue and switched gears; he feigned consideration of the question. "Well, I bring you tidings, and books, courtesy of Elsie and all the women down at the annual Muir Library Book Sale. Elsie was kind enough to feed the meter for your car this morning and said she'd be up to visit this afternoon."

Margaret rolled her eyes.

Fauna stood up quickly. "I bet," she said, "that Mrs. Brewster called Doug 'the Fletcher boy.'"

Uncas was bewildered. His daughter's outbursts rarely failed to take him off guard. They were what reminded him that she was only twenty-two years old, not her defiance over throwing out his old crib or her impertinence in implying that Margaret was pregnant. Elsie *had* called Doug "the Fletcher boy," but that's who he was.

"And I bet you just nodded, as though that were an appropriate way for her to refer to your son-in-law. He has a name. But the woman can't let go. I dumped her pothead son after going out with him for two days and it's like . . . Oh, I don't know." Fauna was looking at him, as though she were waiting for a response, but Uncas didn't know what to say.

"Lord Reticent Taciturn pleads his case. Never mind," Fauna said.

Lord Reticent Taciturn, Uncas thought. An affectionate nickname given to him by his wife and turned on its ear by his children.

"Oh, and, Dad, the doctor—Charley Bisgrove—was here. Mom won't be out for a few days. He wants to talk to you."

"Little Charley?" Uncas asked.

"There's only one practicing Dr. Bisgrove. His father retired," Fauna said. "The nurse at the desk has a question about insurance, and I'm late to meet Doug and the kids." She turned to Margaret. "I'll be back later this afternoon, Mom. While the kids are napping."

On her way out, Fauna stopped and looked at him. "Sorry about that outburst, but Mrs. Brewster really fries my . . . She gets on my nerves." She kissed him on the cheek briefly. "Is there anything I can pick up for you, Mom? Besides a crib."

"No, I don't think so."

Damned, Uncas thought, if she was going to ask Fauna for anything. But then she did.

"If the mail comes in time. Oh, and the newspaper."

Uncas stepped farther into the room with the bag of books. With his free hand he lifted the paper that had been resting on top of the books. "Here's the *Gazette*."

"Oh, bless you. My angel husband."

"You didn't make the front page. I'll phone Steve immediately."

Margaret gave a snort of laughter. Steve Weckstein was the editor of the *Sparta Gazette* and a recent widower who had moved to Sparta with his wife about a dozen years ago. He'd seen the paper through some difficult times, not the least of which was its absorption by a chain. Even so, he covered local news with the attention to detail that some people reserved for their annual Christmas letter. No doubt Margaret would appear in the weekly hospital roundup, "The Stetho Scope."

Fauna patted Uncas on the arm. "See you back at the house. We'll leave some lunch for you."

"Okay."

"Unk, do you want some of this?" His wife indicated her tray of food. "I don't think much of the salad, but the bologna is a treat," she said.

Uncas looked at her but didn't know what to say about her offer of food. He wasn't hungry; the food looked and smelled unappetizing; and he felt that it was important for his wife to eat a balanced meal.

She should have food in her system to absorb whatever toxins her medication threw off.

"It's a simple question, Unk. Would you like half?"

"Not for me," Uncas said. "We missed you last night. You would have been amused to see your grandchildren tackling bagels."

"Bagels?" Margaret said. "Plain old toast isn't good enough? Where did they get bagels?"

Uncas stood up a little straighter in fake pomp and laid his open palm against his chest. "I bought them." Then he relaxed his body as though letting out a little air. "It was a little embarrassing. I walked right by the Menelaus and ran into the Stephenson girl"—Uncas remembered Fauna's outburst regarding the Fletcher "boy." He and his wife, who, he knew, was thinking the same thing, exchanged smiles—"Hannah," Uncas said, "Hannah Stephenson."

As he sat down, Uncas wondered how to describe Hannah's friend, Betty Delafield's stepdaughter, whose name he had already forgotten, so Margaret would get the full effect. Of course, any account would involve the particulars: her hair and boots, the nose earring (that wasn't right, but it wasn't exactly a nose ring either), the combat fatigues. But also there was something else: her direct gaze, her firm handshake, and her appealing smile—all things that impressed Uncas, that might impress any adult, but that weren't calculated. You couldn't really call it charm—it was confidence.

"Her mother said she was working there. She's a peach," Margaret said. "How's Joe?"

The other girl's name wasn't Jo. "Jo?"

"Stephenson. Hannah's father." Margaret poked at the Jell-O and then ate a bite.

Of course. "Fine, I guess." He hadn't asked. He decided to skip the description of Hannah's friend. "What did the doctor say?"

Margaret waved her hand, as if to push the news away from her. "Something about bruised tendons and a sprain." She looked up at her husband. "The miracle is, nothing's broken."

Uncas's shoulders fell. He recrossed his legs and settled further into the chair, in case Margaret noticed the response. He had enough firsthand experience with injury to know that in some cases, a break was preferable. The bone mended and you were on your way. A sprain at Margaret's age could mean months on crutches. But his wife was an optimist: of course she would hear the news as positive.

"Did he say when you'd be getting out?"

Margaret looked at him. She put on a caricature of crossness. "Not today."

He realized she was no longer in traction. Maybe the prognosis wouldn't be so bad. "Your elaborate suspension bridge is gone."

Margaret looked at him, puzzled. Then she snorted in laughter. "They took that off first thing this morning. Good riddance. Actually, I was a little sorry to see it go. I thought the kids might get a kick out of it."

"Who was in to see you?"

"Well, no one. Except for Fauna. I don't think anyone knows. Oh, you mean which doctor? Little Charley came in, and then the new surgeon, the one we met at Malc and Libby's last fall."

Uncas could picture him immediately. A very large man, a former college-football player who combed over the remaining strands of his hair to cover his bald spot, and who was—Uncas could think of no other word to describe him—sullen. His wife had family here in Sparta and there had been a rumor that he'd left his practice in western Massachusetts under some sort of cloud; nothing to do with his competence as an orthopedic surgeon, but more like a feud. He carried himself like a beaten man.

"He's the one who, bless his soul, told them the traction was unnecessary. And I think he's not recommending surgery." Margaret's voice changed to a conspiratorial whisper. "Much as I'm grateful for his diagnosis, he's not cozy like Little Charley. I don't care if Libby does think he's handsome. Oh, and Unk, this is sad: Leila Benson's here again. Her son was by to tell me. She's gotten much worse lately. Gee, I hope they get it all this time. One of the nurses told me they're hopeful. That nice redheaded one, her mother was . . ."

Uncas was suddenly hungry; he couldn't listen to his wife anymore. He'd stop at the desk and see the nurse about the insurance form, and he'd call Little Charley from his office. He wondered if Bagel Falls sold sandwiches. He wondered if Margaret had ever met Betty Delafield's stepdaughter. He wondered if she'd be outside the shop again. Glad he'd thought to bring Margaret the mysteries, he selected three books from which she could choose. She'd be set for a week if necessary. Uncas looked at her and smiled. "I've been meaning to ask you, Mags, why textbooks? Thinking of brushing up on your algebra?" He wanted to protect her. She had her reading glasses perched on her nose, magnifying her lovely blue eyes. It was the eyes and the laugh, he'd always maintained, that he'd fallen in love with.

She looked at him a moment, and he saw her brow furrow. "Oh," she said. "That. You'll be happy to know, I was looking in the poetry section, at the next table. Much more highbrow. There's a book I had years ago. When we lived in Cambridge." She looked thoughtful. "Gee, that was a fun year."

Uncas felt a chill cast on his warmth for his wife. He thought he knew the book to which she referred; it still left a residue of irritation. He had tucked it into the giveaway box himself many years ago, in Cambridge.

Margaret continued, but Uncas couldn't concentrate on what she was saying and caught only every other word or so. ". . . must have given it away . . . look at used bookstores . . ."

"Sounds too highbrow for Sparta," Uncas said. He got up and gave her a dry kiss on the lips. "I'm off. I'll check in with Little Charley." He walked through the hospital corridors slowly; Margaret had taken him by surprise. Maybe it wasn't even the same book she was talking about. It was funny, like their Cambridge night apart, he hadn't thought about the book in ages, and wondered at his strong feelings. He was surprised to find he cared.

TWO

"Well, Margaret seems to be in great spirits, as always." Uncas's sister-in-law Dorothy leaned into him as Doug brushed by with a drink in each hand. The cocktail hour had just begun and already Uncas was exhausted. Margaret was fresh back from the hospital, fitted out with a thigh-to-calf cast, but had insisted that Thanksgiving plans go ahead without her. As tired as he was, he was glad too. Thanksgiving had always been important in his family: after all, Uncas was an Indian name. There had been an Uncas Metcalfe in every generation since the late 1600s. The original Uncas was a brave in the Pequot tribe who later split off and founded the Mohegans. The Metcalfes had settled in what became Connecticut before moving to central New York, and legend had it that Uncas, who was known as a fearsome and aggressive warrior, had saved, with particular cunning and courage, the life of one of Uncas Metcalfe's ancestors, and the man had promised to name a son for him. (The way Uncas saw it, his family had been aware of multicultural histories before all these absurd committees had been formed at the university.) He and Margaret had continued the tradition: Hank, whose full name was Uncas Henry Metcalfe, was the eighth. For his nickname Margaret had opted for a diminutive of his middle name because of the way a tuft on his first head of hair fell. Uncas had had a brief conversation with him today. With his mother laid up in bed, Uncas couldn't understand why he hadn't come home—something about travel and papers that sounded like a poor excuse. As usual, Uncas's brother Dave and his wife, Dorothy, were there, and their daughter and her husband; his sister, Flo, and her son, Tom (a layabout as far as Uncas was concerned); and two of his brother Tom's children—the younger, Emily, had also brought her boyfriend. And then Margaret's unmarried first cousin Cornelius from New York, who always made jokes about visiting his country cousin, and acted, Uncas thought, as though he were doing them all a great favor by spending two days in the hinterlands. In the past, Uncas had heard his children imitating him, in the most offhand and sharp of ways. Hank would say, in an exaggerated English accent, as though British English were the only tongue of snobs, "Well, yes, Hank, we must get you over the next time you have a minute in New York. You get there often, do you? I do love making my annual pilgrimage up here to see you and your cozy family. It can't help but be fresh air so far from New York." Then Fauna would say, in an equally exaggerated sort of English accent, "Yes, Corny, that's just delicious. I heartily concur." And the two of them would laugh, then one of them might abruptly say, "What a jerk," and then they'd launch into news about their lives or what movie they'd like to see. They were clubby, like the fellows down the hall from him in his house at college, who'd all come from the same boarding school. While they were friendly enough, you never really felt a part of their circle because you hadn't been around at its inception. But Uncas and Margaret obviously had been around at the inception of his children's—well, he didn't know what to call it. He'd never mentioned it to her, and wondered if she felt the same way, felt the same exclusion. Uncas was troubled less by his own exclusion than he was by the absolute way his children judged people. The word "jerk," of which he disapproved, fell easily and often from Fauna's lips. Whence had she learned such harshness? He couldn't, however, fault her on her taste—though Margaret and Cornelius had been close as children, and he was one of the few of her relatives who made the trip to Sparta at all, the man was a snob.

Normally they celebrated on the day after Thanksgiving, so that Margaret could hire someone to help her in the kitchen. But Fauna would have none of that. She insisted they have it on the actual day, saying she'd always found the delayed celebration irritating and she didn't want her children growing up thinking that holidays were meant to be shuffled around to make them more convenient. She didn't present it as a choice, the way Marcia might have. And since she was running the show, Uncas didn't have the heart to argue.

"There are plenty of healthy bodies around, Dad," she'd said, "who we don't even have to pay, who'll be happy to cook food and clean up. I bet we can even get old Cornelius to bring smoked salmon and pâté from some overpriced shop in New York."

He stopped himself from saying "whom," "*whom* we don't even have to pay," because he had learned, or relearned, in the week that Fauna had been at the house, that correcting her grammar often led not to increased understanding or more correct English, but to unpleasant outbursts. It bothered him when his children misspoke, and he thought, as he often had, that he and Margaret should have insisted that Fauna go to boarding school, and maybe she'd have a college degree now instead of three sticky children and a fourth on the way.

In the three days between Margaret's release from the hospital and today, Fauna had made a series of calls to arrange the dinner—

she'd seemed to know who could be counted on for a main dish (Dave loved to cook) and who should be asked to help clean up. Uncas had to admit he was impressed with how smoothly the evening had gone so far; it seemed he'd imagined that his daughter's quick temper would affect her ability to organize.

"People like being asked to help out, Dad," she'd said. And it appeared they did. Flo had made a pumpkin pie from a recipe she'd learned from one of the cooks of their childhood, and someone had written out beautiful place cards. Fauna, five months pregnant and already looking as if she were going to have twins, had thought of almost everything. As far as he could see, only the lemon twists for Dave's and Dorothy's martinis had been forgotten.

"When do you think she'll be up and about, Unk?"

Uncas heard Dorothy ask a question, even heard the actual words, but he couldn't make sense of it. Fauna wasn't due for several months, and then he remembered Margaret. He felt as though he needed a sheet of paper with which to answer the most frequent questions: *How did it happen? Where was she? How long had she been in the hospital? Will there be any residual damage? How long would the cast be on?*

"The doctors say in a month, maybe six weeks. It depends on how the leg heals." Uncas drained the last of his nonalcoholic beer into his glass. He focused on Dorothy. "Have you and Dave been out to the Creek recently?" As he watched her face for an answer (which would probably be that Dave had been but that she didn't much like the cold and was content to hear reports), he realized he should check on people's drinks. He'd be seated next to Dorothy during dinner anyhow. They could catch up then.

*　*　*

"Dad, do you want to clank a glass and tell people to sit down, or shall I?" Fauna pushed a straying lock behind her ear.

Shall. It was music to Uncas's ears; this was the way his children were meant to talk.

"Why don't you go ahead." She had done all the work, why shouldn't she call them to the table?

"But, Fauna"—Uncas touched his daughter's shoulder lightly—"I think one of your dirty-footed numbers has switched the place cards around." He smiled, hoping she would be amused as well. Her children had been running around with one of their cousins during the cocktail hour and then had trooped dutifully up to bed. "According to perhaps Janey's plan, I'm seated between Tom and Kirk." Every other year since he could remember Dorothy was on his right and Flo on his left.

"No, that's right, Dad. I decided to play around this year." She lowered her voice to a whisper. "It may be the only Thanksgiving in history that I won't sit next to Uncle Dave and Tom. I took Aunt Flo and Emily, who I never get to see. I figured, let the men talk to each other; we're tired of listening. Look at it this way, at least I separated the couples. And I put you next to Kirk, who's a good guy."

Uncas was flustered. "Now . . ." How he missed Margaret.

"Dad, you had your chance."

"Very well," he said. Margaret had often told their children not to complain about whom they were placed next to; it simply wasn't polite. He sighed and regretted not taking up Fauna's offer of a day ago to seat the table. He certainly wouldn't have put himself between two men, one of whom he considered a ne'er-do-well, a "loser," in the parlance of his children.

Uncas pulled out the chair to his right, then stopped. He'd forgotten: Kirk, not Dorothy, would fill the seat. The twinge of irritation he felt as he left the chair half under the table made him determined to try to enjoy himself. He wondered what Margaret would have done. There would be silent agreement that Fauna could be exasperating, but Margaret, who could have a lengthy conversation with a bricklayer, would be game and act as though it were the most natural thing in the world to be seated between her niece and sister-in-law at a table filled with men. He determined to play her alphabet game where you introduced subjects in alphabetical order until you hit upon one that turned into a conversation. At least Dorothy was nearby—Fauna hadn't totally segregated the sexes.

"Oh, hey, Uncle Uncas. I guess it's you and me. Or should I say you and I? I better watch my grammar, huh?" Tom was dressed in a cardigan and T-shirt, and some kind of boot, similar to what Uncas himself had worn for six months on long marches through the wilds of New Jersey. Then, as though he knew what Uncas was thinking, Tom pulled his chair out and lifted his leg over it. Reserves in honkytonk bars after drills were better mannered. This is a tragicomedy, thought Uncas. Manners and etiquette seemed to be completely a thing of the past. He wondered if his own son, who was just a little taller than Tom, stepped over the backs of chairs, or forwent jacket and tie and wore undershirts to dinner. Something about the boots—they weren't authentic combat gear—struck him as familiar. He'd seen someone else in them recently, though whom he couldn't imagine.

He turned to his right to say hello to Kirk, his niece Emily's boyfriend, who at least had a collared shirt on, if no jacket or tie. As he waited for Dorothy to join them, to pull out her chair if Kirk or Doug, who was on her other side, neglected to, Uncas glanced at Kirk again—there seemed to be a sparkle coming off his left shoulder that glinted off Uncas's glasses. The damn things were probably scratched, having been knocked off by Nik at least twice in the last week.

There was a time when he would have been happy to talk with Kirk, to find out what he had studied in college, to find out what other professors were doing. But at the moment he felt weary, in need of Margaret to carry the occasion. He tried to imagine what kind of student Kirk was. As a professor, Uncas had lasted through the rifts of the sixties and the inclination toward smugness of the seventies, which had culminated in the actual smugness of the eighties. The students—and he knew he was making sweeping generalizations to which there was nevertheless some truth—simply didn't give a hoot about learning. He never thought he would look back on the late sixties as a fertile, blossoming time. His own children had worn clothes that didn't fit—in both size and gender—but never mind, it had been a time when students were still students of something, even if it was of Life (as one of his more exasperating charges had filled in for a major). Now they might have been attending an employment factory, for all the genuine interest any of them took in, say, avifauna, or even basic biology; the fastest-growing department in the sciences was in computer programming. Mostly his classes over the last ten years had been riddled (yes, he thought, like a cancer) with premedical students looking for an easy course in biology; also, there were occasional humanities majors, and these were mostly girls (women, he could hear his daughter say) looking to fill science requirements, who took the class pass/fail. Where would this young Kirk fall?

"Hi, Mr. Metcalfe." Kirk proffered his hand. At least that nicety wasn't completely gone. "I'm honored to be seated here. I thought maybe one of the kids had been screwing around with the cards."

"No. It seems to be intentional."

As Dorothy walked behind him, Kirk turned and pulled out her chair. "Hi, Aunt Dot," he said with a big smile. "How'd I get so lucky?" He kissed her hello and gave her a little hug. He held her for a moment at arm's length. "You look like a million bucks."

Dorothy smiled and pushed him lightly on the shoulder.

"Oh, Kirk. I'm an old lady, and you're a flatterer, but thank you." She looked over at Uncas, who had seated himself. "I guess I've been replaced by the younger generation. I can't remember a Thanksgiving at the Metcalfes'—and this includes when Uncas and Dave's parents were alive and we'd have it at their house— where I wasn't seated next to Uncas. I feel all at sea. And I'm not sure I like it."

"Then please, let's switch seats," Kirk said.

"Oh, no, no, no. A plan's a plan. And Uncas and I could use a little shake-up. Right, Unk?"

"As Margaret is wont to say, 'If you say so, it must be so,'" Uncas said.

"How is she?" Kirk asked. "I understand she'll be laid up for a while. Emily's crazy about her, so if there's anything we can do, please let us know."

"Oh, I don't think so. Fauna seems to have everything under control during the day, and I act as a sort of night nurse," Uncas said.

"Fauna's done a wonderful job here," Dorothy said. "It was clever of her to ask us to bring things. She's got Margaret's flair for a party. Too bad Margaret couldn't see for herself."

"When she awakes from her stupor, I'll report in detail," Uncas replied.

"What about you, Unk? Are you getting enough sleep?" Dorothy said.

"Me? Yes. I always sleep. I have a theory that if you don't you shouldn't worry about it, because you can always get through at least the following day without sleep and you're more apt to sleep that night."

"You've said that before," Dorothy said. "But it doesn't seem to work for me. Oh, I fret so that sometimes I wake Dave up, but he always rolls over and falls back *kerplop* asleep."

"With you next to him?" Kirk said. "I can't believe it."

Uncas wondered what Dorothy thought of this bit of cheek. Young people didn't know the boundaries of flirtation anymore. Time to move on to the alphabet game. A subject this young man was likely to know about that began with the letter A. There was the glint again, coming off his left shoulder. Uncas peered closely. "Excuse me," he said. "Something's catching light."

"Probably my diamond stud, Mr. Metcalfe," Kirk said. "Emily got it for me for our first anniversary." He fingered his earlobe.

Nothing was more mysterious than what was considered fashionable. Ten years ago Fauna and Marcia had fought over his old army jacket, and then for his discarded Brooks Brothers shirts. Now grown men were wearing earrings.

"What do you think?" Kirk asked.

Uncas regarded him. What he thought was that it was something homosexuals might do, and he wondered if men also wore earrings in their noses like Hannah's friend Alex (fully, probably the prettier "Alexandra"). It was she he had seen in the boots like Tom's, and if she wore men's boots, he reasoned, why shouldn't men wear earrings in their ears or noses or any damn place they wanted to? He hadn't seen boys with earrings at Wright, but maybe that type didn't go in for botany. Happily, there was no pressure on Uncas to don any jewelry; others could do as they pleased. In Alex's case,

Uncas could look beyond the nasal jewelry and boots. She had an intelligence that over the years he'd learned to recognize when choosing lab assistants. Of course, he wasn't always right, but he'd been more right than wrong. He wondered what she was studying at Mott.

"I wonder," Uncas said, "who gets the other one in the pair?"

"Good question. I'll have to ask Emily. This is my first. Lots of guys do it now, so you can probably buy a single stud."

"That does seem only fair."

"Interested, Mr. Metcalfe?"

"In an earring?"

"Sure. Why not? Keep your students guessing." Kirk leaned back in his chair as though he were sizing up how Uncas might look with an earring.

Uncas felt his irritation at Fauna grow. There was no need for him to be seated next to Kirk. He chose to ignore the suggestion.

"Now, Kirk," Uncas said, "have you ever traveled in Asia?"

"No. Believe it or not, I've actually never been out of the United States. The farthest I've been from Hamilton, where I grew up, is Ohio, where my older brother was in college for a year. Emily and I are talking about traveling though. Once I finish law school and get a few years under my belt. We're even talking about living abroad."

"I'd forgotten that you're studying the law."

"I couldn't decide between that and business, and then I got into law school, so I decided why not?"

Why not, indeed, thought Uncas. He had been about to move on to the subject of bicycles—both his new stationary model and his stolen Raleigh—when Kirk interrupted.

"I've got a question for you. Where did you get the name Uncas? I've heard lots of names, but yours is the strangest."

It wasn't the first time Uncas had heard the question, but he'd never understand why people felt free to disparage it simply because it was out of the ordinary. "It's an Indian name."

"As in 'Native American'?"

"I suppose."

"Wow, that's funny. I was expecting you to say that it was some ancestor's last name. There's a guy in my contracts class named Covington Batchelder the Fourth."

"Yes." Uncas nodded. "I went to school with his father, I believe."

"I always want to ask him: there weren't enough first names to go around? How did you end up with a Native American name?" Kirk asked.

Uncas told the story as briefly as possible.

"Ironic, isn't it?" Kirk said. "I mean the chances are pretty good that the alliances the tribes made with the colonizers led to the eventual decimation of their people."

"In this particular case, the tribe and my ancestors coexisted peacefully. There was a great respect due the original Uncas, and Richard Metcalfe, my forebear, paid it to him."

"Maybe that's true," Kirk said. "I wonder if the rest of the tribe and his descendants would agree."

Uncas felt Tom tap him on the shoulder, and was thankful to have an excuse to turn away.

"Hey, Uncle Uncas, Fauna wants you." He was pointing to the other end of the table.

"I wanted to drink a toast to Mom," Fauna said. She had cupped her hands and was yelling down the length of the table.

Uncas stood up, annoyed with himself. He should have remembered to welcome his guests. He picked up his champagne glass and gave his father's customary toast. "To those who are here and to those whom we wish could be."

Uncas brought the champagne to his lips, though he didn't intend to drink. In an attempt to cut down on useless calories, he'd sworn off alcohol a couple of years ago.

"What about those who are here and we wish weren't?" Kirk said. "And those who aren't here and we're glad they're not!"

Everyone with glasses raised lowered them slowly, as if uncertain what to do. Uncas stared ahead; he wouldn't so much as look at Kirk.

"We can drink to them too," Fauna said. "It's Thanksgiving. Cheers."

There were shouts of agreement and raised glasses.

Uncas sat back down, fully irritated. He turned toward Tom, less to engage him in conversation than to shift away from Kirk. Apparently he thought he was in a fraternity house. An uneasy silence was broken slowly, as patches of conversation surfaced.

"Uncas," Dorothy said. "Would Margaret like a sip of champagne? I could run one up."

"I don't think so," Uncas said. "They advise against it with her prescription."

"Listen to this," Kirk said. "I'm in a motorcycle accident, and end up in the hospital on painkillers. My girlfriend at the time sneaks in a bottle of beer for me. For the first time in my life, the idea of a beer makes me feel sick, so she drinks it instead. The nurse flipped out when she saw the empty bottle on my bedside table. But my girlfriend was like you, Aunt Dot. She really thought she was doing me a favor by sneaking it in."

"I see," Dorothy said. "Do you still ride a motorcycle?"

Uncas surveyed the room. His eye settled on the portraits over the fireplace of the third Uncas and his wife, a Quaker, who had almost not been allowed to marry him. U. M. the Third had persisted after her first husband had died, and her mother had finally smoothed the way for her father to give his blessing. She was a stern, unadorned woman with her bonnet tied under a prominent chin. His toast included her, as well as those more recently dead, not to mention the absent living. While Kirk's effrontery mocked her, Uncas had no doubt who would buckle were they face-to-face.

As had become usual in the past week, Uncas found himself at the end of the evening sweeping the floor; tonight, he was looking in particular for pieces of glass. Tom had broken Flo's pie plate when he helped with the dishes. Fauna was washing the last of the pots. Doug was in the dining room with the carpet sweeper.

"Well, Dad, we did it."

"Yes. It went off rather well," Uncas said. "Everybody seemed to have a good time."

"Yeah. Even Kirk, who you called Kurt by the way, but even that didn't shut him up."

"Oh, dear, did I?" Uncas said. While everyone was drinking coffee in the library, Kirk, after incessantly interrupting Uncas, had dominated the conversation, going on and on about his fellow students and their spouses and girlfriends, and how they were handling the travails of a law school schedule. And Emily, who, Uncas had always thought, had a good head on her shoulders, kept cueing him. The limit was reached when they described their own first anniversary and how a misunderstanding about where to meet had almost led to a breakup. It felt to Uncas like one of those dreadful television shows where the interviewer asks inane, prying questions. Uncas had left the room on the rather thin pretext that he had to go check on Margaret, who he knew would be sleeping, knocked out by the drugs, mouth open.

"What a jerk he is," Fauna said. "I never knew until tonight. And then he kept interrupting you when you were telling the story about the car. Emily's crazy about him though. She kept saying how smart he is, and how he likes to travel just like she does. He wants to live abroad."

"Who wants to live abroad?" Doug asked as he came in from the dining room, with the large white tablecloth in his hand.

"Oh, Kirk. He and Emily may go when he finishes next year," Fauna replied.

"Maybe he should try marrying her first," Doug said.

Uncas looked up. He was always surprised when Doug was vehement, and especially when it was something with which he agreed. What was so wrong with marrying a woman before you traipsed all over the world?

"Ugh. Maybe living in another country with him will point out what a loser he is, and she'll dump him and then marry some handsome French guy who will charm us all with his accent. We won't be able to tell if he's a jerk or not." Fauna turned back to scrubbing the sink, and then looked up again. "Hey, did Hank ever call? Everyone was asking what he was doing, and I didn't know what he decided."

"You didn't speak to him? I left him talking to your mother, and she was going to yell for you."

"I must not have been in shouting distance. Or Mom and her painkillers forgot. Never mind. It doesn't matter. What'd he end up doing?"

Uncas couldn't remember exactly what Hank had told him.

"Dad, you look pained. Was his choice so bad?"

Uncas felt badgered and a little embarrassed. "He was with George and a friend." That much, he recalled.

"Peter?" Fauna asked. "With George? At Martha's Vineyard?"

"Yes. That's right," Uncas said.

"They're like the Three Musketeers or something. You'd think they'd get sick of spending so much time together. Did you ever pal around like that, Dad? I mean, not come home for Thanksgiving, and just spend it somewhere with a friend?"

If my mother had been laid up, I wouldn't have, Uncas thought. Then he remembered a magical Thanksgiving in New York. "I plead the Fifth."

"The Fifth. This I have to hear."

"Tell all, Uncas." Doug was leaning against the doorjamb.

Uncas smiled. "Nothing to tell."

"C'mon, Dad. I know it was before you were married. We were all young once."

He studied Fauna for a moment. Imagine at the delicate age of twenty-two thinking you had been young once. As it was, his daughter was right. He had been young—a junior in college. He hadn't thought about it for ages. "What makes you so certain that it was before your mother and I were married?" he asked.

"Because Mom would have to be pried from your side for any holidays. And she'd never just go off somewhere for Thanksgiving."

Fauna was right about that. He and his roommate and one other fellow, now dead, had impulsively taken a train to New York and reserved rooms at the Plaza Hotel. With a view of Central Park; invitations to three parties, one of which was black tie; the number of a girl he'd met once at a cousin's house (it was before he'd laid eyes on Margaret); and his parents persuaded that he was working out the details of his junior paper and couldn't be disturbed, Uncas had spent the most carefree four days of his life. He could still remember leaving the Plaza at ten for the dinner dance, with a Manhattan (when in Rome, he had reasoned) under his belt. The following night, at a railroad apartment—a long, narrow affair—in Greenwich Village, where it was rumored that one of the two people fighting in a corner was a famous poet, had felt like an exotic visit to another country.

Fauna pushed her hair back over her ear in what had become a very familiar gesture over the last week or so. Her hair was shorter than when she'd left, shorter than she'd had it since childhood.

"So you're not going to spill the beans, Dad? You're just going to go all silent and dreamy on us." She turned to Doug. "Remember, Douglas, I'm not one to kiss and tell."

Uncas smiled at her imitation of him. He'd grown used to her cheekiness. "So I was able to teach you something," he said.

"Yeah, Dad. I never kiss and tell, and neither will my kids. That's what I'm hoping to hand down to them."

He knew that Fauna was being sarcastic, but didn't lose hope that she would convey that sense of privacy to her children. One could do worse than that as one's life lesson.

"Why the big premium on silence, Dad?"

He wanted to make clear, without sounding as though he'd been falsely judged, that it wasn't simply silence he advocated but a respect for one's own privacy: not so much "mind your own business," but instead the gentler "I'm minding my own business." He wouldn't be lulled into Kirk-like logorrhea by discussing his long-ago nights in New York. He could teach best by demonstration, even where the stories were innocent by today's standards, and chose to smile at his daughter to convey his intention. There was strength in silence, character in forbearance.

THREE

"Hannah, please come here. I need you."

Uncas was in the kitchen picking up his lunch tray (Hannah had prepared roast beef sandwiches), when he heard Margaret's disembodied voice come over the baby monitor Fauna had encouraged him to buy once they had found out that Margaret was going to be confined to bed.

Hannah immediately shut the water off in the sink and turned to go; she gave a start when she saw Uncas. "Oh, my God, I'm sorry, Mr. Metcalfe. I didn't know you were in here. I— I— I sometimes have trouble hearing." She had her hand on her chest in a gesture that looked to calm her pounding heart. "You scared me."

Uncas held his laugh. He knew he had frightened her, but somehow it was comical at the same time. "I thought you heard me come in."

"No. No, I didn't. The water's too loud. Well, I'd better go see what Mrs. Metcalfe wants."

Uncas stepped aside as Hannah lowered her head and moved purposefully to the door, which she swung into the kitchen and propped open, in anticipation, Uncas guessed, of bringing Margaret's breakfast tray down. This girl was a planner. She was blessed with the kind of logic that of his three children, only Fauna had inherited. And with Fauna it came and went. Hannah had been with the Metcalfes for two weeks and daily Uncas saw evidence of a mind he admired, reminiscent of her great-grandfather's. As preoccupied as she often seemed to be with the moods and impetuosity of adolescence—the occasional furtive phone call, the muttering to herself as though she were involved in an ongoing internal argument, and the afternoons of pure elation when she looked like Uncas could remember feeling when he thought he'd discovered a new species—there was a dogged, forceful mind at work that governed her actions. It had been a stroke of genius to hire her. Uncas was unreasonably proud of his quick assessment. She had impressed him the first time he had seen her at Bagel Falls; on his second visit he impulsively asked if she wanted a part-time job. He and Margaret and Fauna had talked about hiring someone once it became clear that Margaret was going to be laid up for several weeks. Fauna was set to ask at the hospital, to find a woman with a little nursing experience. Instead, while he was at the bagel shop with Fauna and Nik, Uncas had without delibera-tion asked Hannah. She reminded him of her great-grandfather, whom Uncas would see on visits to the farm-works factory office his father shared with old Mr. Stephenson and his son; because of the early death of Uncas's grandfather, they were an out-of-sync trio—but they had worked well together. Uncas's father had had a wonder-ful urbanity about him—he was never without a bow tie and silver-handled walking stick. He was a gregarious sort, the perfect foil to the Stephensons, the men who, like Hannah, put ideas to work. Old Mr. Stephenson had given Uncas, almost on the sly, two things right from his desk. A brass-hinged wooden ruler that folded in on itself, and later a paperweight that encased a four-leaf clover. No words of advice had accompanied these presents, no explanation, but Uncas knew they weren't given impetuously. He treasured them. Maybe he had offered Hannah the job because she, without fanfare, except a look at Fauna to see if it was okay, had given Nik a bagel.

Originally, Margaret's leg was put in a calf-to-thigh cast. Then the day after Thanksgiving her foot began to get taut and red—it felt as if it would explode to the touch, she'd said, and Margaret was by no means a complainer. Uncas had wasted no time in getting her back to the hospital, where the doctors, bless them, had immediately diagnosed that she had a clot in her leg. They put her on an IV to thin her blood and replaced the cast with a removable splint, so they could keep an eye on the swelling. Now, she was back home, mostly bedridden, mending slowly, on yet another blood thinner, Coumadin ("a fancy name for rat poison," Margaret said, while she made nibbling noises and scrunched up her mouth so that only her front two teeth were showing). It would be at least a month before she could move about freely.

He was relieved at how smoothly the days at home were passing, despite the hordes of visitors. It was a busy time at work—he'd signed on to teach a graduate seminar in biogeography, and he was advising doctoral students. His presence was required twice a week, but with end-of-term meetings and final undergraduate projects, he ended up going over more often. He had worried that once Fauna and her family moved into the Fletcher house, he'd be unable to cope, unable to get any work done, unable to tend to his wife's needs, needs that Fauna seemed to anticipate the same way she took care of her three young children. But Hannah had stepped into the rhythm of their days. Today Uncas would eat lunch with his wife up in their bedroom.

"Knock, knock," he said, standing at the entryway of the bedroom, tray in hand, watching as his wife hobbled from the bathroom with

Hannah beside her saying, almost chanting, "Weight on the left leg, weight on the left."

"Oh, hello," Margaret said. "Is this the cafeteria today?"

"Did I get the directions wrong? I thought the sign said, 'More seating this way.'"

Margaret laughed.

"Hannah," she said, "I always tell people, even if they, like you, haven't asked, why my husband and I get along. Two people who on the face of it couldn't be more different: my husband makes me laugh, which is more important than anything else in a long marriage. See that you too choose your husband wisely."

Hannah didn't say anything while she helped Margaret bring her legs up onto the bed. She rested the right one on the pillow at the foot of the bed. Hannah adjusted the pillows behind Margaret's head, all, Uncas noticed, without making eye contact. Something had ruffled her; typically, she was an implacable nurse.

"Oh," Margaret said. "That feels wonderful. You have the right touch with those pillows, Hannah. Now that I have the two of you here—let's talk about the Christmas party."

Uncas was puzzled. They'd had a long conversation about canceling their annual Christmas party. It was a Metcalfe tradition, begun by his great-grandparents and continued for decades. It had once been a tremendous affair, thrown ostensibly for children and attended by the staff at Laconia Farm Works and friends and neighbors. In addition, the Metcalfe children were each allowed to invite a friend. After his parents had died, Uncas had been reluctant to splurge on the annual affair—the factory had closed, after all—but Margaret would hear none of it. It wasn't going to fade away on her watch. The party evolved into a black-tie dinner dance, with a turkey and a large roast ham, along with hors d'oeuvres, cocktail sandwiches, and chocolate truffles. For the past five years or so about a hundred guests looked forward to the yearly event.

"Mags, I thought we'd decided not to throw it this year."

"Unk, the party practically throws itself. Hannah"—she looked over at the door, where Hannah was hovering—"can be my legs."

Uncas thought about cutting the conversation short. She'd made up her mind and that would be that. The party was going to happen, he knew.

"The invitations can go out the day after tomorrow. Libby told me about a place that will run them off on short notice. I'm sure Hannah has a friend who can help with the legwork," Margaret continued. She stopped, abruptly, it seemed to Uncas, but he hadn't been entirely focused. He turned to listen to Hannah.

"I can ask a friend I know." She lowered her eyes.

"Wonderful," Margaret said. "If she's half as helpful as you, we'll be able to double the size of the invitation list. Why don't you go get a pad of paper and a sandwich for yourself when you bring up my lunch tray? You can eat with us."

Hannah returned and took down Margaret's instructions—from the cleaning of the silver to the brand of paper napkins to the wording of the invitation—as though she were preparing for a difficult exam. She said she'd eat lunch later. She asked questions throughout: Where should they set up the bar? Where would they get the Christmas tree? Where were people supposed to park? What if it snowed? What if they ran out of ice? What if? What if? Margaret, Uncas could see, had had to stifle a laugh or two. He looked at his wife with wonder, as she detailed the plans, and he realized there was no better cure for her than throwing a party. They didn't discuss how she would get around once they got her down the stairs; planning the party was one thing, but participating in it was another. He'd have to talk to Charley Bisgrove.

* * *

The following day, running late for an appointment at Wright, Uncas heard the front doorbell ring. As he struggled to unlock the old-fashioned dead bolt, built into the mechanism of the door handle, he wondered who it would be. Probably a deliveryman or someone asking directions; someone who didn't know enough to read the note they had posted below the knocker—PLEASE USE SIDE DOOR—and then follow the arrow. Anyone who knew the house used the entrance next to the garage. Since Margaret had been laid up, people had been coming and going—friends calling on the patient, nurses performing weekly blood tests, bearers of casseroles, florists, well-wishers, Fauna and the kids. For the most part they buoyed Margaret's spirits; they made Uncas want to tear out his dressing room floor so he would have access to the back set of stairs and could escape to his office or to Wright. Yesterday a red truck had been parked so close to his Jeep he'd had to climb in via the passenger side and inch out. His home was no longer his castle, if it ever had been.

When at last he wrenched the front door open, there, standing on the step, gazing off into the scrub pine that sat on the side of the stairs, was the girl from in front of the bagel shop. What she was doing here he couldn't imagine. He was embarrassed that it had taken a good three minutes to turn the lock. She must think he was a hermit.

"Hi. Is . . ." She stared at him for a moment. "Oh, hi. I've met you. You're the guy who knows Betty."

Uncas looked at her; that was it—she was Betty Delafield's step-daughter. "Yes," he said. The "guy," he thought; this was the language of his children. He nodded, then remembered her name. "That's right. Uncas Metcalfe. And you're Alexandra. May I help you?" Maybe something had happened. "Is Betty okay?" Uncas asked.

She looked surprised. "She's fine." Her eyes darted to either side of Uncas. "I'm here for— Hannah called, and said, and asked me . . ."

"Sorry, Mr. Metcalfe. I should have told Alex to use the side door." Hannah had come up behind Uncas.

Where the hell was Margaret? he found himself thinking, before he remembered.

"Alex is who can help with the party. Mrs. Metcalfe wanted to meet her."

Despite his irritation, Uncas wondered what Margaret would make of this girl. He remembered the firm handshake, which Margaret also would admire, and he guessed she would be amused by the hair, but wouldn't think it was very becoming. No doubt he'd hear all about it tonight.

"Of course. Why don't you take her up? I'm off to Wright for the afternoon if you should need me. And Hannah, lock that, would you?" He motioned to the front door. As he walked through the kitchen, he took out his billfold and added to the growing list on the index card that sat opposite his credit cards and driver's license. "Oil front door lock," he wrote, and then drew a line through "Pay parking ticket," which he had done, finally, yesterday. He tucked his billfold back into his breast pocket. He was the handyman of his castle—that much was true.

Two days later Uncas watched Alexandra as they sat in Uncas's car outside of Joe Stephenson's house, waiting for Hannah.

"Hannah tells me you're an old pro at these parties."

Alexandra looked at him directly, which was startling. Then he remembered her outside the bagel shop that day—the brief moment when their eyes had met. Her large dark eyes didn't seem to fit with the bleached-blond crew cut. The ferocity was there for about two seconds, then disappeared, to be replaced by the distractedness of their first meeting. As though, Uncas thought, she had caught herself.

"I guess so. My mother used to give lots of parties. I had to help her when I was growing up."

"And where did you grow up?" Uncas was amused. This girl was hardly grown-up.

"New York City."

"New York, my. Are you finding enough to amuse yourself here in Sparta?"

"It's different from New York, but I like it."

He remembered his own first visits to New York. They'd take the sleeper car and arrive in time for a breakfast at Horn and Hardart, an automat where he and his brothers would be given change and free choice, while their father drank a cup of coffee. It was such fun, so unlike the oatmeal they had been served at home. He remembered longing for a hat—a fedora—to match the one his brothers had, and finally one day his father took him to a hatter on Madison Avenue. The man had laughed and put one on that was far too big. His father had laughed too, when his youngest son had swung around and run into the mirror. But Uncas had walked out with a light brown fedora to wear on special occasions. That night they had eaten at one of his father's clubs and then seen a play, probably a musical, but Uncas couldn't remember which one; he did remember waiting for it to be over so he could put his hat back on. He studied Alexandra, in her combat boots and down parka, practical but not snappy, nothing like what his mother, or his sister, would have worn even in Sparta, never mind New York—where they would have donned cashmere coats and fur-trimmed hats.

Alexandra stared out the windshield, with an occasional glance out the side, though she didn't seem particularly uncomfortable with him. The dark roots of her hair were coming through, making the blond part look like a slightly askew wig.

There was a knock on the window, and Alexandra started. Hannah opened the back door and climbed in. "Sorry. My mom was trying to explain some French Christmas dessert to me. She thought we might want to make it for the party. I think she's more excited about it than Mrs. Metcalfe."

Uncas smiled at Hannah. "Bright-eyed and bushy-tailed this morning?"

"You sound like my dad."

Alexandra turned and said hello, with, it seemed to Uncas, a certain shyness, or maybe she just didn't know Hannah that well.

The plans for the party, which was the following Wednesday, were coming along. Uncas would drop Hannah and Alexandra off at the shopping center just outside town, and while he was collecting the papers for his seminar, the girls would pick up some of the things required. Fauna and Janey, who was sick with an earache, were keeping Margaret company at the house.

They rode in silence to the West Side Plaza, which was just past the former plant site of Laconia Farm Works, Uncas's family's business, and also, he remembered, Hannah's family's business. The building deterioration had begun while Uncas's father was still alive. The city had purchased the property with the idea of attracting one of the large chain stores to set up house—everyone knew the land was gold—but they'd had difficulty selling it "as is," and the city council didn't want to spend the money to tear the old factory build-ings down. Uncas had gleaned enough about business to know this was pigheaded and counterproductive—a political vote so as to seem thrifty; in reality, sitting on the lot was robbing the city of needed rev-enue. Finally a fire did most of the work—the blaze was so tremen-dous that he and his children saw it from more than five miles away. They had been on their way back from Poplar Creek on a Sunday night in the early spring—stubborn patches of snow had made the sprawling lawn look like some ill-conceived abstract painting—when they noticed something glowing in the distance. They had settled on a spectacular sunset as the explanation (which was pure nonsense and off by at least forty-five degrees—it rankled him still when he re-membered how long it took to realize this was impossible), and only when they saw the detour signs did it dawn on Uncas that it was a fire. He wondered why it hadn't happened sooner—the place had been empty for years. There were no signs to indicate that it had once been Laconia Farm Works, the business had been absorbed and the factory abandoned by an out-of-state concern years ago before his fa-ther retired, but friends of his father's had commiserated with him, and there were letters to the newspaper reminiscing about the fac-tory. Hannah had told Uncas that she was thinking of doing an inde-pendent study next year. She wanted to write a brief history of the business for her father. Uncas said he'd be glad to help in any way— it was the kind of scholarship he enjoyed. He was tempted to suggest she use him as an adviser, but it wasn't his area and it wouldn't have made sense anyhow—she was a student at Mott.

"Did you see the old factory burn, Mr. Metcalfe?" Hannah asked.

The girl was a mind reader. "Oh, yes," he said, "I was coming back from the lake with my children. Strangely, it took a while to piece together, but as soon as I realized it was a fire, I somehow knew it was the factory. Though that wasn't so surprising—it was one of the few old buildings left in town." Most of the others had been knocked down to make room for businesses like the new Laconia Bank. A mass of concrete and unpaned glass. Uncas had picked up his father, knowing he'd want to see for himself. They had driven as close as they dared.

When Uncas and the children had finally arrived home an hour or so after they were expected, Margaret's initial fear that something had happened to them had already turned to fury. She'd called his father's and had found out where they were from his live-in maid. Her wrath was coldness, a chill that took hours, sometimes days, to thaw. She'd refused to accompany them back to watch the fire.

"I drove as close as I dared," Uncas said, "and we watched it burn. We finally left at about eight or nine—the children were riveted and begged not to leave. As I recall, it burned most of the night."

"My parents drove me and my younger sister down," Hannah said. "My brothers weren't born yet. There was all this noise, and it was so hot. But it was cool too."

Alexandra laughed. "Cool *and* hot?"

Hannah pushed her shoulder. "It was."

Until Hannah said her father had been there, Uncas hadn't recalled seeing Joe Stephenson, but suddenly the memory was vivid. Uncas remembered stepping out of the car to shake hands. While they'd been thrown together frequently as children, they'd never been particularly close, but Joe was the only person who might have understood what the burning meant to Uncas. Joe too had elected not to follow in his father's footsteps, and instead of running the factory, he sold insurance. He carried Uncas's policies, and occasionally they played poker together, but Joe wasn't a regular at the monthly games. Neither of them had said a word as they stood and watched the fire dart out of windows and take down beams, but Uncas had never felt, before or since, so certain of what another person was feeling. Despite the sadness that he sensed from his father, relief was what Uncas felt. Relief that there was no longer the possibility of following in his father's, grandfather's, and great-grandfather's footsteps. Though realistically that option had long since been unavailable, he realized that the factory no longer taunted him on his way to the university. The remarkable thing was that he only recognized it as relief now. He had never tried to name the feeling before. What he *had* remembered from that night was Margaret's clenched jaw and his father suddenly seeming terribly old.

"Mr. Metcalfe?"

Uncas glanced in the rearview mirror and then back at the road. "Yes, Hannah?"

"If we're going to the West Side Plaza, you just drove by it."

Uncas frowned. He disliked his recent absentmindedness.

"Oh, dear," he said, "I guess you'll have to get out and walk. You won't mind that, will you?" He looked for her reaction in the mirror.

Hannah's mouth dropped open and she looked almost hurt. When she saw him slow and put on the blinker to double back she smiled. It was gratifying to see her get the joke; Alexandra, on the other hand, never even reacted. She seemed as ready to walk as to tolerate his humor, so composed was she. He would hate to play poker against her.

Uncas parked the car in front of the Fletcher house, behind his wife's station wagon. Fauna and Doug were using her car while theirs was in the shop—the long trip from Illinois had practically done it in. Only this morning, Uncas had parked across the street in front of the Stephensons' while he and Alexandra waited for Hannah. Everything had gone smoothly after he'd dropped them off at the plaza; he'd remembered to pick them up upon his return from Wright. Margaret seemed pleased with their initial purchases; she was beginning to relax, as though she were a professor who realized he could trust his graduate-student section leaders. Uncas braced himself for a moment before going into Fauna and Doug's house; it had been a long day, hurried at the university; his mailbox was littered with memoranda about when grades were due and holiday parties and performances. Margaret had encouraged him to have dinner at Fauna's. He was reluctant to leave his wife alone and had suggested that Hannah and Alexandra stay with her until he returned, just in case something happened. Margaret had scoffed at having "babysitters," and conceded only when he said that otherwise he wouldn't go.

Fauna was outlined in light as she stood in the doorway waiting for him to make his way up the short walk and steps. He wiped his feet on the welcome mat and cast a glance to his left, where there were several empty packing boxes among the porch chairs—not a sight Joe Stephenson would be relishing from his own trim house. The boxes were temporary; once settled, Fauna and Doug would be good neighbors, keeping the property neat and the house in good repair. Doug was handy and for the most part practical, despite having left the place empty for several months. As Uncas stepped through the front door, he recalled another time he'd been inside. Delores Fletcher, Doug's mother, had invited them to dinner after Fauna and Doug had announced their engagement. It had been the five of them, and they had spent a good amount of the evening looking at Delores's wedding album, as though she hadn't been bitterly divorced from Doug's philandering father, Ray. Margaret, who was masterful at handling such awkward situations, had played along—

asking about the bridesmaids' dresses and the ceremony. She had even tried to match Delores drink for drink, out of sheer politeness. Fauna, sensing the delicacy of the situation, was on her best behavior, nodding cheerfully at the photographs. Uncas had mercifully been spared most of them when Doug, who had looked as though he were about to cry, asked him down to the cellar to seek his advice about some foundation work. Uncas had returned upstairs to see Delores slam the album shut, look Margaret in the eye, and say, "Fuck Ray!" And Margaret had said, "Well, Delores, I'd have to agree with you there." What a relief it had been to leave that night.

"Hi, Dad. Janey and Tommy are so eager to show you their rooms they've forgone their television hour. Better get up there."

Uncas made his way upstairs. It was probably small-minded of him to want his wife to get better so she could handle requests like looking at her grandchildren's bedrooms. The two older children came out of separate rooms into the hallway. Each was in pajamas and, judging by the look of their slicked-back hair, fresh from a bath. Models of good behavior. Janey ran toward Uncas.

"Poppy!"

Tommy echoed her. "Poppy!"

Uncas stopped at the nearest door and watched as his eldest grandson walked across the room. He stopped near his desk and turned around, as though he were a docent in a historical house, but a docent who had forgotten his lines. "My room," Tommy said, and spread his arms.

"Show him the train," Janey said.

Tommy looked at his sister for a moment and walked toward a chest under the windowsill. He knelt down and lifted up the lid, resting it on his head.

Uncas surveyed the room. It was small—an upstairs sitting room, not really meant as a bedroom. It had a kind of parlor feel to it. Uncas felt a pang for his daughter, having to live this way. The five of them, with the sixth on the way, living in a house made for a retired couple. There were bunk beds along the near wall—he supposed Nik would move in once the baby was born. There were milk crates filled with toys, and a bookshelf with a few books resting on their sides. Fauna was still young. Her resourcefulness and her pride would ensure that she made the best of things. Three children, Uncas thought, and she'd barely broken stride.

"Hi, Mr., uh, Uncas. Nice to see you." Doug extended his hand, and Uncas clasped it in a brief handshake.

"Daddy!" Tommy ran to his father.

"Hi, sweetie pie."

Uncas stiffened when he felt Janey take his hand and then tried to loosen up as she pulled him toward her room. He would like to be able to relax, to enjoy being alone with his young granddaughter, but he had little idea how to behave with her.

"Oh, what a nice room."

Janey sat on her bed and picked up a doll. "You and Granny gave this to me for my birthday." Her bed was half-covered with stuffed animals. It was a metal bed; one that Uncas had painted off-white years ago for one of his own children's rooms. It needed a fresh coat. "Granny cried today."

Uncas felt his insides seize up for a moment, but he didn't know what to say. He wanted more information, but he could hardly quiz such a little girl; he wasn't good at probing adults, much less four-year-olds. He was considerably surprised that Margaret had cried in front of her granddaughter. She hadn't said a thing about it when he'd gone in to say he was off to dinner.

"Sorry to interrupt, but, Dad, would you like to read them a story?"

Fauna too had probably been there when Margaret had cried.

"Dad?"

"Yes?"

"Story. Read. Aloud. Sorry to interrupt space travel."

Uncas followed Fauna back to Tommy's room. Janey trailed behind. He stopped at the door and she squeezed between him and the doorframe. Doug was seated in the armchair, with Tommy perched on one of the arms; Janey climbed into her father's lap.

Doug offered the book to Uncas. "I get to do this every night, Uncas."

"Dad was an old pro in his time," Fauna said.

"No. Keep reading, Daddy," Tommy said. "Keep reading."

"Yes. Why don't you keep going, Doug. I can be called out of retirement another day." Uncas ducked his head and turned to go out the door and downstairs. He had an adolescent urge to call Margaret and asked her why she had cried. More likely he'd never learn the reason; it would be too awkward to bring up, and there was the added indelicacy of having learned it from Janey. And he was quite certain Margaret would never mention it; she wasn't one to chart her emotions.

"Dad, sorry, you're not off duty yet. I promised Nik you'd say good night."

Uncas slowed and stopped. He couldn't remember his own parents ever setting foot in the upstairs of his house, much less admiring their grandchildren's bedrooms. He and Margaret would have called the children down to say good night; but this, he had to keep reminding himself, was, as Fauna would say, a new generation.

"Of course." He put his head into Nik's room. His youngest grandchild was standing in his crib, clutching the rail.

* * *

Uncas sat in the living room slowly sipping his nonalcoholic beer. Through the window he could see out to the porch and packing boxes and across to Joe Stephenson's window, which was festooned with lit-up Christmas lights. Insurance and botany—Joe and he had certainly chosen different paths from the one their fathers had taken. Both had opted for independence, freedom from a nine-to-five schedule. But in Sparta neither job bestowed the stature their fathers had enjoyed. That was a sacrifice that had little troubled Uncas. Nor, probably, Joe.

"Need another beer, Uncas?"

Uncas looked up, startled to see his son-in-law standing in front of him, with an apron on.

"Yes. Yes. That would be nice. Nonalcoholic."

"Coming right up."

Doug returned with a bottle and a beer stein. Uncas reached for the bottle, and waved off the glass. He preferred the old-fashioned glass, which he'd helped himself to in the kitchen earlier. It was less clunky and, because it wouldn't hold the contents of an entire bottle, he drank more slowly.

"We frosted this for you specially."

"No need to dirty another glass."

Doug looked at the stein, and then at the stairs. "One more glass is nothing, but okay. Dinner will be soon. I don't know what's taking Fauna so long. How's Mrs. M.?"

"Mending nicely. It'll take more than used textbooks to keep her down."

Doug gave an appreciative laugh. He stood there for a moment, his hands on his hips, with the empty bottle and stein each jutting out. Uncas sat back in his chair, trying to remember if he had ever worn an apron, and thought it very unlikely.

"Let's eat. I'm starved," Fauna said. "Are we ready? Everything ready, honey?"

Uncas looked over as Fauna came down the stairs. When she said "honey," she sounded as though she were making fun of someone, as though she were disdainful of endearments and people who used them. This was her sense of humor.

"Ready and waiting," Doug said. "Uncas, we'll eat in the kitchen if that's okay. We've been using the dining room as a kind of catchall for things we're not sure where they're going to go."

"'Catchall.' Now there's a word I haven't heard in a long time."

Doug laughed. "It was my mother's name for my room."

The kitchen was small, considerably smaller than his own, and Uncas wondered again how they would manage. He was pleased to note that Doug had already built two benches with backs, almost like pews, that met at a corner of the kitchen. They were still rough, but Uncas could see that with a coat of paint and some cushions they were going to look as though they'd always been there. A large round table sat in front of the benches; chairs, including a high chair, completed the circle. It was a fine use of limited space; he was impressed.

He sat next to the high chair. Fauna sat on one bench, Doug on the other. All the food was on a lazy Susan, which Doug turned. He stopped it so the chicken was in front of Uncas, who speared off a breast, and spooned some sauce over it. He took some rice, and moved the lazy Susan back for some more sauce, then moved on to the peas, which were laced with grilled onions.

"So how was Mom when you left?"

"Oh, fine. Not best pleased at being babysat, but otherwise cheerful."

As they sat and ate, chewing their food almost in a kind of rhythm, Uncas remembered Margaret's crying. He wondered if Fauna would bring it up, and half-hoped she would. It wasn't like Margaret; she was stoic. She had been watching the news when Uncas left, and had asked him to take the newspaper downstairs. The crossword puzzle had been half done, in his wife's distinctive hand. There was nothing to indicate that she'd been upset.

"I think," Uncas said, "it galls her to pay Hannah to do 'nothing.' But when I suggested she and Alexandra could tend to some party plans, your mother said they needed a break."

"It's Alex, Dad."

Uncas looked at Fauna. "Pardon me?"

"It's Alex. It's not Alexandra. Hannah's friend prefers Alex."

"Does she?"

"Yes, Dad. I asked her."

"I would swear that Hannah introduced her as Alexandra. It's so much prettier, don't you think?"

"Nevertheless, she prefers Alex."

"In any case, your mother felt they needed a break. Presumably, they're watching television. Is there another beer?" Uncas held up his glass.

Doug got up and got one from the refrigerator. "How are the plans for the party coming along?" he asked.

"I think splendidly, and Little Charley thinks Margaret may be up and about by then."

"*Little* Charley? I wonder if that nickname bugs him, or it's just me. He towers over his father. What does that other guy say, the one with the bad haircut? Do either of them know what went wrong? Do they get why it swelled up? Could it happen again?" Fauna asked.

"I'm not sure. I'm in charge of her medication and a nurse comes in once a week to check her blood."

"I know what's being done. I'm there every day. I just wondered— Oh, never mind. I'm sure they're trying to figure it out. I just feel like you need to rattle cages. When Nik was sick last year, I swear if I hadn't, if one of us hadn't been there constantly, they would have drugged him every time he started to cry. And it was the crying that finally tipped them off to the lactose intolerance. But I guess it's different— I'm worried, that's all, and I feel like Mom's getting totally dispirited. What's she like when it's just the two of you?" Fauna looked at him.

Uncas watched Doug move his peas from one side of his plate to the other, and resisted telling him to stop playing with his food. What was she like? She was Margaret. Little had changed. "She's very optimistic, and she even allows as to how Little"—he paused— "as to how Charley is doing a good job, though she can't resist telling almost everyone that he cut his hair with play scissors when he was at Miss Margaret's." Uncas smiled.

"Yeah," Fauna said. "Cute."

"Does she ever consider running a nursery school again?" Doug asked.

Uncas saw Fauna's face, which said, *Are you bereft of all reason?* Exactly what he himself was thinking. But his own expression, which reflected back to him from the kitchen window, hadn't changed.

"Well, she's nearing sixty, Doug. Don't tell her I told you that, but I don't think she'd have the energy. She'll have to make do with her grandchildren." They're almost a nursery school unto themselves, he thought.

"Were either of you around this afternoon, when Janey—" Uncas started to say.

"I haven't seen Mrs. M. for about a week, I'm embarrassed to say. There's so much to do here, and with looking for work—"

"When Janey what?" Fauna cut Doug off.

"When I was just upstairs in her room, she—"

Fauna looked impatient. "Not just now, Dad. You were saying she did something this afternoon."

"Well, yes. She told me she saw your mother cry."

"Oh, that," Fauna said, shrugging. "I wouldn't worry about it. It's probably just the first time she's seen Mom cry."

"What do you mean?"

"What I said. It's probably the first time Janey's seen Mom cry. And it made a big impression. It can be a little scary to see an adult cry."

"But, Fauna, you make it sound as though your mother crying is an everyday occurrence."

"It *is* an everyday occurrence. It's like the littlest thing sets her off." Fauna looked up. "She says she doesn't want to worry you with it. That you have enough on your mind."

"Why doesn't she take one of her painkillers?"

"She's not in that kind of pain. She's scared. She keeps asking me if I think she's going to lose the leg, and she's told me the story of her mother's death almost every day. Like she forgets from day to day that she's told it before."

Margaret's mother had died suddenly of an undiagnosed heart problem, while Margaret was on a year abroad, between school and college. It was a sad story, of course, but not one he had heard her mention for a long time.

＊　＊　＊

There was a light snow falling as Uncas drove home. A dusting gathered on his coat as he opened the garage door. He stopped when he
remembered that the rental chairs for the party were being temporarily stored there. He pulled the door back down and parked the
car beside the house. He hung up his coat in the hall that ran alongside the garage, and paused before going inside the house proper to
look through the window of the door, into the darkened sunroom,
which was lit only by the pixels of the television set. He could see the
backs of the girls' heads as they sat close on the sofa. Uncas could see
that on the television was some kind of situation comedy, with its
brightly lit, antiseptic kitchen and its neatly groomed inhabitants.
Shows like this infuriated his eldest daughter, Marcia. "Just for once,"
he could imagine her saying, "I'd like to see a mother scream, really
scream, at her kids." A commercial came on and the television was
muted. The door to the sunroom was ajar, and as he stood in the
hall, he could hear Alexandra's low, serious voice. She was describ-
ing waking up one night to see an orange light cast on the wall in
front of her. She kept hearing glass break; as she walked to her window, her mother came into her room and shrieked when she saw
Alexandra next to it. She yelled at her to come away from the window
just as Alexandra saw a column of fire tip out of the building across
their courtyard. "The sounds were scary," she said to Hannah, "but
the fire and the colors were beautiful. The flames were so quick and
unpredictable. I've never seen anything like it." She was right,
thought Uncas. Exactly right. *Hot and cool.*

When he opened the door to the sunroom, Hannah jumped up.
She looked at him with her hand on her chest. A now familiar gesture, only this time he couldn't help smiling.

"I'm always scaring you, aren't I, Hannah?"

"It's you," she said.

Alexandra craned her neck around and nodded her head at Uncas.

"What's on the box?" he said.

"The box?" Hannah said. Then she looked at the television. "Oh, some show."

Alexandra stood up and turned it off.

"Mrs. Metcalfe went to sleep around eight o'clock," Hannah said. "I kept checking, and then I went up there, and her book— Well, I put a bookmark where it was opened to and took off her glasses, and shut off the light. But I left the one in the bathroom on so you could find your way. Which you probably already know." Hannah looked suddenly embarrassed.

"Guess we should be going," Alexandra said.

"I'll give you a lift home. I think Mrs. Metcalfe can be left that long."

"You will?" Hannah said. "That would be great."

"But—" Alexandra said.

"Oh, that's right," Hannah said. "Thanks, Mr. Metcalfe. But we'll walk. It's not that far. I mean, neither of us lives that far from here. I was going to sleep, to have a sleepover, at Alex's house tonight anyhow. I mean, we thought it might be late, so it seemed better than waking up two families."

"Nonsense. It's snowing. I feel responsible." He turned to go. He didn't care how sleepy a town Sparta seemed, he wasn't going to let two young girls walk home at ten at night.

As he backed down the driveway and turned left onto the street, he realized that it would be the third time that day that he'd made the trip to Fauna and the Stephensons' street.

"Mr. Metcalfe, we're going to Alex's house. She's living with Betty's mom, old Mrs. Delafield. On Stanton Ave."

Uncas turned to her in puzzlement, and then said, "You don't want to take the scenic route?" He had never been so distracted in his life, and he couldn't blame it on Margaret's leg. "There's a spot where I used to take my children each year on the day of the first snow. It overlooks the library and the pond. I thought we'd swing by there and then I'll drop you. I'll bet Alexandra has never seen it, even if you have."

"Okay. You mean the sledding hill. Okay."

"Yes. That's it."

He'd rather have them think he was up to something fanciful than that he was, as Margaret would say, touched in his upper story.

Uncas drove back through the center of town. The fresh snow and tired Christmas decorations that stretched from light pole to light pole made Sparta look trapped in time, a textbook photo of a bygone era. Even the virtually new buildings—fifteen-year-old urban-renewal projects, structures whose ribbon-cutting ceremonies he had attended— looked outdated and unnecessary. Uncas felt enormously tired and yet dreaded his bed. He wanted life to be as it was before Margaret's accident, when he didn't have to go to Fauna's alone and then shepherd "babysitters" home. The girls hadn't seemed to mind taking a detour to see the sledding hill (Hannah had said it was "cool" to see the snow falling on the pond), but otherwise they had both been silent during the drive to Lizzie Delafield's house, coming to life only to say good night at the bottom of her driveway, and Hannah thanked him again for giving her the following morning off. Uncas had watched them walk up to the house, with Alexandra leading the way. Hannah had turned and waved just before she stepped inside. He dreaded these nights when his wife was lost to the world of sleeping pills.

He climbed the stairs slowly, trying to remember what it was that

Fauna had said to him just as he left—was it something that she wanted to borrow? Hannah also mentioned that a man had called saying that Uncas's bicycle was in the playground at Lincoln School. Uncas would retrieve it tomorrow before the snow buried it. He was trying to keep both thoughts in his head so that he could write them down once he got to his dressing room. Even if he couldn't remember what it was that Fauna wanted, he'd at least be able to ask her.

"Out gallivanting, Mr. Metcalfe?"

"No one you know," he replied to his wife with a familiar joke. He continued to walk to his dressing room, until he remembered to be surprised—she was supposed to be asleep, the light was supposed to be off. He stopped and turned. "But Hannah said you were asleep."

"Oh, Unk. I got so sick of her peeking in the door that I just pretended I was so she'd stop. Is there such a thing as being too conscientious? I don't think I've ever met someone who's more responsible. Maybe you."

He studied her face for a moment, to see if there was evidence of sadness. He wondered if she cried when she was alone, or in front of Hannah; he couldn't remember the last time he'd seen her in tears.

"Well, I'd much rather that than come home to evidence of a wild party or to find they'd been completely remiss in their duties, with you in a crumpled heap on the floor." He said this with a smile and she smiled back at him. The Margaret he knew had a sense of humor about her physical ailments. He stood silent for a moment and then walked to the doorway opposite the bed. He found himself wondering if the book on her night table was a book of poems, and again he had to tell himself not to be ridiculous.

"Oh, I don't know. A wild party sounds good about now. At first I thought it would be lovely to lounge around in bed, preferably eating bonbons, but it's plain boring."

Uncas hung up his jacket and trousers and folded his sweater; he put everything else in his laundry basket, and then stepped on his scale—one hundred ninety, five pounds more than when he'd graduated from college; he wrote it down on the chart next to the mirror. He removed his pajamas from the hook on the back of the door and dressed for bed. He added "Bicycle at Lincoln" and "Fauna?" to his list of things to do; he crossed off "deposit checks" and "prescription."

"Mags, don't you think the party next week is going to be plenty wild for you?"

His wife didn't answer—she was asleep.

FOUR

Uncas awoke with a feeling of well-being. He had fallen asleep as soon as he climbed into bed and felt as though he hadn't moved all night. Margaret's eyes were closed when he slid out from beneath the covers and still had not opened by the time he had knotted his bathrobe and headed out their bedroom door. As he walked down the stairs he could see through the small windows that outlined the front hall door the snow tumbling down—eight inches of big flakes must have fallen overnight. They'd pick up a foot if it continued through the morning. At times like this he considered taking up tobogganing again. The half-mile down the Poplar Creek driveway, with its curves and short steep hills, seemed as though it had been designed for sledding. Really, he couldn't have asked for better conditions to chop down the Christmas tree. The snow would make it easy to drag through the woods. He and Alexandra would drive out after her shift at the bagel shop, after he had retrieved his bicycle from Lincoln School; he wondered if he'd even be able to find it under all the snow. Hannah would stay with Margaret. He could feel the tingle in his bones at the prospect of going out to the lake. Iroquois wouldn't be frozen yet, but the untrammeled new snow and the bareness of the trees along the shore would give the place a spareness that appealed to him. As much as he loved the late spring and early summer, when Poplar Creek was at its peak botanically, the snow relieved him of the pressure to observe plants and answered the side of him that preferred an uncluttered life.

The phone rang once and then stopped. Uncas hoped that the caller had hung up, rather than awaken Margaret. He heard a voice, Fauna's, in the kitchen; she must have answered. Then he remembered what it was she had said she wanted to borrow—him. He had promised last night to help Doug adjust their boiler early this morning. He didn't know why they'd bought a secondhand boiler to begin with; it was the kind of thing that you spent more money fixing than you'd originally saved. Fauna caught sight of him, and he could see her face fall in surprise and then wrinkle in hurt.

"Dad, I was just coming up to get you. I can't believe you're not even dressed. Doug's waiting."

"I forgot. If you could fix me some herbal tea and toast and yogurt with some of that granola cereal, I'll go up and change." He started to turn and then remembered the phone. "Who called?"

"Mrs. Brewster, practically salivating to tell you she'd spotted your bicycle out at the Lincoln School playground. I'll bet she's been up for hours, waiting by the phone, wanting to make sure she told you first."

"That was thoughtful of her. Apparently someone called last night and told Hannah the same thing."

"I hate to tell you this, but you should skip breakfast. Doug has to leave in half an hour. Maybe you should call him and tell him you can't make it."

Uncas sighed. "There's no other time?"

"Dad, it's freezing there; after all that noise after dinner, the boiler finally conked out around midnight. Doug needs your help. I almost called you in the middle of the night and brought the kids over to sleep."

"Is he sure this isn't a job for Mr. Wildner?"

Fauna's face clouded. "Why'd you say you'd help out if you didn't want to? I gave you a chance to say no." Fauna lowered her voice when she heard one of her children yell, "Mommy."

"Dad, you don't seem to get it, so I'll be blunt. We're strapped for cash until Doug gets steady work, which is where he's going in half an hour for an interview. He thinks it'll just be a minor adjustment, and that it'll save money and time if he does the work."

"Why don't you call Henry Wildner and you can have him send the bill to me." He didn't like to give his children money casually, but he couldn't have his grandchildren freeze.

"Jesus, Dad. Can't you see? Doug doesn't want more of your money. It's bad enough that we borrowed to make the move and bad enough that we had to spend two weeks here while Doug readied the house and found a decent secondhand boiler. We can't take any more."

Uncas couldn't understand what got Fauna so mad so quickly, or what made her—he supposed he was old-fashioned—take the Lord's name in vain. It wasn't how he and Margaret had raised her. He thought he saw tears in her eyes, but he didn't want to stare.

She swallowed. When she spoke her voice changed. "Dad, we're so grateful you let us stay and that Mom has loaned us her car, but I can't ask Doug to accept anything more. He'd rather us all freeze."

We, Uncas couldn't help thinking, *we all freeze.* He turned as he felt his own eyes dampen. "Why don't you call and tell him I'll be right over. I'll just change."

He hadn't supposed things were so bad. On his way up the stairs he adjusted a picture that was askew—a drawing of Margaret when she was a child. It was next to a similar one of him, done by his mother. They must have borrowed money from Margaret for the move; it was the first he'd heard of it. He pulled on his dungarees, a long-sleeved union shirt, and a sweater that was unraveling at the elbows. He was tugging on his thick wool socks, when he heard Margaret yawn.

"Unk, is that you?"

"Who else, Mrs. Metcalfe?"

"Oh, I seem to be seeing a lot of Hannah recently. How about a lift to the john?"

Uncas knew he should ask Fauna, so he wouldn't be any later for Doug. *That* had been their agreement last night. She'd come over and help her mother out of bed and tend to her breakfast, while Uncas was giving Doug a hand. But Margaret was his wife, and the least he could do was help her to the john first thing in the morning. They were halfway there when Fauna came in.

"Jesus Christ, Dad. What does it take?"

Uncas could feel Margaret stiffen. "Please do not use that language," his wife said. Uncas looked over his shoulder to see Fauna stalk out of the room. He turned back to find Margaret looking at him. "What was all that about?" she said.

"I promised Doug I'd help him with their boiler this morning, and I forgot, and it seems he has a job interview for work."

"Oh, Unk, you didn't? The house must be cold as ice. You should go." But they both knew that he couldn't: they were midway; returning her to bed would take as long as continuing.

"This won't take but a minute. Then Fauna can come up for the return trip."

"This damn leg. I've been nothing but trouble for everyone."

"Now, Mags, you can't blame yourself."

They both fell silent as Margaret hobbled across the floor, resting her weight on her good leg and on Uncas's arm.

There was no sign of Fauna when Uncas went downstairs. The keys to Margaret's car were on the floor just inside the door, as though they had been pushed through the mail slot. The car was parked in front of the garage. He saw several footprints—big and little—mixed in with tire marks on the driveway. Fauna must be daft. It looked as though she had walked home and had made the children walk too. Maybe they were taking a walk around the block. He got into his own car, when he remembered Margaret, stranded in the bathroom. Thank heavens, he thought, I remembered. He'd figure out a way to fix the boiler himself. There would be no money involved. Why did Fauna get so angry about these things?

Uncas hurried upstairs. This wasn't the way the day was supposed to go.

"The prodigal husband returns." Margaret was lying in bed, breathing deeply. He heard the chilliness in her voice. How had she gotten back to bed?

"Mags, your daughter has chosen this moment to go for a walk."

"Go take care of the boiler. I expect Hannah will be here shortly and she can tend to me."

Uncas nodded and left. He walked slowly down the stairs. He was hungry and wanted his breakfast, but knew it would have to wait. He followed a plow for two blocks and then turned onto Sycamore Street, where Fauna and the Stephensons all lived. Doug was standing on the porch shaking his head. He hurried down the stairs when he saw Uncas.

"Uncas, I hate to ask you this, but I've got forty-five minutes to get to an interview that's an hour away, and . . ." He paused. "I forgot that Fauna was taking Mrs. M.'s car. Can I take yours? Would you mind?"

May I take yours, Uncas thought, but caught himself. Yes, he would mind. He fingered the keys in the ignition. He could walk home; getting out to Poplar Creek to get the Christmas tree would be a different matter: Margaret's car would never make it down the hill. Though he could probably pick up his bicycle in it. He looked at Doug. "Yes. Why don't you take it? How's the boiler?"

"I got Joe Stephenson to come over and take a look. He jiggled the thermostat, and the tank jumped back to life. Made me embarrassed that it was so easy. I didn't touch the thermostat yesterday because the guy said it was new. But Joe says different basements can make a difference and a move can too. He says the needle's off-kilter. Simple as that. That guy knows a lot. Sorry I didn't wait for you."

"That's all right." Uncas got out of the car and Doug got in.

As Doug was about to pull out, he waved to Uncas, who nodded back. Doug rolled down the window and Uncas leaned his ear toward him. Doug was testing his patience. He'd be late, if he didn't leave immediately.

"Thanks, Uncas. I really appreciate this. I'd give you a ride but it's the wrong direction and I'll probably be late as it is."

"That's all right."

"I'll bring it by on my way home. Probably before lunch."

"That'll be fine."

Uncas set out for his own house. He was dressed for driving, not for walking in a snowstorm. He had put on a jacket, but no gloves or hat or scarf. *Hut, two three four.* There was the old rhythm. The army would get him home. He climbed over a bank formed by the snowplow and walked in the empty street, where the going was easier. As he turned off Sycamore, he could see Fauna and the children walking toward him. They were strung out across the street, like some scene in a musical from his youth. Or a B movie Western, with a showdown on main street where the good guy and bad guy walk slowly toward each other.

"Howdy, pardner," he said.

"What?"

"Do you remember the old Westerns where they faced off in front of the saloon?"

"Sure, Dad. Who doesn't?" Fauna stared at him. Her jacket wasn't quite closed over her protruding stomach. "Why are you walking?" she asked. "Where's your car?"

"Your husband has the loan of it. He had no other way to get to his interview."

"He's not at the house?"

"He just drove off."

"Oh, right, we forgot how he'd get— Okay. Bye."

Uncas paused. "Goodbye," he said. The children looked cold. But the snow was abating and the sun was coming out. Uncas relaxed his shoulders. He made to head off and then stopped. "Listen, why don't you come out to Poplar Creek this afternoon? I think the sledding will be terrific. We're picking up a Christmas tree."

"Who's we?" Fauna asked.

"We is Alexandra, Hannah's friend, and myself."

"Oh, Alex, whom you insist on calling Alexandra. Sounds like fun, Dad, but maybe some other year."

"If you change your mind, we're going out at about one o'clock." He wanted to insist. He knew she was being stubborn, that she was mad at him, as she seemed to be at least half of the time. He could take her softer chidings and her cheekiness—he viewed them as her way of showing him affection—while her coldness stung. It seemed directly passed down from Margaret, and only served to make him want to duck and cover.

Uncas fixed himself breakfast at home. As he was eating it, he realized that there was still no sign of Hannah. It wasn't like her to be late, and then he remembered he'd given her the morning off. He boiled water for coffee and made some toast. Margaret never ate much early in the morning. He put these on a breakfast tray along with the *Gazette*. Her eyes were closed when he stepped through the doorway but her glasses were on; she must have drifted off.

"Oh, hello."

"Order for Mags Metcalfe. That'll be a dollar even."

"Highway robbery, but you can charge it to my husband's account."

He waited while she shimmied herself up in bed to eat.

"Where's Hannah?" she asked. "I'm surprised she hasn't at least called. I'm famished."

"She's not due till noon. I forgot to tell you, she looked tired last night so I gave her the morning off."

"How generous of you."

"Rather."

"Where are Fauna and the kids? Did you find them?"

Uncas sighed. "We had a showdown on Elm Street. Fauna and her posse making their way slowly from the south, while I strode in from the north. You would have been amused. Your daughter was not."

"Strode in? What happened to the Jeep?"

"Doug needed it to get to his interview."

"Honestly. What about my car? Where was that?"

"It was still here and Doug was in a hurry."

"How's the boiler?"

"Operating. There was a problem with the thermostat."

"But Unk, she's downstairs now, right? With the kids? Their house can't have heated up yet."

"Well, no. She left in a bit of a snit."

Margaret picked up the phone and dialed. "Hello. It's your mother. We were just worried that you weren't warm enough."

Uncas lingered near the door; he wanted to retrieve his bicycle. He wondered if he could leave Margaret by herself.

"Hold on a sec and I'll ask." Margaret covered the mouthpiece of the phone, more out of habit, Uncas supposed, than to hide something from Fauna. "She wants to know did Doug say when he'd be back?"

"Before lunch. He'll drop my car here."

"Did you hear that, Faun? Before lunch," Margaret said into the receiver. "No, no. Hannah will be here while your father plays Santa Claus and gets a Christmas tree, though I think we should just get an artificial one and be done with it. Why don't you and the kids go with him? With all the snow I should think it'd be fun. And you can come here for dinner."

Uncas could see Margaret begin to spin a plan for the day. She was feeling better, that much was evident. He wondered if Fauna would say no to her too. He watched as Margaret's expression changed from enthusiastic to concerned to cold, and had his answer.

"Okay," she said, "we'll see you when we see you."

Margaret hung up the phone. "She said to ask *you* why they aren't coming." She smiled at him expectantly.

He shrugged. "Say good night, Mrs. Calabash," he said. It was an old joke of theirs. They used the Jimmy Durante line as shorthand for the inexplicable acts of their children.

"Good night, Mrs. Calabash," Margaret replied halfheartedly. "That's too bad." She looked at Uncas and smiled. "But they'll have other chances. It's not as though they're leaving tomorrow anyhow."

Uncas didn't answer.

"Oh, Unk, while you were gone, Malc called about your bicycle. He thinks he saw it at the Lincoln School playground and wondered if you were 'making a statement.' Those were his direct words. He wouldn't elaborate, but he certainly sounded amused." She laughed. "I wonder what that means."

"Possibly that it's still visible under all the snow. I was worried this storm would bury it. Elsie Brewster called."

"Oh," Margaret said. "What did she want?"

"To report a sighting of my bicycle. My spies are everywhere. I had requested that she stay on the alert. I think you're too hard on the poor woman, Mags."

"The 'poor woman' doesn't know what to do with herself since her children left, and when young Floyd does come back to visit, she pesters him so that he always leaves early. She does drone on about it. He doesn't want to take over Floyd's shop because he's worried about his mother's interference. Not that that boy could ever fill his father's shoes. Imagine. The woman's never worked outside her home a day in her life."

Uncas smiled; he enjoyed baiting his wife. It was a game they played. "She hasn't had your opportunities. I thought she conducted herself quite nicely at the book sale."

Margaret snorted in derision. "Why don't you go get your bicycle, Unk? I'll be fine here for the time being." She picked up the *Gazette* and looked immediately engrossed in the front page. Their game was finished for the time being.

Uncas drove his wife's car over to Lincoln School, which his children had attended. The building no longer served as a primary school, but on the weekends an arts group used some of the empty classrooms; it was slated to be torn down in the spring. The land would be sold in lots and Uncas could already picture the houses that would be built—squat and unimaginative, but affordable. The inhabitants would shop out at the mall, no doubt. Several of the large windows had Christmasy construction-paper shapes taped to them: snowmen and evergreens and stars. One had a huge misshapen Santa Claus whose limbs varied wildly in size, as though each child had constructed a single body part oblivious to what the others were doing. The head was grapefruit-sized and one of the legs was the size of a fire hydrant. He pulled around the back of the building where the playground was. He remembered retrieving a tearful Fauna once, after she'd fallen from a seesaw because she was showing off, if you believed her classmate, or was knocked off intentionally, if you believed Fauna. She had bitten her lower lip severely and the teacher got worried when the bleeding and crying wouldn't stop, and had had the nurse call Margaret, who in turn, with Hank home sick from nursery school, had persuaded Uncas to pick her up. He sometimes wondered if every square inch of Sparta wasn't filled with memories waiting for him to happen by and awaken them. He looked around the base of the jungle gym and swing sets, but the ground was flat, nothing to suggest a bicycle. Then he saw it, the Raleigh he'd gotten secondhand over forty years ago in college, suspended from the main bar of the largest swing set. The pedals had four inches of snow on them; in fact the entire bike was outlined in snow. It had caught on the chain guard and settled on the fenders and crossbar. Even the spokes had snow balanced precariously on them. The child's seat, unused now for years, was filled with snow. Uncas walked closer and studied it, and wondered how it had been attached and how he would get it down. Someone had gone to a lot of trouble. Maybe Malc? Doubtful. He wouldn't have left it up there in a snowstorm.

A woman with a dog on a leash walked through the field toward Uncas. "A winter wonderland, isn't it?" she said.

Uncas looked at her. She had several scarves wrapped around her neck, and a couple on her head.

"I live over there," she said, pointing to a small, green house with white trim on the edge of the playground; Uncas knew it well: the former house of the Misses Henry, home for several decades to two teachers, one first-grade and one third-grade. They had fascinated his children and then had become objects of derision. Uncas remembered Marcia saying to Fauna when they were teenagers, "Don't ever count on sharing a house with *me*."

He realized the woman was speaking to him.

"I've been wondering if anyone was going to come and claim this. It seemed dangerous, but I guess that's not a problem on a swing set in winter. So I figured it would be all right for what, another six months?" She laughed. "Winter sure lasts a long time around here. At least it did last year. My first. How will you get it down?" Her dog pulled on its leash. "Hold on. Hold on. I'm talking to this nice man." She turned back to Uncas. "Wolfie gets a little excited by the snow. I bet the kids are happy; they love the snow." She pointed to a small hill in one corner of the playground. "They'll be all over that any minute." As they both looked a young child—

Uncas couldn't tell if it was a girl or boy—came up to the crest of the hill from the back dragging a sled, and then another child appeared, and then another. "What did I tell you? When they get bored there they'll come over here and hang on your bicycle. It's yours, right? I'd get it out of here before it falls on top of some kid and you're held responsible." The woman's arm shot out as the dog tugged again at his leash. "Gotta go. Nice to talk to you, Pops. Good luck with the bike!"

From below, he could see that plastic cord tightly wound around the piping held the bicycle in suspension. Without a ladder, it was going to be difficult to untie. Uncas pulled his wife's car snug up along the outside of the low chain-link fence that surrounded the playground. He stepped onto the car's front bumper, then onto the fender. He grasped one of the legs of the swing set's A-frame and tested his weight on the horizontal bar; it was solid. He pulled himself up and established his footing. He then took off one of his leather-palmed mittens and leaned over the top of the swing set, and dusted off the snow. He uncovered the rope that held the bike in place. The knots were taut and frozen; the ends of the cord had been melted to prevent fraying. There was no slack with which to work.

Who would do this? So elaborate and possibly amusing if it weren't so cold and snowy. It reminded Uncas of pranks from his college days at Wright. In Sparta it was different—there was standard petty vandalism; he remembered coming back from the lake at the end of one summer to find that the windows of the house had been graffitied with the most repellent words he could imagine. He remembered too relocating his college roommate's bed and dresser to the green, and he'd heard about cow tipping on local farms. But those were all impetuous; this was planned, it wasn't the work of a giddy schoolboy. He covered the nearest knot with his mitten and pressed down, trying to warm the rope up, but he could see he would need a knife and a ladder. He climbed down and tucked his hand into his armpit. The bicycle would keep. It wasn't going to come down easily. Even if a child were to hang on it, it wasn't going anywhere. The snow had stopped and he could feel the temperature dropping; there was no sign of the sun he'd felt earlier. Uncas drove past the Misses Henry house. He couldn't remember where Libby had said they had moved, someplace in the South, he thought, or maybe Canada. He brightened when he realized that Alexandra could help him. He looked in the rearview mirror and saw the woman who had talked to him earlier waving her arms. He slowed to stop, but instead fishtailed on the ice. He drove out of the spin and pumped the brakes. She was at his window when he stopped.

"Fancy driving, Pops." She leaned into the window, almost cozily, as though she were an old friend.

"It comes with practice," he said. "May I help you?"

"Sure can. You're not just going to leave that, are you? You're not just going to leave it hanging there? That's a playground, Pops. For kids. You should know that."

"No, no. I'll be back."

"You need help? I can call the fire department. You can use my phone."

Uncas cringed at the idea that the fire chief might be called to cut down his bicycle.

"That's not necessary. I'll be back in a few hours."

"No problem, Pops. I call them all the time when Wolfie chases cats up the tree. That tree there." She pointed to a large elm in the Misses Henry front yard. He wondered how it had escaped the Dutch elm disease that had taken so many fine trees in the area a decade back.

"I'm sure the cats are grateful, but it's really not necessary in this case."

"Well, you could at least say thank you, Pops." She turned sharply from the car window and smacked the back fender with her open palm, as she walked by it.

Uncas checked his rearview mirror to make sure she was safely away from the car. Thank you for what? he wondered.

Awaiting the return of his Jeep, Uncas brought the aluminum ladder, a broadax, a handsaw, and some plastic cord from the cellar to the garage. He then went back down to sharpen his father's old knife. His father had worn it under his suit jacket, which was highly incongruous given what a natty dresser he was, but he also liked that element of the unpredictable. True to form, the knife was of the highest quality. Uncas imagined that Hank would pass it on to his own son. He put a few drops of oil on the blade and whorled it along the whetstone. Grateful that his father had taught him how to take care of tools, Uncas tested the blade, scrapping it against the grain of his thumbprint. He fed his belt through the loop of the sheath and snapped the leather band around the handle.

As he started up the stairs to the kitchen, he found he had regained the lightness of feeling with which he had awoken. Despite his annoyance at having the Raleigh subjected to snow and cold, he was looking forward to his projects for the day: cutting the bicycle and the Christmas tree down.

"Hi, Mr. Metcalfe," Hannah said. She was at the top of the stairs. "You won't scare me today." She sounded positively bubbly.

He smiled back at her. "I'll have to plan more carefully," he said. "I was hoping to sneak up on you. You haven't seen Doug, have you?"

"Here I am," Doug answered as he walked through the kitchen door. Hannah jumped. Hannah's start made both Uncas and her laugh. Doug came around the corner, with a smile on his face.

"Hi, Hannah," he said. "Here's the car, Uncas. I mean the keys. It's parked next to the garage. Thanks for helping me out. I really appreciate it."

Uncas was about to ask how the interview went, but decided not to. He'd know soon enough if Doug had gotten the job. No need to talk about it if things had gone badly.

"Why don't you take Margaret's car back with you?"

"I thought I'd run up and check on Mrs. M. first, if that's okay. Is she asleep?"

"I don't know. I haven't been up since breakfast," Uncas said. "I'm off. Tell her, will you?"

"You don't want lunch, Mr. Metcalfe?" Hannah asked.

"Well," Uncas said. He was unable to decide. He'd be late for Alexandra if he ate.

"I know what. I'll call Alex. She can make you a bagel sandwich at work," Hannah said.

"A bagel? Trying to fatten me up?" Uncas asked.

"Don't you have to eat?"

"If I must, I must. Tell her I'm leaving now and I'll be waiting outside. And I'd like a cup of Sanka too." He wondered if he should specify low-fat milk.

But Hannah was already dialing the phone.

As a rule, Uncas disliked eating in the car. It struck him as uncivilized, but he knew it would save time. He didn't want to be dragging the tree through the woods as they lost daylight. Just past Bagel Falls, at a red light, he unwrapped his sandwich and took a bite. Chunks of tuna salad fell on his thigh and he was glad that he was wearing dungarees. Alexandra ate potato chips and licked her fingers off after every handful. Through a straw, she sipped from a drink still in its brown paper bag, as though it were alcoholic and had to be covered up.

"That happens with tuna," she said. "It's not the best filling for bagels, but it's the best-tasting sandwich they sell there. Besides the roast beef, which we're not allowed to take for free."

Uncas stopped himself from saying that he would have gladly paid. He didn't want to sound ungrateful.

"It's very tasty," he said.

"That's good. I get sick of it."

On his way to Lincoln School he drove back past his house; his wife's station wagon was where he'd left it. As he drove a little farther, he saw Fauna and her children, and slowed down; if they'd planned it, he wouldn't have run into them as often as he had today.

Alexandra rolled down her window. As Fauna approached the car, she told Janey and Tommy to stay on the sidewalk. She was carrying Nik.

"Hi, Alex," she said. "Hi, Dad."

"Off to visit your mother?" Uncas asked.

"No," Fauna said, "I thought I'd trot the kids over to your house and back in the freezing weather for exercise. It's just the thing for a pregnant woman and young children. Yes, we're on our way to visit Mom. She sounded lonely." She turned to leave. "I've got to get them inside. See you."

"Bye," Alexandra said.

Uncas gave a wave of his hand, but Fauna was already on the sidewalk urging the children to walk quickly.

*   *   *

As they pulled into the Lincoln School playground, Uncas pointed out his bicycle, which was swaying gently in the wind. He had to laugh.

"Thar she blows," he said. "Now, if you would reach into the glove compartment in front of you and take out the camera, I'd like to record this."

Alexandra had opened her door to get a closer look, and was half out of the Jeep. She was staring at the bicycle. "It's beautiful," she said. "It's so strange looking." She ducked her head back in and got the camera and handed it to Uncas, almost in a daze. "Wow. I wish Hannah could see this. It's even on the spokes. She'd love it."

It *was* beautiful, Uncas realized. And also amusing in its way. He got closer to the swing set and focused on his Raleigh. He took a few pictures and put the camera in his jacket pocket, and returned to the Jeep for the ladder. Alexandra stared at the bicycle without saying a word. He balanced the ladder between the two knots.

"I'll climb up, but I'm not sure if I've got proper purchase here, so I'll ask you to steady this from the bottom." Uncas indicated where Alexandra should place her feet. He climbed up until his waist was even with the swing-set bar and set about slicing through the braided plastic cord. He used the knife as a saw and the individual plastic strands gave way one by one to reveal the piping. Holding the bicycle so it wouldn't drop, he unwound the cord and tied one end around the crossbar of the bicycle and loosely knotted the other around the bar of the swing set; he did the same at the other end once he'd sawn through the knot. He replaced the knife in its sheath.

"What's that?" Alexandra said.

"What's what?" Uncas looked across to the Misses Henry house, apprehensive of a visit from the woman with the dog.

"That. It fell off your bike."

Uncas steadied himself, craned his neck around the bicycle and saw her pointing to something on the ground, below the ladder; it looked like a piece of folded paper but he couldn't really tell. "Well, we can't worry about that now. I'm ready to lower this. I think I'll be able to lower it all the way down, using the cords as a sort of pulley, if you can be ready to catch it once the tires touch ground."

"Catch it?" Alexandra said.

"Steady it, so it doesn't fall."

Uncas lowered the bicycle slowly. As the Raleigh knocked against the ladder, the snow fell off in clumps. The rope was too short for it to reach the ground, so Uncas leaned over the pipe and stretched out his arms. The bicycle was heavier than he'd expected. His jacket was open and he could feel the cold of the metal pipe through his sweater and shirt. The knife handle dug into his hipbone and the sheath point into his thigh. Reaching around the ladder, Alexandra held on to the seat and handlebars and guided the bicycle to the ground. Uncas let go of the ropes, and lifted himself back up. He was sweating and felt an uncomfortable chill as he climbed down the ladder.

He swung back his leg as though he were going to climb onto his Raleigh and pedal through the snow; he expected at least a smile from Alexandra, but there was no reaction. She was busy picking up what was indeed a piece of paper that had fallen off his bicycle. He liked it that she knew enough not to leave trash on the ground; she had collected the ropes too. He held the handlebars toward her. "Why don't you take this, and I'll get the ladder," he said.

He led the way to the car and laid the ladder on the roof, securing it to the rack with bungee cords. They put the seats down in the back of the Jeep and with a little maneuvering managed to fit his bicycle in. The whole ordeal had been easier than he expected. He hoped getting the Christmas tree would prove as easy.

Uncas turned the heat and blowers on high. His union shirt was soaked with sweat and he was chilled. His Sanka from Bagel Falls was lukewarm, but it was something.

"Can I open this?" Alexandra asked. She held up the folded piece of paper that had fallen from the bicycle.

May I? "I don't know," Uncas said. "It's probably a flyer. Perhaps we should throw it away." Occasionally he'd find them tucked into the spokes or slipped between the brake cable and the cross bar.

"And not read it?" Alexandra said. "It says 'Prof. Metcalfe.' Aren't you curious?" He could hear her puzzlement; she didn't know he was kidding.

"Okay?" she asked, holding it up again.

"Go ahead." He stopped at a red light and watched her.

The paper was folded into quarters and started to tear diagonally from one of the corners as Alexandra pulled on it. She stopped and took off her gloves, and carefully unfolded it. A car behind Uncas honked. The light had changed. He turned left toward the lake road. Alexandra was silent.

"Let's see," he said, keeping his eyes on the road. "Let me guess. 'Summer fun. Two watermelons for the price of one. Sale ends tomorrow.'"

"No," she said.

He stopped at another light.

"I'm sorry, Mr. Metcalfe. It's really not nice." Alexandra handed him the sheet of paper.

He looked at the note: YOUR TOO TALL FOR YOUR OWN GOOD ASS-HOLE!! WHY DON'T YOU SAY SOMETHING? YOUR AN ASSHOLE—ASSHOLE!! FROM SOMEONE WHO KNOWS. He felt sick to his stomach. Who would use such language?

FIVE

They drove along in silence. To assuage the sting, Uncas concentrated on who would have written such a note. Was it Fauna's idea of a joke? No, not likely. His daughter might have made the grammatical errors, and as a teenager she'd certainly spewed vulgarities, but she wouldn't write down the word "asshole" on paper. He'd heard the expression used casually, and wondered if people ever stopped and thought about exactly what it was they were saying. The good old-fashioned "ass," as in "the man's an ass," had a Shakespearean lilt to it, and could be apt and cutting, but not crude.

"I'm sorry, Mr. Metcalfe. I was just really curious. I should have let you read it first. I shouldn't have opened it," Alexandra said.

"That's all right." Uncas felt sickened. The vitriol was sickening. Whence it sprang, he couldn't for the life of him imagine. The exclamation points he didn't think were Fauna's style either.

"Such a beautiful image, and such a mean note," Alexandra said.

It wasn't as though Uncas expected everyone to like him. His lab assistants for example—he need not be their friend to be their mentor; it didn't matter to him if they liked him. They learned by deed, not affection; this was the case even with the reluctant few he'd had to steer to other fields.

"But I guess whoever did it had no idea it would snow and that it would make the bike look so beautiful," Alexandra said.

From someone who knows. That was the part of the note that galled him, that made it impossible to shrug off. Probably it was just some nut, someone a little off. Uncas knew that. It was nonsense to think that the man (or woman, as Fauna would no doubt point out) who had written the note knew Uncas, in the way that his family or friends did, but the words themselves made Uncas uncomfortable. He'd have liked to forget about it here and now, but he couldn't seem to.

"Who do you think wrote it? Do you have any enemies?" Alexandra asked.

The note was demeaning. Uncas saw no reason to dignify it. He would neither discuss it, nor take it to heart. He was embarrassed that Alexandra had seen it. But he didn't want to appear shaken. It was merely one person's foul opinion. "Let's leave it, shall we? It deserves no more time and attention than a puppy fouling a rug," he said.

Still, he too wondered if he had an enemy. Whoever left the note had to be the same person who had laced his bicycle to the swing set. He considered the woman with the dog who now lived in the Misses Henry house. Certainly she hadn't been responsible for the bicycle; she seemed more likely to respond impulsively than in any premeditated fashion. She'd slapped his car, not stolen his bicycle; she'd yelled at him, not written an unsigned note. Whatever her imagined provocation, she wasn't likely to suffer in silence.

"C'mon, Mr. Metcalfe," Alexandra said. "Wouldn't you want to teach the puppy a lesson?"

Uncas was startled. He didn't think he had said anything aloud about the woman with the dog. "What puppy? That big pussycat of a dog she was walking? What could he have had to do with it?"

"No." Alexandra looked confused. "I'm talking about the— the metaphorical puppy. The one that went on the rug. Wouldn't you want to yell at him? I mean, we've cleaned up the 'mess,' now don't you want to teach him a lesson?" She paused. "Can you really just forget about it? There's no way I could."

"Forget about it?" Uncas was surprised by her question. He'd had no trouble forgetting all kinds of things lately, but it was highly unlikely that he'd forget this; he could see it pushed to the recesses of his memory the way his night away from Margaret had been. There was no such thing as forgive and forget; forgiven, maybe, but never forgotten.

"Did you ever hear the story about Tolstoy and his sister?" Alexandra asked.

It was strange that since Margaret's accident he'd been thinking about their time in Cambridge. There had been a note involved there too.

"Whom?" Uncas asked.

"Tolstoy." She paused. "He wrote *War and*—"

"Of course. I didn't hear his name."

"He had this game he played with his sister. Not like a regular game, but that's what my English teacher called it. Tolstoy would bet her that she couldn't sit in a corner and *not* think about a white horse." Alexandra paused again. "Try it," she said. "It's practically impossible."

"But that's different," Uncas said, "from not talking about it."

Alexandra winced. "Sorry."

"Whereas, in the army I was told I wasn't paid to think." He tried to sound less sharp; it was unreasonable to make her suffer for someone else's misdeed.

"My boss at Bagel Falls says that to me sometimes."

They drove along in silence, until Alexandra began again. "My dad, if he ever got a note like this, he'd be ranting and raving. We'd have to hear all about who he thought it was, and then he'd start calling them up and asking them, and I bet they wouldn't have any idea of what he was talking about, but still if he thought they did it, he wouldn't shut up about it until someone confessed, and then there would be World War Three while he yelled at whoever did it." Alexandra put her hand over her mouth. "Oops. I'm still talking about it. Aren't I?"

Uncas had never heard her say so much at once. She sounded more like one of his children talking to another in their clubby, intimate way than the taciturn young woman he'd been observing over the past week. She had relaxed; she sounded less stiff, less afraid of conversing with him. He liked her easy tone.

"Indeed you are. Maybe I should call your father. Perhaps he could get to the bottom of this little mystery." Though he could no more imagine ranting and raving about the note than he could conceive of writing it. Why would you want to call that much attention to yourself?

"He might not be so helpful. He's only visited here once, after he married Betty. But that wouldn't stop him from decreeing exactly what you should do."

"And what would he decree?"

Alexandra was silent. Uncas was amused. It was as though she were really trying to figure out how a man whom Uncas had never laid eyes on might solve this mystery, which seemed more of a sort to be solved by a child detective — *The Case of the Swinging Bicycle* — than the full-blown mysteries Margaret devoured. Uncas was surprised to find that they'd already passed the high school and the Catholic cemetery and were on the lake road. It was well plowed here, and the sun was out again. The pavement showed through in patches, while the banks were high with the crumbly snow that the plow had thrown up.

"Well," Alexandra said, "first he'd want to know what was your first thought? Like, when you first read the note, who did you think it was?"

Uncas paused. He was embarrassed to answer.

"My dad," Alexandra said, "would say that it's someone you know. I mean, when you think about it, who would spend so much time doing something so elaborate to mess with someone they don't even know? It's probably someone who wants your attention; I mean, that's pretty obvious. So it must be someone you know."

Watching Alexandra, whom he'd once thought of as poker-faced, warm to the mystery was like watching Margaret plan a party.

"But," Uncas said, "are we sure it's the same person?"

"What do you mean?"

"Is it the same person who left the note as hung the bicycle from the swing set?"

"Definitely. Otherwise, it's too much of a coincidence."

"And you seem to think it was a man," Uncas said.

"Sorry, Mr. Metcalfe, but no way did a woman do this. There are definitely women out there who are strong enough, but it just seems more like something a guy would do."

"My first thought was Fauna." He said it abruptly, immediately regretting that he'd implicated his own daughter. Once he heard it aloud, he knew it was absurd.

"Fauna?" Alexandra said. "Your daughter?"

No, Uncas thought, the other Fauna I know. He was embarrassed at how surprised she sounded.

"No way. I mean, aside from the fact that she's, she's one of those,

I don't know, 'let it all hang out' people"—Alexandra talked as though Fauna were an entirely different species of human being, separate and far older than herself, though in fact Fauna was twenty-two; no more than two or three years older than Alexandra. He supposed it was the fact of her having children that made her seem older—"I mean I don't know her as well as you do, I mean obviously, but she just doesn't seem like the type. It's too, too . . . complicated."

Uncas didn't say anything.

"You thought Fauna," she continued, "because she's on your mind because she's pissed at you." Alexandra drew her gloved hand up to her mouth. "Sorry, annoyed. It's none of my business, except that it seemed like she was annoyed or something when we saw her on the street. I should probably just shut up."

"That's all right. Fauna did seem annoyed with me"—what else is new? he thought. And that was surely why he had thought of her—"and you're right, I don't think the note was hers." It was a relief to dismiss the idea firmly.

The lake appeared to his left. It was the first open view on the road from town and Uncas never failed to find it breathtaking. It was one of the narrowest parts of the eight-mile lake. On the opposite shore, you could see the evergreens that outlined farmland, and the red barns bright in the new snow. The water was slate-blue today, and the fresh snow covered the shale stones of the beach and met the choppy water right at the edge of the lake. He'd heard his colleagues complain about the dreariness of the winter landscape, and he had a strong desire to present them with the scene as empirical evidence from the opposing camp.

As Alexandra began to quiz him about possible enemies, Uncas adjusted the blower in the Jeep. She went through different categories, and he didn't resist. He found himself relaxing into the conversation. She tried to jog his memory like an experienced police detective: Your kids' friends? Your students? Any of them local? ("Loco?" Uncas had asked and her serious expression had given way to a half-smile.) Lab assistants? People you work with? Your friends? Their kids?

"People can be incredibly sensitive," she said. "You never know who you might have offended by some stupid comment that you didn't even mean."

"Whom," Uncas said.

"What?"

"Whom you might have offended."

"Okay," Alex said. "Keep anyone you think could have done it in your mind, and I'll read the note out loud line by line. 'Your too tall for your own good.' What does this tell us?" she asked, as though she were breaking a coded message. "I mean, aside from the fact that he doesn't know contractions." She laughed, then said, "It's probably some short guy. Otherwise who cares about how tall you are? And as for 'Why don't you say something?' Well, I mean, anyone really could say that. Hate to be blunt, Mr. Metcalfe, but it's true."

He'd heard it many times from Margaret, and from Fauna for that matter. *Lord Reticent Taciturn.* He laughed. He couldn't say what struck him as funny, but there was something about the absurdity of the whole situation—the bicycle, the note, and even the tuna salad on a bagel—that made him laugh. "I've heard that before, Alexandra."

"Look, Mr. Metcalfe, would you call me Alex? Please. I really hate my real name. Only my dad calls me Alexandra."

Fauna had been right, after all. While "Alex" seemed unnecessarily masculine, it hardly mattered what he thought in such a case. It was a small request, and he would do his best to honor it. "Of course," he said. "Alex."

She continued through the note, making it seem less terrible. "It's the 'From someone who knows' that's intriguing. I think this guy wants you to know that he actually knows you. He wants to let you know that he's not just some guy who's seen you ride by. Hannah told me you ride your bike a lot, so lots of people must have seen you. But this guy sounds pissed."

She smoothed the note out on her leg. "It's kind of a little strange," she said. "I wrote an anonymous note once." She looked over at Uncas. "It wasn't mean like this. But I definitely wanted the person I wrote it to to respond."

"Did you steal his bicycle?" Uncas asked.

"Nah," Alex said. "It was to someone I had a wicked crush on."

A love note, Uncas thought.

"I didn't sign it," she continued, "but I was sure they would know it was from me. It was obvious. We were, like, friends. Really close friends. I mean, I thought for sure they'd at least recognize my hand-writing."

They? Surely it's he. But he held his tongue.

"Well, I wrote the note to this person, and it was all about how I was sick of pretending that we weren't attracted to each other." She paused. "And then I found out from another supposed friend that the person had no idea who it was from. And the thing is, I thought we liked each other but were just too shy to say so, and that the note would force them to at least acknowledge it. But it didn't turn out that way. So—and this is the reason I'm telling you this—afterward, after they never responded, I said some really mean things. God, I was so mean, even though I really liked this person. But I never told them face-to-face."

He listened patiently through the "theys" and "thems," resisting the urge to correct her.

"Why don't you say something?" Alex said.

They both laughed.

The truth was, he didn't know what to say. It didn't seem as if it were his business. He watched Alex smooth the note over her knee again. Maybe hers had also come to its recipient completely out of the blue. "Why didn't you tell him? Why did you leave him guessing?" Uncas asked.

She hesitated. "I don't know. I guess because I was too, oh, it's stupid. I was too embarrassed. Especially since supposedly they didn't even like me that way. We're not friends anymore. If we were, I might. Besides, that was in high school. I was a little immature."

She said this with an air of the incident having happened decades ago, instead of a few years. He knew she felt worldly wise. How that would change as she aged, he thought.

"I used to think that the absolutely worst thing in the world would be to have someone say they didn't like you that way after you'd just spilled your guts," she said. "Now, it feels like it might save you a lot of embarrassment. All the intrigue—do they like me or not—will only carry things so far. It's better to know."

Uncas knew the sentiment well. The lack of clarity could dog a person.

"I mean, let's take my parents. If they had just been honest when they first met, maybe my mom wouldn't have had affairs. Of course, my dad can be a total weirdo, but I just keep feeling either they should have split up earlier, or never gotten together to begin with."

"My, you sound positively old-fashioned," Uncas replied, trying to maintain lightness, and distance from a conversation about cheating spouses. "What happened to free love and women's lib?"

Alex laughed. "Now *you* sound old-fashioned. It's not even called 'women's lib' anymore, and 'free love' is from the Beatniks, I think. Get with it, man! It's the eighties."

"But they wouldn't have had you either," he said. "And who would have helped me get my bicycle down and who would help me chop down the spruce?" His glasses clouded, as he got a little misty-eyed. This happened to him sometimes; he teared up at the ends of movies or books. His children and wife teased him about it, but he took it in stride. There were worse things one could do than tear up at a poignant moment. Still, he hoped she wouldn't notice.

"Are you sure it's not *whom*, Mr. Metcalfe?"

"Quite."

"Seriously, Mr. Metcalfe. I mean, divorce just sucks. Sorry, but I can't think of a better word. I mean, I don't blame my dad for leaving. And it's hard to blame my mom either. She was just super unhappy and lonely. I just wish it weren't so hard for people to stay together." She paused. "And I wish no one ever"—her voice faltered—"cheated on anyone. It makes it worse. And you never get away with it. It's always just *there*." She cleared her throat. "Take your wife—" She stopped abruptly, and started again in a slower voice. "It's so stupid. I know she wouldn't. I know I sound like a weirdo. And I know it's none of my business. Obviously, you don't have to answer me. I just don't have anyone to ask about this. None of my friends are here, and the ones at Mott are friends of the person, well—let's just say I can't talk to them. And I can't talk to my friends in New York because my stepmother told me I basically can't use the phone for more than a few minutes at a time, even if they call me."

Uncas couldn't explain it, but Alex seemed very small and very large at the same moment. She sounded as though she were about to cry *and* about to burst. As if she were coursing back and forth between humiliation and anger. He knew the cocktail mix well.

She seemed miserable. As she talked about her parents and about her mother's affairs, he had the feeling she was talking too about something closer at hand.

They passed the dilapidated little grocery store where his children had bought candy when they were younger; the roof was caving in now—it got worse and worse with each passing winter. A growing number of abandoned eighteen-wheelers, now snow covered, had found their way into the fields behind and around the little store and the owner's house. Eyesores and a nuisance, and probably dangerous, and all opposite the Poplar Creek driveway. He had wanted to buy the land, or at least help dispose of the growing junkyard, but the owner had declined both offers. Happily, the half-mile driveway down to the lake meant that at least the truck carcasses weren't visible from Poplar Creek.

Alex broke the silence again as though she were thinking aloud. "I mean, suppose all that had happened was one kiss. You knew the person you love kissed someone else—they told you, they confessed!— and you still loved the person but you couldn't get it out of your mind. Even if you knew that the person they kissed didn't mean anything to them." As they rode down the driveway, she stopped talking.

"I know," Uncas heard himself say, "what you mean."

He felt Alex's eyes on him.

"You do?" she said.

He did know what she meant. Driving down the hill, surrounded by all that Alex had said, Uncas replayed the betrayal in his own marriage. And he could show her, by example, that it wasn't the end of the world. He wasn't one to dispense advice per se, but she had asked and his own story could perhaps serve the purpose. He pulled into the parking space next to the house and turned off the car. Uncas stared out the windshield as he talked. "During our third year of marriage, my wife and I moved to Cambridge, Massachusetts."

Uncas had been awarded a fellowship at the botanical museum there. Margaret was thrilled. Her father still lived in Boston, as did friends from her youth and cousins she hadn't seen since her move. As happy as she'd been in Sparta, she was delighted at the thought of living near Boston. She had found a third-floor walk-up. He remembered her quoting the notice, *Unk, it's a tree-lined street.* He'd replied, *Every street's tree-lined in Sparta. If that's a feature, let's stay here.* Why would he willingly uproot himself? But his mentor at Wright had encouraged him to accept the honor. So he and Margaret had rented out their house in Sparta, and had set up on Billings Street, near the Square. A friend of Margaret had kept the nursery school going; the move felt to both of them like a honeymoon. Seeing Margaret with her old friends, Uncas fell in love all over again.

Margaret kept house and arranged their social life, and tutored occasionally; they lived off his fellowship. She was thrifty but knew how to entertain, and she stretched their budget to include lots of simple dinner parties. Mostly they saw friends from Margaret's childhood and schooldays, but there was one fellow from the museum she'd taken to. Uncas could remember the year almost fondly. She would select concerts she thought they'd enjoy; Uncas took her to the movies. On Friday nights they might meet one of her friends and they'd all split a pitcher of beer. Their Sunday roast beef lunches at Margaret's family's house were a respite from the budget-conscious meals of the rest of the week. They ate in the high-ceilinged, drafty dining room; Margaret, as the eldest daughter, sat at the foot of the table opposite her father, responding to his stories as though she were hearing them for the first time.

Uncas's fellowship project had been exciting: organizing and editing a monograph on the tiger lily. He'd selected it because it grew so plentifully at Poplar Creek. He liked its common name and its looks and the fact that it grew wild. This wasn't a fussy flower. He threw himself into his work. The series was unusual—they wanted literary references and engravings and lithographs, as well as the more scientific, botanical aspects in which he was better versed; but the whole gamut appealed to his scholarly instincts. (In recent years at Wright there had been a push to teach "across the curriculum"; he had pointed out more than once that this wasn't exactly a new idea and that professors who needed to be directed to include other disciplines might fare better teaching in the vocational or technical schools.)

Uncas had felt a part of something and independent all at once. He liked the other fellows and his professor at the museum; he enjoyed his solo evening runs along the river. As the spring came he had been forced to cut back on the gaiety. He wasn't used to the synthesizing of such a vast amount of material, and he'd found the work in other disciplines slower going than he liked. He'd also done far more socializing than he was used to.

"I'd been awarded a yearlong fellowship. My wife was pleased; she had spent her girlhood in Boston, hence we saw a great deal of her two closest friends, Myrna and Peg, whom she'd known her entire life and who still lived in the area. These two and Peg's husband, Ted, and Philip, also a friend from Mrs. Metcalfe's childhood, were our most constant guests. Then, as now, my wife loved to entertain. I worked hard, and also played a little—my wife's dinner parties tended to last into the wee hours." Philip had been seeing Myrna, but both Margaret and Peg said he would never marry her. According to their gossip, he was in love with someone else. "Before I knew it, and let this be a lesson to you, spring had arrived and my deadline loomed. I knew I had to turn my head toward work and began to put in late hours."

He found he could get more done at the museum if he brought lunch and dinner and worked through. Margaret and he had what his father used to refer to as "active discussions" about this, but they'd worked them out. Margaret stayed home, reading, writing letters to friends in Sparta; occasionally she'd go out with friends. She'd been ill for a month or two; she had been pregnant and had miscarried. Uncas had urged her to quit her job tutoring. For Uncas life fell into a rhythm closer to the one he had been used to at Sparta. He would bring Margaret tea and toast in bed on mornings when she felt queasy. They would talk for a little while and then Uncas would be out the door by eight twenty and at the museum at eight thirty. He'd leave with a light heart; sorry to be away so long, yet pulling the monograph together was exhilarating.

There were two others who were also working late: Fred Manning, who was cataloguing the museum's resources, and the sole female fellow, Helen Mynes, an accomplished illustrator, who would sketch for hours. At the end of their long days, the three of them— they called themselves "the Night Bloomers"—would often stop at Ferrelli's for a drink before heading off to their respective apartments. Uncas had never worked so closely with a woman before; he admired Helen's drive and scholarship. She wasn't quick to laugh and curious like Margaret, but she wasn't wary like some of the other fellows. She had an appreciation for the fact of what she was doing as opposed to where it was going to land her. He couldn't understand why Margaret didn't welcome her, though she had never complained when he'd come back from drinks a few times later than planned; she seemed to encourage his friendship with Helen, without wanting to embrace it herself.

"One night—" He interrupted himself. As he sifted through the story in his head he found he was less willing to go into detail. It felt too intimate to describe his wife in bed. Uncas had returned to their apartment rather later than usual. As was her habit even then, Margaret had fallen asleep with a book on her chest. She hadn't yet started wearing glasses, but the light was on and the book was a new store-bought hardback, which was unusual—she always borrowed from the library. He had picked the book up gently, so as not to disturb her, and marked her place with one of the flaps. He had noted that it was new, but didn't consider whence it came. On another night, he picked up the book and a note fell out, which Uncas had read without thinking. He could practically still feel the texture of the stiff card, and see the line drawn through the last name printed along the top. M, the card said, THANKS FOR LISTENING, AS ALWAYS. YOURS EVER, PHILIP. Margaret had woken up and reached for his hand. Normally he'd have embraced her, but that night he leaned over and kissed her and said, "You need your rest." It was poetry, but not the old reliable ballads and sonnets, not even A *Shropshire Lad*. No, this was modern—the poet hadn't even capitalized his own name. Uncas had closed the book on the card and left both on her nightstand. It wasn't an interest of which he'd been aware.

About a month later, Margaret had organized a dinner party for their usual group; Uncas had thought to include the Night Bloomers. Margaret had said to bring Fred; she was eager to match him up with her friend Myrna; but not Helen. Like the new, hardback modern poetry book, this wasn't like Margaret. Their meals at home had a "come one, come all" feel to them; they were almost always potluck. Peg and Myrna would each bring at least one dish, and, of course, Philip could be counted on for a jug of wine. Helen wasn't a regular visitor to their apartment—she ran with an artier crowd—but as she was a third of the Night Bloomers it had seemed awkward not to invite her. And in the end, he had. As usual, the three of them had a drink after working a long day. He planned that he and Fred would drop her at her apartment and then walk on to his, but, when the time came to part—and maybe it was the influence of the alcohol—he felt it was unfair of Margaret and he extended the invitation to Helen as well.

Margaret greeted the three of them with a big smile and glasses of sangria—"if it isn't the Deadly Nightshades," she'd said, and everyone had laughed. Which might have been some sort of warning, he supposed. The theme that night had been Spanish food and Margaret had filled a Dutch oven with paella; Myrna had brought flan. It was strange, the details he remembered. Smoothly, Margaret had gotten a plate from the kitchen for Helen; it was unlikely that she ever realized that Fred had been expected and that she hadn't been.

"One evening," Uncas said to Alex, "we had a dinner party combining our two sets of friends. I invited two of my colleagues from the museum—Helen and Fred—to join our usual group. At about ten the party began to break up." Peg and her husband departed; then Fred had offered Myrna a ride home. Only Philip and Helen were left. "When Helen got up to leave, my wife insisted I call her a cab, but Helen declined, saying firmly she would walk." *I have no money for cabs*, she'd said. Uncas had expected Philip would offer to escort her.

But Philip was in the kitchen, mixing another batch of sangria. In retrospect, it wasn't so strange that Philip had seemed perfectly unbothered by Myrna's defection and had even given her a goodbye peck on the cheek and had shaken Fred's hand.

"I couldn't see Helen walking alone late at night, so I let my wife know I would accompany her." On the pretext of needing to take out the garbage, Uncas had followed Helen down the stairs. "I walked with her a few blocks, until she declared in no uncertain terms that she was safe. So I returned home."

Uncas tried to tell the next part as though he were merely bringing the story to an end, rather than articulating an evisceration. He ran his finger along the bottom ripples of the steering wheel.

"I found," he said, "my wife and Philip—I got back sooner than expected—and there they were, they were exchanging a kiss in the doorway of the kitchen."

He could hardly believe he'd said the words aloud.

The rest he relived in silence. He'd backed out and closed the door, and tiptoed back down the stairs. Minutes later he had returned, making as much noise as he could without making it seem as if that were what he was doing. He'd hung up his coat and hat, said a quick good night to Philip, who was putting on his coat, and left him with Margaret, and had gone into the bedroom and cried. He was ashamed of the tears that now fell down his cheeks. Any hope that Alex wouldn't notice was erased when he felt her hand on his shoulder; after some moments she withdrew it. As casual as he'd tried to make it sound, as unimportant as he'd come to feel the incident was, the heat and the anger felt fresh; the betrayal palpable.

He had heard the front door open and Philip say, "Farewell, goddess," and he hadn't known what to do. By the time Margaret came into the bedroom, he had composed himself. Margaret was surprised to see Uncas sitting on the edge of their bed still in his clothes. *Farewell, goddess.* The fatuous lout.

"You got home quickly," she'd said, in a cold voice that would become familiar over the years. "What happened to Miss Mynes? 'I've no money for a cab,'" Margaret had said, lowering and exaggerating her voice. "I told you not to invite her," she'd said. Then her voice had become more pleading. "I begged you, Unk."

He hadn't been able to say anything about Philip, or to him; he hadn't seen him since that night, and there was never a moment of confessional guilt from Margaret; it was as though it had been a harmless friendly embrace. But he'd seen it for what it was, and she, by never mentioning it, corroborated her betrayal. The picture of them standing in the doorway repelled him. Margaret had sat next to him in tears asking what it was that he saw in Helen. He'd gone back to the office that night without a word and slept at his desk. The next evening he returned home. He stopped going out for drinks with Fred and Helen. Within the month, he and Margaret had moved back to Sparta. He'd never said a word to his wife about Philip; nor she to him.

"So you see," Uncas said, breaking his own silence. "I do know what you mean."

Alex was silent for a moment, then spoke. "But he was her old friend, right? I mean," she said, "she must have told you it was a friendly kiss, right?"

Oh, yes, he wanted to say, this was a most friendly kiss. The friendliest kiss he could imagine. "It was a single kiss, just like your friend," Uncas said.

Uncas knew that several conversations with Philip had followed. For the next several months Margaret always had news of him, which she passed on in the same manner she told him about Peg or Myrna. The truth of the matter was that Uncas had felt that by walking out and spending the night at the museum he'd lost his right to any indignation. He'd been a coward. Even after they'd returned to Sparta he'd played the kiss over and over in his mind more times than he cared to remember, and then, gradually, with the birth of their children and his increasing duties at Wright, he hadn't.

"Mr. Metcalfe, you should talk to her," Alex said. "Ask her. Please. It's better to know."

Uncas suppressed an urge to say, "Say good night, Mrs. Calabash," which he knew would mean nothing to the girl. He got out of the Jeep and opened the back to get the broadax and the saw. "O Tannenbaum," is what he said instead, and led the way to the path that followed the glen.

Uncas and Alex hiked in almost complete silence as they made their way up the path to the grove of blue spruce. For the first time since his father had died, Uncas felt as though he wanted to cry, not just a few tears; it was as though a full-blown sob were building. But he didn't feel miserable—he felt relieved. But there was no chance that he would cry again in front of Alex. Much as he trusted her, he couldn't imagine, now, half an hour later, what had compelled him to talk about his night apart from Margaret with such abandon. He felt embarrassed to have said what he'd said and to have heard, almost in exchange, her confessions. But that wasn't how it went. She had spoken first, and he'd imagined he could reassure her. In the end, it was she who had reassured him. It was curiously as though Margaret's injury had weakened something in him also. He looked around at the snow-covered spruces and thought, not for the first time, that he might have fared better as a tree. No one expected trees to sort through the wreckage of suppressed history.

They tramped along; the sun and the exercise felt freeing after having sat in the car talking for a good forty minutes. Uncas could hear the "hut, two three fours" in his head. Alex knew nothing about trees, virtually nothing about the outdoors. She'd admired the color of the lake and had listened carefully when he'd told her about the geese, who came later in the season and kept a circle of water from freezing over by paddling in it constantly. She was outfitted in her favored footwear—her work boots. They couldn't be keeping out the cold, but she didn't complain. There was something physically substantial about this girl, and her more ethereal side—as when she'd been trans-fixed by the bicycle covered with snow—only seemed to add to her substantialness. As though she didn't care that the various parts of her didn't add up to a more typical person. Uncas himself was wearing felt-lined snow boots that were making his feet sweat. He could see that a few trees had fallen into the glen during the storm and would create temporary dams in the creek below come spring. One had got-ten wedged between the banks above the water, creating a bridge that was impassable because of the roots at one end. All projects for the spring. At the edge of a clearing he saw the perfect spruce.

Though the species wasn't indigenous to the area, a blue spruce, with its short, wide needles and pleasing shape, made an ideal Christmas tree and had become part of one of his and Margaret's fa-vorite jokes—that it was going to be a blue Christmas. It had thrown their children into a tizzy; Fauna had fully believed that the tree was going to be blue; even when he'd shown her the picture in the field guide, she doubted him. When she saw the tree for herself, she had announced that it was a silly name.

"No way that'll ever fit in the house," Alex said, when he pointed to the one he had in mind.

"Of course it will."

"I guess you would know."

The tree was ten feet high, but he knew from experience that he'd lose some at the bottom for the stump and that some of the branches would have to come off so the tree would set properly in the stand. It was a dwarf compared to those he used to chop down with his father; the ballroom in the house in which Uncas had grown up was propor-tioned for an eighteen-foot tree. Those had been grand Christmas

parties, but in later years they had also been shabby; as the house became more expensive to heat, his father had put up clear plastic tarps
to seal the French windows, and the room had seemed diminished.
Uncas's own house, several blocks away, was large but not grand.

After he sawed off a few branches at the base, and determined
which direction it should fall, Uncas hefted the ax in one hand and
then the other. "Why don't you take a whack?" he said. Alex looked
at him in surprise. "Why don't you go ahead and chop it down?"

Alex took the ax from him. "Okay."

With her first stroke the blade cut in. Uncas was impressed. On
her second swing the blade missed; instead she hit the trunk with the
shaft just below the blade, and Uncas could see the sting register in
her hands.

"It's like baseball or golf, keep your eye on your target and pretend you're going to follow through," Uncas said.

"I hate golf. That's my dad's obsession. Third swing," Alex said,
and the blade dug in again. She felled the tree in a relatively short
time. On its descent, it caught on a neighboring maple. Uncas
pulled on the tree butt and the spruce fell into the clearing. They
each took hold of branches at the base and dragged it down the path.

The ride home was in blessed silence. He left a shivering Alex in the
kitchen with Hannah, with orders to revive her with hot chocolate
laced with a dollop of medicinal cognac and to find a dry pair of
wool socks, while he went up to check on his wife. Margaret was
asleep when he went upstairs, but she had left the *Gazette* at the foot
of their bed. On the front page was a picture of his bicycle, looking
as though it were made from snow, suspended from the swing set.
Underneath the caption—RIDIN' HIGH—she had inked in HIYA

SWINGER, GOING MY WAY? She woke up as he was reading it and laughed till she cried when he described the woman with the dog (she knew exactly whom he meant; said she was known as a loon, but harmless) and how he and Alex had managed to free the bicycle. Uncas played the story for laughs and told his wife about the Dutch elm in the Misses Henry's yard too. They'd lost a beautiful one in their own backyard not too long ago. He didn't mention the note; he saw no reason to concern Margaret about another loon. And of course he made no mention of his conversation with Alex.

In their bedroom, objects from their Cambridge apartment were mixed with furniture and lamps and rugs accrued over the next thirty years. A bed inherited from Margaret's father was flanked with the old side tables. A flea market print of a purple iris next to one of his mother's watercolor seascapes. A mystery instead of poetry. How Uncas longed, as he studied his wife's sleeping form, to be swept up by her vulnerability into forgiveness, to feel helpless with compassion. In telling the story to Alex, he'd meant to be instructive, to show how insignificant the incident had been when weighed against decades of marriage. But it still gripped him. As she slept on her back, with her leg propped up, her steady breathing interrupted occasionally by a hesitant intake, he saw himself taking a few deliberate strides to her side of the bed, and then standing with his feet about eighteen inches apart, looking down at her. He would be steady when he struck her with his backhand, even as she lay there peacefully with an injured leg and a propensity to develop clots.

SIX

A browse at midnight through his photo album of Poplar Creek species had brought Uncas no comfort. He awoke the following morning feeling he hadn't slept at all but that lying in bed longer would just be marking time. He was surprised to see that Margaret was already awake, reading. Again he had to suppress the urge to verify the book's contents. He imagined discovering that it was the book of poetry Philip had given her years ago. He would tear it out of her hands and throw it across the room.

"Well, sleepy, I guess you're not as young as you used to be," Margaret said.

Uncas found he had no reply. There were mornings like this; mornings where he felt enveloped in blackness. He tried to contain it within himself until it passed. As much as he loved his wife, he couldn't bear to be in the same room with her. The idea that he'd imagined striking her sickened him. He found his idle fury despicable. He felt disquieted; he had betrayed her by talking to Alex. No matter what Alex had confided in him, no matter how much he felt she could be trusted, he shouldn't have said a word. And at the same time, he wanted to shake Margaret, to ask her why she'd kissed such a shabby specimen as Philip, to tell her that he knew and that he'd always known.

As he brushed his teeth and shaved, he tried to get hold of himself, to will himself into complacency, into a husband who would get breakfast for his temporarily crippled wife and then into a professor who would grade his final papers. Stop it, Metcalfe, he said to himself, you're being melodramatic. Nothing's changed in the past month. Margaret's herself and so are you. He could hear Alex: *Ask her. Please.* And despite himself he smiled. It warmed him to think of her, how she'd turned to him, as though he might be some kind of authority (based, he supposed, on his thirty-plus-year marriage to Margaret) on how you moved ahead with someone once the person disappointed you, how kindly she'd listened, and how she hadn't said a word against Margaret. How she wanted to believe that it was a misunderstanding that could be cleared up with a conversation. Maybe that would work for a generation raised on the notion of chatter, but the idea that solace would come from a discussion with his wife about a kiss that took place thirty years ago was ludicrous.

When he walked back into the bedroom from his dressing room, his wife looked up and he saw worry on her face. It was a look he knew well. Next would come a tentative question, a little joke, to fix what kind of mood Uncas was in, and with the response she would then know how to proceed. To say as little as possible, to tell him about a phone call, to ask after his plans for the day. He couldn't bear it. He wanted to tell her to stop worrying, he wasn't going anywhere, that he had no more demands of her than he had of most people. He slowed by the door and leaned against the frame, a pose of attention. I'm here, he wanted to convey, to give you my attention. He couldn't speak, or smile. A lean on the doorjamb was all he could muster.

"I forgot to ask yesterday if it's going to be a blue Christmas," Margaret said.

"Of course," Uncas said. "What other kind is there? There's a nice ten-footer ready to be trimmed." He paused. "I'll be back with your breakfast."

"If you like. Hannah's working today; so is Alexandra, after her shift."

"It's Alex."

Margaret looked at him. "They'll both be here. There's still so much left to do."

Uncas ignored the sudden chill, arrived at when her playfulness didn't work. "In that case, maybe I'll make myself scarce and head down to the office first thing and slog through seminar papers." He made it sound as though he had more than four papers to read and that they were going to be tough going. In fact, these were papers from the strongest graduate students he'd had in five years. He was looking forward to seeing their work on biogeography—an area that wasn't his specialty but had always interested him. Normally, Uncas would have done the first read in front of the fireplace or on their bed while his wife was doing the crossword puzzle. Occasionally, she'd ask him clues, mostly related to the natural world. Today he didn't think he could bear to be near her. Like as not, she'd ask him some innocuous question, and he would explode. He needed to get over this hump, over this renewed feeling of revulsion for a misdemeanor that had occurred decades ago. He was being absurd. It wasn't as though she had committed a capital offense. His complaint would be laughed out of any lawyer's office and not solely because of the statute of limitations, but for the triviality of the infraction. Not to mention the unmistakable fidelity of the subsequent years, her knack as a mother and as a support. Commonplace strengths perhaps, but no less important for that.

As he pushed off the doorjamb with his shoulder—his hands in his pockets—he felt a twinge; something that said *you're being unfair, she has no idea whence this blackness falls.*

"I'm off," he said, "like the bride's pajamas."

"See you at lunch then?" There was the slight warming that made it easier to leave.

"I expect you will," Uncas said.

Uncas settled in at his office. He wondered if his father had ever retreated here on a Sunday. There was a steady drip from the gutter seam above one of his windows as the snow melted. The day was unseasonably sunny, and the roads and sidewalks were completely cleared. He'd started down the driveway on foot and decided instead to ride his bicycle. He'd propped his briefcase in the child's seat and found a plastic bag to cover the bicycle seat. The padding had absorbed water after spending who knew how many nights on the swing set. The chain could stand some oil and the gearshift was loose, but otherwise the Raleigh continued to defy time. He wished he could say the same of himself. A month ago he'd felt spry, or maybe it was that he just hadn't had reason to give his corporeal self a thought. With not sleeping and having Margaret laid up, he combed over each little ache. On his way down through the woods yesterday, dragging the Christmas tree, he'd felt suddenly unable to bend his knee. The feeling came and went quickly, but was part of an entire catalogue of tender spots. He tried to get comfortable in his desk chair. Normally, he'd lean back and rest his legs on the writing slide: as he slid lower into his chair his toes would end up higher than his shoulders. He could read like that for hours. Today, he couldn't get comfortable; the bones of his pelvis dug into the chair and his elbows seemed to be in the way.

Halfway through the first paper, breakfast smells—coffee, bacon, and doughnuts—rose from the Menelaus Café; getting ready for the postchurch crowd, Uncas supposed. He'd hurried through his own breakfast, not wanting to run into Hannah, and considered a mug of hot chocolate, or maybe even some toast and bacon from downstairs. The waitress had often told him that though they didn't normally deliver takeout, the busboy as a courtesy to their neighbors would run things up to people in the building. Uncas had always preferred to fetch his own. He talked himself out of the bacon as unnecessary, but he was hungry for something. As he read, it occurred to him that a bagel would be just the ticket, and a walk to the shop might loosen the kinks.

As Uncas opened the door of Bagel Falls he heard the now familiar bell, but what he wasn't expecting was the line. There must have been ten people waiting, and he found it irritating. They should be home on a Sunday morning. He had assumed he would be the only customer.

"It's the brunch crowd," someone said. Whatever that could mean in Sparta. He'd never seen anyone else in the shop before. He could feel his face cloud. This was exactly what he didn't want. What in God's name was he doing in a bagel shop on a Sunday morning?

Then Alex waved to him, and he didn't feel he could leave. The man just ahead of him turned around. Uncas was surprised to see Floyd Brewster.

"Hello, Floyd."

"Hello yourself." He stepped back away from Uncas, as though to take all of him in. Uncas looked past him and into the mirror. He was startled to see his normally impassive face look like a teenager's, glowering and drawn. But Floyd didn't seem to notice.

"Now, Uncas," he said, "I didn't picture you as a bagel man."

Uncas smiled, trying to lift the weight on his brow. "We can't let the world pass us by, can we?"

Floyd studied him for a moment. "Now me, I'd be just as happy to, if it meant I could go straight home after church and smoke my pipe like I've done for the last several decades. But Elsie's mad for these and has to have them fresh. I'd just as soon have a doughnut. How's Margaret? We got your invitation, and of course we'll be there. I think Elsie called up to say so as soon as she saw the envelope. She'd as soon miss it as miss a visit from the Queen. I'm looking forward to it myself. If his mother can convince him, Floyd Junior will be there too. He comes home for the holidays on Tuesday."

Uncas nodded. Floyd had been a great favorite of his father's, and Uncas had found him as steady a man as you could ask for. The line seemed to be moving quickly. Uncas took off his glasses to polish off the steam. What a fool he had been to come here; a waste of time and money.

"Fauna was just through here, with one of the little ones. Margaret must be glad to have her back. Elsie can't get enough of ours when she comes to visit."

"Next," Alex said.

Floyd turned and placed his order. Alex quickly selected the four bagels. The boy behind her was fixing someone else a sandwich. Uncas saw the picture of his bicycle from the *Gazette* taped to the wall just behind the counter.

Floyd shook Uncas's hand goodbye and said he'd see him Wednesday. "You give our best to Margaret. Elsie will be by sometime this week to see what she can do to help."

"What are you doing here, Mr. Metcalfe? You just missed Fauna and Nik," Alex said. "Better hurry, she's headed to your house with a baker's dozen. I guess Hannah sold Mrs. M. on them."

"I'm here for myself, Alex. Doing a little work at the office."

"Tuna salad, Mr. Metcalfe?" Alex asked, leaning toward him with a smile.

Uncas felt his eyes mist, so grateful was he for her warmth. He didn't trust himself to respond to her joke; he was utterly resolved not to choke up in front of this girl again. "A Sanka and one of those ones with the sesame seeds." He stepped toward the end of the counter, and she mirrored him.

"Anything on that?"

Uncas could hear the tentativeness in her voice, and it reminded him of Margaret: *I forgot to ask, Unk, is it going to be a blue Christmas?* So unlike her confidence and expressiveness of yesterday.

"Maybe a little jam if you have it."

"Grape, raspberry, or strawberry?" He could still feel her eyes on him, though he himself couldn't look at her.

"Whatever's most plentiful."

"Are you all right, Mr. Metcalfe?" Alex said this quietly, almost in a whisper, for which Uncas was enormously grateful. "You really don't look so good."

"As right as rain."

Alex wrapped the bagel in wax paper and started to put it in a bag with his Sanka. "Or maybe you wanted this to stay," she said. "Maybe you should sit down for a minute."

"I'll take it to go. What's all that add up to?"

"On the house, Mr. Metcalfe. My treat."

"I couldn't." Uncas heard his voice crack. He thought of Floyd
with his pipe and Alex worrying that he was okay and Fauna passing
like a ship in the night. He was tired; he needed to be by himself. He
took the bag and left two dollars on the counter and turned and
made his way to the door. The bell jangled when he pressed his
thumb on the door handle and pulled. Through the glass he saw
Doug and Fauna on the sidewalk opposite. Doug had a paper, probably the Sunday *Times* for Margaret, under his arm. They were walking toward Margaret's car, with Nik in tow, eating a bagel. Uncas
turned left out the door, and walked with his head down, hoping to
avoid notice. No doubt he'd see them all at lunch.

It was a harebrained idea, Uncas knew, but he felt lighter than he
had in twenty-four hours, make that twenty-four years, as he pedaled
across the small bridge and onto Iroquois Road. The day was only
getting warmer, and he'd decided the seminar papers could wait—
they weren't due till Tuesday anyhow. He would bicycle out to
Poplar Creek. He loved the sound of the tires as they made their way
through the wetness of the melting snow, as through light rain. The
higher stretches of asphalt were already dry. He felt like Huck Finn
off on an adventure. He hadn't even gone back up to his office; he'd
walked in the door of the Menelaus Building, and started past his bicycle, which he'd stowed underneath the stairs. At that moment it
seemed like the exact cure. He'd put his bag from Bagel Falls in the
child's seat and had ridden off. No one to answer to for hours. No
one would miss him until dinnertime. Plenty of time to ride the ten
miles out to the lake and back, though it had been a good long while
since he'd ridden that far. He pedaled hard in third gear for the
length of Iroquois Road. He wanted to join the lake road as quickly

as possible; then he would feel he was on his way. He concentrated fully on the four or five feet in front of him. He might as well be on his stationary bicycle for all the interest he took in the world passing by. He nodded as people waved or honked horns, but never looked directly at them. He didn't want to know who was watching; he simply wanted to feel that his world was behind him.

Finally, he was on the lake road, riding hard for the break in houses where he'd see the open water, and stop and eat half his bagel. The Sanka would be lukewarm, but that seemed to be par for the course from Bagel Falls. He reached the break more quickly than he expected. He was dripping with sweat, but he felt exhilarated. He hadn't ridden so far or so quickly in ages. He sat on the guardrail tugging at a bagel half. He thought about Alex: as absurd as it was to compare her with Margaret, he'd found an expansive warmth in her that seldom seemed to absent itself. He played over and over in his mind scenarios where he asked Margaret, as Alex had counseled, about kissing Philip, and where he asked her for a divorce. He'd always seen divorce as something weaker sorts did. Men like Philip, who were perpetually waiting for something better to come along. He tried to think of it in a different light, of how an accountable man might justify it. It wasn't just the errant kiss, as much as that grated against his idea of what marriage should offer. It was that the wound had proved to be as fresh yesterday as the day it was inflicted. Pushed to the periphery as it had been, it had nevertheless colored what had come afterward. Once Hank was out of college, his responsibility to provide a home for his children was through. Of course they'd be welcome wherever he landed.

He climbed back on his bicycle and at a slower pace resumed his ride. The idea of starting fresh, a new life without Margaret, intrigued him. He downshifted to first gear as he began to climb the long gradual incline where the road veered off from the lake and no longer ran between shore and cabins, but ran between fields. The shoulder was wider, and the wheels dug into the soft gravel. Such a feeling of spring pervaded the air that Uncas expected to see glimpses of forsythia and the first green leaves of cow corn, but the fields were still blanketed with snow. He was thirsty. Who was he fooling except himself? His inarticulateness in the face of his wife made him want to rage. What was his plan? To remind her of a single kiss from years ago? To accuse her of retreating into coldness? How had he come to sound so feeble? There had been low points, similar periods of blackness when he hadn't known what to do; he'd seen his father similarly affected. Still, the desperation always passed. Yet, after so many years, he had opened his mouth to a virtual stranger. What a foolish man he was. He hadn't had the respect to leave the solid mass of his marriage to Margaret alone.

As he neared the crest of the hill he was moving the pedals so slowly that he had to get off and walk. He swung his leg over the seat and dismounted. As he pushed the bicycle he ate the other half of the bagel. A teenager had unsettled him with the kind of advice he heard his children give each other about employers or professors. ("Talk to him. He's nicer one-on-one." Or "Talk to her. She must have misunderstood what you meant.") Soft. Soft. Soft. People should say what they meant and behave themselves. The kind of dallying that went on in the guise of "I'm just being honest" was the sure mark of an insipid parasite, one who gathered sustenance from attacking the chinks in the armor of those stronger than himself. No, he didn't want to be "free," or to "find himself," the very words made him feel ill; this was the kind of convenient reasoning his children were partial to when they were looking for a way out of something. There had been little to justify abandoning Margaret then, and less now. He couldn't rightly consider it. Her injury had thrown his world into a maelstrom, and he'd allowed himself to reveal a long-dead secret in the name of aiding an unhappy nineteen-year-old girl who had then countered with sympathy. He stared at the bagel in his hand. What a sop he'd been. Since when did he eat bagels? He'd dodged his own daughter.

He paused at the top of the hill and leaned his Raleigh against a boarded-up fruit-and-vegetable stand. This was the highest point on the road around the lake. He would be able to coast down the hill almost all the way and walk down the driveway to Poplar Creek inside of a half an hour. But riding back up the hill to home would be an effort he knew might well exhaust him. Still, he could probably heat up some canned soup at the house. The water was turned off, but the stove would work. He'd be able to rest a bit, though he wasn't feeling as tired as he had a half-mile back.

Uncas swung his leg back up over the seat and let gravity whisk him down the steepest part of the hill. He resumed pedaling and found himself at the top of the driveway even more quickly than he'd estimated. Though he was in excellent shape for a man his age, his heart was pounding. He was already dreading the ride home. He leaned his bicycle against a tree and made his way down to the house on foot through the soft snow, packed by yesterday's tire tracks. Gone was the Huck Finn feeling. He was a tenured professor at a respected college, and he felt as confused as he ever had in his life. He was exhausted and would have left immediately if he'd had something more with him to eat. He walked gingerly as he felt his muscles tighten up. As he neared the house he could hear the rushing of the creek. The melting snow would affect the level just enough to speed up the flow. His and Alex's footprints were still visible in a circle around the spot where the car had sat. They had strapped the tree to the roof of the car. Uncas had taught Alex how to tie a clove hitch and a square knot, and she'd secured the top of the tree to the front of the roof rack. As they were taking the tree off, he saw that she had re-sorted to granny knots, several of them, which he had in turn cut through because it was too cold to try to loosen them.

He let himself into the house and rummaged around in the hutch. He found a can of beef stew that asked for one cup of water, but he would do without. He emptied the contents into a pan and set it on a burner to cook. He'd boil lake water after lunch so he'd have something to drink before his ride.

The stew was just bubbling on top when Uncas heard the door blow open. He thought he had pushed it tightly closed, and won-dered how a day so calm had suddenly become windy. As he crossed the room, head down, he became aware of another person. He felt his heart jump as he looked up and saw a figure in the doorway, sur-rounded by sun. Uncas squinted at the light streaming in. It outlined a dark figure; he couldn't see the person's face.

"Professor?"

A man stepped in and shut the door. Uncas shook his head and found he was backing up. His visitor was a young man, considerably shorter than Uncas, but stocky and muscle-bound. Uncas could see that in his neck, and in the way his down vest seemed to be straining to cover his torso. A bulky hand-knit sweater fit tightly around his arms. But he had a smile on his round face, which made him look like a jack-o'-lantern. It was as though the wrong head had been stuck on his sinister body, like the cutout Santa Claus at the Lincoln School.

He didn't look familiar. That he had called Uncas "Professor" might have suggested that he was a student at Wright, but lots of people in town called him that as well.

"Professor, it's me. Carl."

"Forgive me," Uncas said, "I can't place you."

"That's not a problem. We have time."

It was as though his visitor were trying to sound both friendly and menacing, as though he were in control. Uncas was weak and tired and hungry. Until he figured out who Carl was, he decided to treat him as an invited guest. He could almost hear his father reminding him: *Politeness provides a handsome refuge.*

"I suppose we do," Uncas said. "Will you sit down?" Uncas motioned to a chair. "I'm just having some stew. Would you like some?"

"All of it, please. Hand me the pot and a spoon."

Uncas tried to swallow but his mouth was dry. He set the pan of stew on a trivet and got a bowl from the cabinet.

"A spoon only, Professor."

Uncas stopped to take a breath. He was confused; he wished he were at home eating a sandwich. The day had been too much, and now he had to deal with this cryptic man.

"I've been following you, Professor. Since the bagel shop, but just like always, you didn't notice a thing."

"You're right," Uncas said. "I didn't see you."

"You didn't see me. Your own daughter across the street you didn't see."

Uncas thought to correct him; to tell him he *had* seen Fauna, but decided against it. He would bide his time. The young man knew Fauna. The kitchen went in and out of light as clouds passed between the sun and the house. Uncas tried to will Carl's face into his memory, to find some match. He was so distinct looking, and spoke so carefully and slowly, that he felt sure he would have remembered him if they'd met before. Uncas looked out the window and saw a red pickup truck. There was script painted on the door that Uncas couldn't make out.

Carl ate delicately. Small spoonfuls, and he chewed several times.

"You are hungry?" Carl asked. He looked around the table, then tugged on the cuff of his shirt and blotted his mouth with it.

"Yes," Uncas said.

"Ask me for some of mine."

"Very well." Uncas's heart started to beat a little faster. He could ask, or he could refuse to play this man's game. The former seemed safer. "May I have some of your stew?"

"Get your own."

Uncas's appetite vanished in irritation and worry. He wanted to call Margaret and have her pick him up.

"You see, Professor," Carl began, "I want"—Uncas looked at him. Before he finished the sentence Uncas knew he was going to say, "I want to make a point." And he would say "point" as though, in fact, the word had quills. The way he stretched out the word "see," to command the room's attention before continuing, was familiar. Uncas had heard Carl's voice before. Two pictures flashed in his mind—the Burleigh lecture hall where every third year Uncas taught the Introduction to Botany course, and answering the old rotary phone in the kitchen at home. Uncas was relieved to have placed him. He had been a student. He didn't know why he'd thought of the old kitchen phone; Margaret had gotten rid of it years ago—"to make a point."

Uncas relaxed his shoulders. He tried to place him. The classes were big, but not so big that a student who spoke regularly wouldn't stand out.

"You remember me," Carl said. "Or you think you do. From where? I'm interested."

"You were a student at Wright."

"I took your course. Yes." He paused. "You can do better, Professor."

Uncas wanted to bury his head in his hands. How he wished Margaret were here. She could handle this young man.

"Do you love the plants, Professor?"

Uncas started to stand up. He needed to eat something. There was other canned food. He'd even risk one whose "serve by" date had expired. .

"Please sit down, Mr. Professor." Uncas heard the first touch of anger.

"Excuse me," Uncas said. "But I'm famished." He tried to say it politely, to appeal to Carl's sympathy.

"Office hours are now in session. Your students do not watch you eat, do they? Then do not eat here." He said the last words forcefully, and then he paused. "Your bicycle was heavier than expected."

Uncas sat down and studied his intruder. "It was you?" This made him uneasy; it meant Carl had also written the vile note.

"Who else?" Carl smiled proudly. "You see, I want to make a point." He continued. "I am sorry for that trouble but I thought, this man will listen to his bicycle."

Uncas could see Carl relax. He wanted to risk a smile at the thought that he would listen to his bicycle, but it could too easily backfire. He felt guarded, as though wherever he turned there were higher expectations than could be met.

Just then the phone rang and Uncas reached for it.

Carl got to it first and held the receiver down on the base. "No. Do not answer it," Carl said. "Let's listen to it ring." He paused while the phone rang several times.

Uncas was hopeful and then anxious. It was probably Margaret, and she wouldn't be surprised that he hadn't answered. She'd think he was outside working. There was no one who knew for sure he was here. He began to be afraid.

"Because, you see, Professor, you do not listen so well to your students. I am but one example. But you will listen to me now."

Uncas bristled inwardly. A malcontent, he thought, a grade-grubber who felt he should have gotten an A and was lucky to get a B minus.

"I admire you. You are so thorough and fill the classes with rigor. I waited until it was your turn to teach the beginning course. I knew that here was a man who loved the plants."

Slowly Uncas began to remember Carl's rambling comments in his class, but he still couldn't picture him in the room.

"You would walk into the classroom, to the podium where you would take out your lecture for the day, and you would take off your glasses. You never looked at your papers; to me the feeling was that you were speaking from your head. And your heart. I was right to wait for you."

It was true, Uncas supposed. He kept the notes there in case he lost his place, but like most professors, he assumed, one knew the basics of one's field.

"You sat in the back, in the center," Uncas said.

"Always," Carl replied.

It explained why Uncas could place only his voice. Without his glasses, the rows past the first few were a blur. Not being able to see his audience had steadied his nerves when he started lecturing so many years ago; it was a habit he had found hard to break.

"What do you want?" Uncas asked. He needed to start home or they'd miss him come dinnertime.

"What I requested several years ago."

"A higher grade?"

"Oh, Professor, you can be so ignorant. How did you obtain such a lovely wife with such ignorance? Mrs. Metcalfe is a lovely lady."

Uncas began to get nervous again. "You know my wife?"

"We are friends." Carl smiled again, as though he knew he was keeping Uncas guessing. "On Wednesday you will have a tremendous party."

Uncas had only glanced at the final list, but he couldn't fathom Margaret inviting this Carl. He was trying to fluster Uncas. But knowing the Metcalfes were throwing a Christmas party wasn't exactly classified information. He was convinced that this man was playing a game, though not one where Uncas would get hurt. He even contemplated asking him for a lift back to Sparta. He felt as though he were caught in a bad detective novel. Only nothing was tidy.

"Come," Carl said, standing up, "I will show you."

Uncas stood up; he felt he had no choice. He felt his world crumbling, but he still needed to protect his wife. They both turned as they heard a car coming down the driveway. They waited in silence on opposite sides of the table. Uncas felt his eyes fill with tears when Fauna, her down jacket straining around her protruding belly, stepped into the kitchen.

"Dad?" She looked confused. "My God, Dad, you look awful. We all got worried when you weren't at your office and your bike was gone and the Jeep wasn't. And you didn't come home for lunch. Alex said you looked terrible. Dad, what's going on?" She looked again at Carl and then at Uncas. "We had no idea where you were. Why didn't you call and let us know you were here? Why didn't you answer the phone? Thank God you're all right."

"How do you do, Fauna? After so many years." Carl extended his hand. Fauna ignored him and walked around the table to Uncas.

Uncas could do nothing to stop the tears that were falling. They were divorced from sobs or keening or grief or hurt. They fell seemingly of their own accord. It was as though he were sweating from his eyes. He let Fauna shepherd him around the table toward the door. He felt old and feeble.

They stopped and she looked at Carl. "What are you doing here?" She sounded as though she couldn't believe who was in front of her. She turned to Uncas. "Dad?"

Uncas could only muster a slight movement of his shoulders. He didn't know.

"Calling on your father. I have confirmed the great professor is nothing more than a great, tall weed tree." Carl faced Uncas.

"Carl," Fauna said, "I don't know what the hell you're talking about or what the hell you're doing here, but I want you to leave immediately." She left Uncas and crossed to the phone.

"As you wish. I will force no one." Carl walked directly to the door. He turned as he went out and said, "I look forward to hearing from you, Professor." They watched him get into his pickup. He waved as he backed up to turn around.

Fauna dialed and said into the receiver, "He's here. I'm bringing him home."

Uncas picked up the pan that had held the stew and the spoon his visitor had used. Left behind, the food would attract animals.

Fauna drove Uncas's Jeep up the driveway and stopped to get his bicycle. Though she hadn't brought gloves and he was stiff and chilled, Uncas wouldn't hear of leaving it. Between the two of them they barely managed to get it into the back. The leftover Sanka tipped and spilled. Fauna sopped it up with some napkins as naturally as though she were cleaning up after one of her children. The tears had stopped flowing from Uncas's eyes, but he didn't try to speak. They caught up with and passed Carl's pickup. Fauna sped by him in a no-passing zone muttering, "Nut job." Uncas had no doubt the man was off, but he didn't have the feeling that he was truly crazy. Carl had played games and so forth, but Uncas had the idea that there was some specific wrong Carl thought he was righting.

Fauna had the blowers on high, but he could hear she was singing quietly to herself; it was a song she sang to her children. Periodically she would reach over a hand and squeeze his arm or his shoulder, and tell him they would be there soon. Halfway back to town he saw that she had tears in her own eyes; it dawned on him that he must have scared her, that she must still be scared. He ran his tongue across his dried lips; he was thirstier than he ever remembered being, even during the long marches in the army. He was warming up slowly. He found himself staring into the stewpot. The congealed juices were liquefying as the car got warmer. The smell made Uncas feel ill. He began to shake again, and he felt tears come to his eyes. He must have caught pneumonia on the bicycle ride out. All he wanted was to crawl between clean white sheets and have someone pile lots of heavy blankets on top of him, and he wanted Margaret at his side asking him what was another word for wood sorrel? Did he have any idea what a "costard" was?

Fauna slowed down as the speed limit dropped on the outskirts of town. She'd look at him now and again as though she wanted to ask a question, but thought better of it. He didn't encourage her. He couldn't have explained the day if he tried. It didn't even feel as though Carl were the oddest part. He was a mystery though. His pickup truck with the script on the door meant he probably ran a local business, probably one that Margaret used. But how had he come to be so familiar with Fauna? Uncas barely had the energy to think

about it, much less ask questions, which he knew would invite questions of him. He didn't think Fauna would mind if he shut his eyes
for a moment. She might even be grateful.

Uncas heard someone calling from far away. The voice was insistent.

"Dad, wake up. You went out hard." Fauna was shaking his shoulder gently. "We're back. We're home."

Uncas opened his eyes. Disoriented.

"You look gray, Dad. I'd go quietly up the stairs and maybe take a
bath in the guest bathroom. I'll see if I can get you some dry clothes
without Mom noticing. I think it would just alarm her."

Uncas nodded. He needed this, he knew. Someone else to make
decisions while he collected his thoughts.

He handed Fauna the stew pot and opened the door. His legs
were stiff but he managed to swing them out of the car and to extend
his feet to the ground. The house would be warm. He made his way
slowly. He stopped in the kitchen and drank two glasses of water.
Lifting his feet to climb the stairs was an effort. But he did it quietly,
following Fauna's advice. He could hear Hannah's voice in his and
Margaret's bedroom. She was asking a question, which he heard
Margaret answer. He wondered if Alex was there too, and then he
heard Hannah say in a playful voice, "Oh, Alex. That's not true," and
then he heard all three of them laughing.

After washing a few spiders down the drain Uncas ran the hot water
to fill the bathtub. He was still cold, but he felt calmer. He found a
hardened square of bubble bath, and even though it might make
him smell like a "lady of the night," as Margaret would say, he

dropped it in under the running water. He couldn't find a bar of soap, and plain hot water wasn't what he'd had in mind. He peeled off his clammy clothes, all layers at once from the top and then the bottom, and then lowered himself into the bathtub. It reminded him of Poplar Creek where the master bedroom still had no shower. In town he rarely took baths, but it was what Fauna had suggested. It hadn't occurred to him until he was enveloped in hot water and bubbles that a shower might have done the trick as well.

Uncas heard a knock on the door.

"Dad? Everything okay?"

Uncas started to answer but his voice caught. He swallowed. His eye rested on a small red airplane on the bathtub ledge; it looked as though it were poised for takeoff. Probably Tommy's.

"Dad? You okay?"

"Fine. Yes, I'm fine."

"I'll leave your clothes outside the door. I'll be downstairs heating up soup. Take your time."

"Good. Okay."

When he woke, the water was lukewarm. He climbed out of the tub and wrapped a towel around his waist. He opened the door and saw the pile of clothes Fauna had left. He slid them across the threshold with his foot. These would be temporary. All he could think of was sleep.

After dressing, he ducked his head into his bedroom; the girls were gone and his wife was dozing. As he headed down the stairs— he didn't feel so stiff as he had—he saw Fauna come into the hallway.

"I was just headed up to make sure you hadn't drowned," she said. "Soup's on."

He followed her through the living room, where the couches had been pushed against the wall and the rugs rolled up for dancing. The band would set up at the far end.

"You wouldn't rather have stew?" she said. "Sorry, that wasn't nice."

Uncas felt slightly nauseated and wondered if he'd ever be able to eat stew again. He ate his bowl of soup while Fauna sat kitty-corner from him at the table. She'd made toast for him too.

"Has your mother eaten?" Uncas asked.

"No, it's still early. I sent Hannah and Alex home. I'll come back in an hour or so, once the kids are in bed, but only if you'll promise to go to bed yourself." She looked away, then down at the table in front of her. "And I didn't mention Carl to Mom."

He nodded. "What did you tell her?"

"That you got a flat tire at the top of the driveway. I arrived as you were walking down to call."

He nodded again.

"I'm glad you're all right, but you scared me. When I walked in and saw Carl— We can talk about this tomorrow."

"Okay," Uncas said. With the soup and toast under his belt he began to feel back in control. Tomorrow there would be no tears, no spur-of-the-moment bicycle rides, no visits to the bagel shop, no baths, and, he devoutly hoped, no unannounced visits by former students. Uncas hoped for an ordinary day.

SEVEN

Uncas opened his eyes slowly and blinked as he took in his lamp and night table and glass of water. He shifted his weight to his right side in an effort to lift himself out of bed; he was so stiff he felt he might strain something if he moved too quickly. But as agitated as he'd been the day before, he had fallen asleep by seven-thirty and felt rested for the first time in two days. Except for the stiffness, he might have bounded out of bed. He turned his head, and from the corner of his eye he saw the outline of Margaret's body. He squinted but couldn't tell if she were awake or asleep, probably the latter because he hadn't heard a page turn. He reached for and put on his glasses, and was considering whether he should slip out of bed or reach over to her when he saw her on Fauna's arm, coming through the hallway from their bathroom. He had been contemplating a pile of bed-clothes.

"Rip van Winkle, up from the dead. Call the *Gazette*," Fauna said. "Dad, you slept for more than twelve hours. I got worried you'd never get up."

Margaret had a faraway look in her eyes and a half-smile, as though she were amused by what Fauna was saying, but Uncas knew better than to test those waters. He didn't know what she'd make of yesterday's adventure; it was best to let her break the silence. He didn't want to risk a rebuke in front of Fauna.

He studied his face in the mirror as he shaved. He moved aside his ongoing list of Poplar Creek projects that he'd stuck in the frame. His eyes were puffy—a look he remembered from when he used to drink—but otherwise sleep had restored him enough that he was embarrassed by his behavior of the day before. He'd as soon forget the whole thing—from the bicycle ride to Carl's visit—and move on; he wished none of it had happened. He regretted not calling Margaret, regretted that she hadn't known where he was or what he was doing. It was likely she saw his absence as a slap in the face, but after all it was her actions, albeit from thirty years ago, that had driven him away. He might eventually have called her from Poplar Creek if Carl hadn't been there, but there was no way to explain that. Everything had gotten so complicated.

He would have liked to ask how Carl knew her, what their connection was, but he doubted he could explain his interest without revealing Carl's unusual behavior, which didn't amount to much. He had followed Uncas to Poplar Creek and asked him for stew and then beaten around the bush about some wrong he felt Uncas had committed. If Uncas could figure out how to ask about Carl without mentioning yesterday's ordeal, perhaps he'd find out that there was a reasonable explanation or similar incidents that made this one part of a pattern and would therefore reduce its potency. Maybe he'd learn what it was that Carl wanted. No doubt Margaret would be a font of information, but he simply wasn't sure the unknowns made it worth asking her. First he'd find out more from Fauna. She had pressed to talk right after breakfast, but Uncas had said he needed to finish correcting papers; he wanted to show there was no urgency, no need for concern. Carl's was nothing more than a curious visit. Not the kind of incident that warranted alerting the police or his wife. Better to deal with it all quietly.

By the time Uncas had finished shaving, his wife was alone in their room. "How's the patient today?"

"We missed you at lunch yesterday."

At least, Uncas thought, she had waited until Fauna left to chastise him. Uncas didn't reply. He didn't know what to say.

"May I inquire what on earth led you to ride your bicycle out to the Creek?"

"It was spur of the moment," Uncas said. "A whim, I guess."

His wife looked at him, unblinking, until Uncas looked away.

"Without so much as a by-your-leave. Would you have the courtesy to let Fauna know if another should strike? She was concerned. We all were." She picked up a book from her bedside table and opened to the bookmark.

Uncas, wishing he knew what to say to clear the air, said goodbye.

Downstairs the house seemed to him a small, poorly designed factory. Doug was carrying a rug down to the basement, and the children were playing in the library, using chess pieces as townspeople on the Parcheesi board, as far as Uncas could figure out. Alex and Hannah were at the kitchen table cleaning vases and silver. He picked up the newspaper and sat at the opposite end; he would discourage conversation. It felt like ages since he'd had a quiet breakfast. Fauna had left him a note saying that Charley Bisgrove had promised to make a house call today to check on Margaret. She hoped he could be there. He'd come back for it if he got the papers done; if not, Margaret could tell him the highlights. Also, Fauna had said, the caterers were going to come by with samples of food. Uncas would leave that up to Margaret and the girls. He had almost forgotten about the other note, the note Carl had left on his bicycle. Alex had been right about Carl being short, but the rest of it still made little sense. He carried his mug and cereal bowl to the kitchen sink and threw Fauna's note away. He was making a sandwich for lunch when Hannah said she would do it for him. He told her he could manage, that there was probably a better use for her time than waiting on him. He felt cross and unsettled and wanted to be left alone; he was looking forward to concentrating on botany; he'd had enough of emotional folderol.

At his office, Uncas set to work. He pulled out the papers and began to read with a red pen. He moved along quickly and decisively. The first two papers, as he'd expected, were impressive first drafts; he gave advice for their final drafts, crossing out whole passages and asking for elucidation of others. He stopped and ate his sandwich and looked at the clock that sat in one of the cubbyholes of his desk. It was taking more time than he'd expected, but reading them felt restorative; a decided antidote to the whining he'd done the day before yesterday. Occasionally his mind would wander and he found himself longing for a return to more normal days, to a time when his wife was up and walking around, to a time when a thief would have left his bicycle behind an abandoned building and the police would have returned it, to a time before he'd felt compelled to babble about his wife's thirty-year-old indiscretion. Still, once he finished, Uncas felt exhilarated. Work often had this effect, he thought. It sharpened his mind; whereas idling over what he'd said to Alex dulled it.

He felt almost lighthearted as he walked back to the house. He'd forgotten his briefcase, but in a way that added to his enjoyment.

Nothing to weigh him down. He thought about Alex. He hoped some boy had the sense to snatch her up. It was true, she wasn't your conventional feminine beauty, but that shouldn't stop a discerning eye; she was handsome, and beyond that she had brains and a sense of humor and kindness and integrity, and, of course, warmth. He found himself hoping that she might choose to settle here in Sparta, but he feared that it would feel too small for her. He was glad that she and Hannah seemed to be such close friends. Hannah was a solid citizen too, but knowing her parents, knowing Joe Stephenson, that surprised him less. Alex was majoring in women's studies; studying women seemed a hopeless pursuit; Uncas found it far easier to understand plants. But he knew that times were changing. Even his colleagues in botanical studies were looking into genetic modification. Nothing would remain as it was.

"I like walking my old route to Lincoln and seeing what's changed," Fauna said as they walked the streets to the school she had attended as a child. She'd been waiting for Uncas when he returned from the office. He was glad he'd put their conversation off. He felt sharper now, and Fauna seemed less combative. He didn't exactly know how he was going to answer her questions. As honestly as he could, he supposed, without betraying Margaret again. The weather was still sunny. Driveways that hadn't been cleared the day before were by now a slushy mess.

"It's strange that my kids will be going to Lincoln in a couple of years, and will have their own route and stops along the way. And dogs to avoid and yards to cut through."

Uncas listened to Fauna's voice and marveled, as he had many times, at how much the cadence and pitch were like Margaret's, except that it wasn't like Fauna to talk on about nothing. She was usually driven by specific information or indignation.

"They've decided to close Lincoln," Uncas said. "They're tearing it down in June. I think your children will go to St. Francis, or what used to be St. Francis. The city's combining three elementary schools."

"Oh, well. So much for nostalgia." Fauna paused. "So, what was Carl doing out at Poplar Creek? You're not having him do work out there, are you?"

"No. He won't be working out at the lake. I don't know what his work is. I don't know him. Though apparently he was at Wright and took—"

"Dad." Fauna stopped and looked at him as she interrupted. "His family owns Benson's Nursery. Or what's left of his family: his father died of some strange disease three or four years ago, and his mother, well, you learn a lot about why Carl is the way he is once you meet his mother. They've only run it for about a billion years. Mom gets flowers and plants there all the time." She started walking again. "How could you not know who the Bensons are?" Then she laughed. "Plants, Dad. You must have biked by it on your way to Wright a million times."

Uncas didn't say anything. He'd never paid much attention to nurseries. He preferred what grew naturally. It would never have occurred to him to plant a new species out at Poplar Creek, especially one that had been forced in a greenhouse—which he saw as an intensive-care unit for plants. At the lab greenhouse it was different—those species were raised for research, not for landscaping. If it was on the way to Wright, it had to be the nursery on the outskirts of town that abutted the property of his aunt's first husband.

"So how did Carl end up at Poplar Creek, if you don't know

him?" Fauna asked. "Just a friendly face by the side of the road that you thought might enjoy a bowl of stew on a sunny winter afternoon? That kind of thing?"

Uncas took a deep breath. "He followed me there."

"What? Why?"

"I had biked out there and got hungry." Uncas wanted to be careful. He didn't want to reveal more about yesterday than necessary. For all Fauna knew, he did it all the time. "I put on some stew, and the next thing I knew, there he was at the door. But he seemed to know you. Do you buy plants there?"

"Yeah, Dad. With all of our extra money, Doug and I buy plants at the most expensive place in town. We feel like it's better to have exotic cactuses than new winter coats for the kids." Fauna shook her head. "Do you remember anything from my childhood? Carl was in my sixth-grade class and would call all the time with that bizarre formal voice of his. And you wouldn't lie and say I wasn't home. I had to be polite to him. He thought I was his friend or something just because I was forced to talk to him on the phone. Our class went on a field trip out to the nursery. Mom was one of the mothers who went with us. It wasn't nearly as big then as it is now. Of course, she befriended his father and mother and still buys stuff there."

But it wasn't her regular nursery. He'd recognize that name. Probably Margaret threw them a little business when her regular place was closed; or if she happened to be passing by, she might stop in to maintain a connection. She was like that; she collected people.

They walked along in silence until they came to the store from which his father had ordered groceries to be delivered. It was a real estate office now. Fauna took a left onto Lincoln Street.

"Sorry, Dad. It's just that sometimes I can't believe what you don't remember. Not that I've got the greatest memory, but— Oh, I don't know, I get the feeling that it doesn't matter . . ." Her voice trailed off. "So what'd he want?"

"I don't know. He took my Introduction to Botany class, and from what I could gather he thinks I owe him something."

"Are you sure? I don't know how he could have been at Wright. He dropped out of high school in tenth grade, after his father got sick. He's the one who hung up your bicycle, isn't he?"

"Yes," he said. He looked at Fauna and wondered how he could ever have thought it was she who had written the note. "How did you know?" He wondered if Alex had told her about it.

"I put two and two together. So he has some kind of beef with you?"

"Yes. I think he does."

"You should call the police."

"I don't think that's necessary."

"For one thing, he was trespassing, and for another—"

"Strictly speaking, it was trespassing, but nothing came of it. He left when you asked him to. I think it's best not to create a stir."

Uncas knew he should offer something more, but he didn't know what to say. He couldn't explain, for example, why he didn't think Carl was a "nut job" or why he hadn't been able to stop his tears from falling or why he'd cried in the first place.

"He must have really scared you, Dad." The tenor of Fauna's voice had changed. She sounded the way she did with her children. "You looked really upset when I walked in."

"I think I was quite tired after my ride. It's interesting," Uncas said, "as peculiar as he was, I never really felt I was in danger." This wasn't strictly true, but for the purposes of his discussion with Fauna, it was.

"I guess it depends how you define 'danger.' I don't think he would physically hurt you, but he had you trapped yesterday. What do they call it? False imprisonment."

Uncas laughed nervously. "I think that's a little strong. Though he did kidnap my bicycle."

"Dad, you were a wreck when I got there." She said "wreck" with a shrillness that was familiar to Uncas. "There's such a thing as psychological torture," she continued. "I don't know what he did, but you— Dad, you— I really was worried about you this morning. When Mom was in the bathroom, I checked to see if you were still breathing." Fauna kept starting and stopping.

"Honey," he said, "it wasn't all his fault."

Fauna turned to him with tears in her eyes. "Jesus, Dad. Sorry, I mean gee. You really scared me yesterday." She brushed her eyes with her gloves. "Whose fault was it?" She paused. "Was it my fault? Because I yelled at you about the boiler? I'm sorry about that. It's just that Doug and I, well, it's hard right now. But I know I shouldn't blame you."

Uncas laughed. "No. It wasn't about the boiler." As much as he longed to blame his difficult day on a technical problem, he knew that wasn't the case. There were many options to choose from: lack of sleep, loquaciousness, infidelity. But the truth was he didn't know—it seemed to begin with the table falling on Margaret's leg, but that certainly didn't explain Carl's visit or his conversation with Alex. He was used to operating on his own, without worrying about how Margaret spent her day; it had been a couple of years since the children had been around full-time; in that time patterns and schedules and expectations had been adjusted; now they had changed again. Nothing was clear or simple anymore. The day's events underscored that truth at least.

Uncas pointed out the Santa Claus in the window at Lincoln,

without saying that he thought it bore a resemblance to Carl. As they walked back to the house Fauna asked about his term at Wright and whether he had interesting students. Uncas felt relaxed, relieved that the discussion about Carl was over, and that Fauna seemed satisfied. He was still troubled about his wife: how he would like to solve that unease.

"What's this? What kind of factory is this? The workers taking an un-scheduled break?" Uncas asked as he and Fauna came into the kitchen, back from their walk.

Hannah, Alex, and Doug looked up from the table, where they were eating sandwiches. "It's our lunch, Mr. Boss. You'd better watch it or we'll go on strike," Alex said.

"Doug, where are the kids?" Fauna asked.

"In your mother's room. Nik's asleep on the rug, and she's reading to Janey and Tommy." He paused. "Don't give me that look, Faun. She volunteered and it's only been about ten minutes. We just sat down here. I fed them and your mother first." Fauna turned and walked out of the kitchen. Doug shrugged and continued to eat. "A mother's work is never done, I guess."

"Now," Uncas said, "I understand I'm needed to pick up some booze. You two aren't old enough, I hear." Margaret had sent Alex and Hannah off to Sparta's Liquor Picks to get the alcohol for the party, and they had been turned away because of their age. Uncas found it annoying, if understandable. Margaret had put in the order with Clarence Granger, the owner, himself. The girls had called from the shop, but no amount of reasoning would get him to change his mind.

Doug put his plate in the sink and left the kitchen.

"If you two would set up the bar while I'm gone," Uncas said, "you can stock it when I get back."

Hannah and Alex looked at each other and then back at Uncas, and then both cast their eyes on the ground.

"I'll come with you, Mr. Metcalfe," Alex said, lifting her eyes to meet his.

"That won't be necessary," Uncas said.

"Well, I hate to tell you this, but Fauna said one of us should go with you, and your wife too," Alex said.

"You mean my wife should come with us?" Uncas said, smiling, though he was a little put off by the thought that he needed company for a trip to the liquor store, or anywhere, for that matter.

Alex smiled. "Nah. Just me."

"Well, in that case, hut, two." He hadn't realized that Fauna was such a worrier, but it didn't seem fair to put Alex and Hannah in any more of an awkward position than his daughter and wife already had. Of monitoring his physical endeavors.

Alex saluted him. "Reporting for duty, boss."

Uncas smiled, but he was distracted. He found Margaret's and Fauna's concern an overreaction.

Alex seemed nervous when she got in the car. "I'm kind of a little worried, Mr. Metcalfe. My dad is going to be able to come to your party with Betty. I want you to meet him, but, well, he can be, like, kind of loud and obnoxious. That doesn't sound so great, but it's true."

Though Peter Miller had married Betty Delafield, who was as no-nonsense a woman as one could ask for, he didn't sound like the kind of man with whom Uncas would be comfortable. Nonetheless he would welcome him. "I look forward to it."

"I could show him the note," she said. "I mean if you wanted me to."

Uncas could feel Alex's eyes on him. "That won't be necessary."

"He's really good at it. I mean it's his job and all, and I know he's my father, but he's really—"

"Your father's a detective?"

Alex laughed. "No, no. He's a psychiatrist. I thought you knew that. I thought I told you. No, he's a shrink, but he hates it when people call him that. I bet he could help." She paused. "Wait. Do you already know who did it? Who wrote the note and who hung up your bicycle?"

As he listened to Alex's voice build with eagerness, Uncas wasn't sure how to respond. He kicked himself for not having anticipated the conversation. He should have been ready with an answer, or he should have avoided being with her when no one else was around. As much as he liked and trusted her, he would keep the information to a minimum.

"Yes. I do know. It was a former student. Your guess was a good one. He was disgruntled."

"How did you find out? Was it before you came into Bagel Falls yesterday? You looked freaked out. I was worried about you."

Uncas was embarrassed at the reminder that he had caused Alex concern, and at the same time he felt touched by it. "I found out yesterday," he said. "So it's all cleared up. No need to bore your father with it all."

"Are you kidding? He wouldn't be bored for a second. But if you don't want me to tell anyone, I won't. I didn't even tell Hannah. I started to, but then I stopped. I didn't tell her even when she got mad." Alex started to laugh. "She gets that way, but it never lasts with her. She never stays mad."

"Probably best to keep it between us."

"Okay. Probably she'll just forget about it anyhow."

"Will you girls bring anyone to the dance?" It wasn't the kind of question that Uncas normally found himself asking, but it was as good a way as any of changing the subject. Margaret had suggested that since the caterers would be handling most of the work, Alex and Hannah might bring dates. Uncas agreed it would make the party more fun for them; their contemporaries, who used to attend when it was a children's party, weren't yet interested in the black-tie event it had become. Hank and Marcia would be back for Christmas, but both had begged off the party.

"You mean guys? I don't know hardly anyone around here."

Uncas didn't press the issue. He could see he'd made her uncomfortable. She followed him into Sparta's Liquor Picks without a word. Uncas greeted Clarence Granger, who was standing behind the counter. A wiry man with big ears and small spectacles.

"Uncas, don't start on me," he said, though Uncas hadn't said anything but "Hello, Clarence, nice to see you." "A rule's a rule, and we've had trouble with boys from Wright and from that girls' school, so I can't take anyone's phone say-so any longer, even though I'd recognize Margaret's voice if she were talking through a tin can. Still, no exceptions. I'd tell the mayor that, and you, all the way down to the lowest bum. No exceptions. I don't want the sheriff in here any more than you'd want him in your classroom, or this girl"—Clarence jerked his thumb toward Alex—"would want him in her home." He leaned toward Uncas and lowered his voice. "When she and that other girl, Joe's girl, came in I thought without a doubt this one was a young man, but they set me straight. Time was"—he raised his voice again—"when you knew who was a young man and who was a young woman and you knew who was buying whiskey for his father, and who was pretending that her mother was sick."

Uncas supposed that a cursory glance that took in only Alex's combat boots and short hair might lead one to think she was male. An old joke of Margaret's that she still trotted out now and again when she saw a young man with long hair or a young woman wearing men's clothes was to point and ask "Boy or girl?" as though she might catch Uncas confusing the gender. There *were* a few students every year whose gender wasn't immediately apparent to him, and like plants whose leaves were similar, you only had to study them more closely to discern the facts. He'd forgotten Clarence's propensity for nonstop chatter. It had been a good long while since he'd been dispatched to Liquor Picks. He reached inside his jacket for his wallet.

Clarence continued, "But I suppose you see all manner of behavior over at the university. When our youngest was there, we made certain sure he knew what was up and what was down, and that it didn't leave any room in the middle for any sideways behavior."

Uncas found himself nodding in agreement. He always found it difficult to interrupt, but finally there was a lull. "What do I owe you, Clarence?"

"What's that? Oh, money. Put your wallet away. We send Margaret a bill every month. We do that for a few of our most trustworthy customers. We used to do it for any respectable-looking sort who had a thirst that needed quenching, but a few too many of these"— Clarence indicated with his thumb some bad checks that were taped to the glass around the cash register—"and plain old nonpayment of bill stopped that courtesy. Still, there are a few law-abiding souls left, and your Margaret is one of them. I remember the first day she walked in here."

This was a story that Uncas remembered from years before, when he regularly stocked the liquor closet himself. (In the interest of maintaining his weight, he'd given up drinking, and Margaret had taken over that task.) It was a story he'd heard almost every time he'd walked in. Margaret had introduced herself ("a real class act," Clarence said) and had asked his advice about Scotch.

"Said her father-in-law drank Scotch and maybe I knew what kind. Did I know what kind? Are death and taxes the only sure thing? Do we all put our pants on one leg at a time? You bet I knew what kind of Scotch Mr. Metcalfe drank."

Johnny Walker Black Label. Uncas smiled. "He liked his Scotch, that's true. That's the order, Clarence? Back there?" Uncas motioned with his head to the back door, where Alex was standing next to a stack of boxes.

"The young man"—Clarence said as he winked—"knows which are the right boxes. Let me give you a hand."

Uncas returned Clarence's smile.

There were six boxes in all—red and white wine, champagne, and hard liquors. Uncas felt the strain on his muscles as he picked up one of the reds, and carried it out the door, behind Alex. He set his box down on the bumper of his Jeep and lifted up the back hatch. Alex and Clarence slid their boxes in and the three of them went back to the store for the second load. Clarence had moved on to zoning laws, and was talking about the farm-works factory and the large department store that now sat on the site.

After they'd loaded the other three boxes, Uncas shook Clarence's hand goodbye. As they drove off, Uncas looked in the rearview mirror and saw that Clarence was talking to himself. Uncas looked right as he prepared to pull out into traffic; he was surprised by the angry set of Alex's face. She hadn't said a word the whole time at the liquor store.

She turned to him and then faced front again. "Guys like him piss me off. Hannah says just to laugh it off, but she never gets called 'young man,' and especially since that old guy knew that I'm a, that I'm not a guy."

Uncas laughed. That "old guy" was a good ten years younger than he. "He doesn't mean anything by it," Uncas said. "When he was your age—"

"I'm sorry, but I really don't think it's funny. I mean, how'd you like it if people called you 'ma'am'? Plus, it's just basic courtesy that you don't stare at people and talk as if they aren't there. It's like he's never seen—" She stopped and then started again, "At least in New York they aren't so infantile when it comes to what someone's wearing or how they cut their hair."

Uncas smiled again. The way she said things like "infantile," when she was so young herself amused him. "How do you know he wasn't complimenting you?"

"Ha, ha," Alex said.

Uncas was surprised by her irritation.

They were halfway home when she turned to him and said, "Do you know what I mean, Mr. Metcalfe?" almost angrily, and he said yes and no more.

As he drove up the driveway, Uncas saw Charley Bisgrove climbing out of his black Mercedes. He had completely forgotten that Charley was coming to pay a house call, and found that he was relieved, after all, not to have missed it. There was no need to exacerbate the uneasiness between Margaret and himself that he'd felt when he'd left this morning. Uncas parked, and left Alex to unload the car.

He walked over to the Mercedes as Charley was getting his bag—
an actual old-fashioned black doctor's bag—from the back.

"Hi, Mr. Metcalfe," Charley said, greeting Uncas with a wave.
"I'm sorry to be late, rounds took longer than I'd anticipated."

He had known Little Charley's father since they were boys, and it
was remarkable how father and son were physical replicas of each
other, except that Little Charley was a good head taller than his father. It was as though the nickname had stuck around long enough
to mock its giver. Still Uncas found it difficult to think of him as anything but Little Charley, who was as affable and unassuming as they
came, the opposite of his brusque and opinionated father.

"I'm running behind, myself," Uncas replied, offering his hand.

Charley's hand encircled Uncas's, but there was no pressure, no
clasp. It was a butterfly kiss of a handshake.

"Patient's upstairs," Uncas said. "I'll follow you up in two minutes.
Or would you like longer to examine her?"

Uncas was seized by a worry that Little Charley would say Margaret shouldn't come down for the party. He simply had to say she
could; no other response seemed possible. He found the idea of giving the party without her by his side unimaginable. She'd been gone
long enough.

Charley smiled. "I guess there's nothing I can't do or say in front
of you, Mr. Metcalfe."

Uncas drank a glass of water and then another and then found
some crackers in the cupboard and cheese in the refrigerator. He was
suddenly ravenously hungry. He'd cancel the party if Margaret
weren't allowed downstairs; no one could begrudge him that.

Charley Bisgrove was thumping on Margaret's back when Uncas
came into the bedroom. He was leaning over the bed, with his
stethoscope planted just below her shoulder blade. Uncas sat down

heavily in the armchair at the end of the bed. Charley helped her turn over, then stepped back away from the bed. Both Uncas and Margaret turned toward him expectantly.

"Well, I hate to tell you this, folks, but I don't have a definite answer." He looked from one to the other. "My strongest guess, Mrs. Metcalfe"—Charley turned to face her—"is that you won't be on your feet in time for the party." Uncas steeled himself to block out the disappointment.

Little Charley continued, "And we can almost certainly rule out your dancing with Mr. Metcalfe. You're out of any immediate danger, but I want to continue to monitor the Coumadin. The correct dosage fluctuates, which is normal. It's possible that . . ." And here Uncas stopped listening to Little Charley covering his bets. Better safe than sorry was a good motto, he supposed, if, in this case, a frustrating one. He stood up quietly, while Charley was talking to his wife, and went to his dressing room. He wanted to change into his sweatpants and T-shirt, so he could exercise. He found that the more doctors learned, the less they knew. He'd have to get used to the idea that his wife wouldn't be at the party. He'd tell her tomorrow to cancel it; he wouldn't host it without her. Thanksgiving had been difficult enough. He knew she would argue, but he was resolved.

As he finished changing, he could hear Alex and Hannah and Margaret in the bedroom. They were laughing, and Margaret said, "Oh, I don't know, I think it might be rather gay, don't you?" This brought on a fresh round of laughter. It seemed like a long time since he had thought anything was gay, but he was relieved that Margaret wasn't taking the news badly.

He stuck his head out the door. "What might be rather gay?" he asked. "I couldn't help but overhear."

Margaret looked at him with what could only be described as a grin. "Why, wheeling around the dance floor, Unk. Don't you think I'll be the belle of the ball? 'Ridin' Low,' as it were?" She looked at him expectantly.

Riding low? Wasn't a lowrider a souped-up car? Uncas was troubled, as well as confused. But if Charley could be responsible so could he. "Now, Mags, you don't want to get your hopes up."

Margaret's whole demeanor changed; she started to say something and then turned to the girls. "Until tomorrow, then?" she said, somewhat sharply. Hannah and Alex said their goodbyes quickly.

After they'd left, Margaret turned stonily to Uncas. "I knew you weren't listening. I don't know why I thought this might be of some concern to you, but you stood up and left in the middle of Little Charley's diagnosis as though the whole thing bored you."

"I hardly think—"

"Oh, Unk, I know this has been a rotten bore for you"—her voice softened, to Uncas's relief—"and you've been an angel through it all, but really. You should have seen the look on his face when you disappeared into the bathroom."

"What did he say?"

"Little Charley?"

"Your daughter finds that nickname, I think she said, 'irritating.'"

"Well, he doesn't mind it. Which is good enough for me."

Uncas was silent. He tried to quash the urge to pick a fight with his wife. "He did say you wouldn't be on your feet for the party. I think we should cancel."

"I'll be there in a wheelchair," she said, "which sounds awfully nice to me."

"Oh, that is good news," Uncas said. It wasn't ideal; he didn't like the notion of Margaret in a wheelchair, but it was far better than having her in bed.

"You don't sound pleased," Margaret said.

"Oh, no. I am. I am pleased. I expect we can learn the ins and outs of a wheelchair." Maybe Alex and Hannah could take turns pushing it.

"Well, that's only so I can get around. I could sit in the same armchair all night for that matter; I'm sure Little Charley would approve that."

Uncas thought for a moment. He had to admit that if she were in an armchair it would be less obvious, probably some people wouldn't even notice that anything was wrong. Or maybe she could settle on one of the couches, like some kind of grande dame for whom people queued up for a visit.

Uncas heard his wife laugh, but it was contemptuous, not merry.

"I can't believe my eyes," she said. "My own husband is considering whether or not I should have freedom through the use of an eyesore. That's what you're worried about, isn't it? Or be confined to one place for four or five hours? Why not seat me next to the band? Then I won't be able to hear or be heard either."

"Now, Mags . . ." It wasn't like her to exaggerate. He knew he shouldn't care if she were in a wheelchair, but he found he did.

"Perhaps you'd rather I didn't come at all? I should have thought you'd be happy to have me there. Perhaps you'd like to cancel the whole thing?" She kept a biting edge as she spoke. "Who knows, I might be rather good at maneuvering a wheelchair. Poetry in motion."

Poetry. The word hit Uncas like a sledgehammer. "What does poetry have to do with anything?"

"What do you mean?"

"Maybe you can tell me what you mean by 'poetry in motion.'" Uncas knew that he sounded foolish, but he couldn't stop himself.

"It's an expression, Unk. Rather a nice one, I think."

"You ended up in the hospital because you were browsing through poetry. Hoping to replace the book your paramour gave you. And now suddenly you're 'poetry in motion.'" Uncas found himself filled with fury.

"Uncas Metcalfe, what *are* you talking about?"

What aren't *you talking about?* would sound fatuous, Uncas knew, but it came closest to what he wanted to say. He couldn't look at his wife; he had been afraid of this, afraid that it would be he who had to articulate the humiliation. *Why don't you say something?* He found he couldn't stomach the thought, and he strode toward the door.

"And how nice to think that I have a paramour. What's his name?" Margaret asked.

"I'm talking about Philip."

"Whom?"

"Philip." He closed the door of their bedroom. In addition to wanting the conversation to be as brief and emotionless as possible, above all he wanted it to be private. As feeling fled his body, he felt coldness settle in.

Margaret looked genuinely puzzled, then he saw her realize.

"Philip Sargent." She smiled. "What makes you think of him?" She was silent for a moment. "Oh. His obsession with poetry. He was the tedious one that year in Cambridge. Myrna always says how glad she was she dodged that bullet: a gloomy Gus who could lock you into conversation and—*poof!*—there went the fun for the night."

She seemed to be avoiding Uncas's eyes. As she spoke he had the feeling that she was distracted, that she was grasping for things to say, to fill time in the hopes that she'd hit on something that would placate him.

"Not much of a worry for men; it was women he preyed on." She drew out the word "preyed"; her tone of voice made a joke of what she was saying. Smiling expectantly, she looked at Uncas. "Well, it's true! And half the time you weren't there to rescue me. Myrna had had enough and Peg had always steered clear and you weren't home half the time, so it fell to me to entertain our Mr. Sargent."

She looked expectantly at Uncas, but he declined to make the agreeable noises that would make the conversation an easy one.

She continued. "Oh, I know he was our friend. To turn him away would have been like turning away family. What a sad life. And what an albatross." She sat quietly for a moment. "He used to tell me that poetry gave him what people couldn't—a feeling that life mattered."

Sentimental claptrap, Uncas wanted to say.

"I remember once saying 'oh, bananas,' after he'd made that or some similar pronouncement, and he looked at me as though I'd kicked a dying dog. I felt terrible. Every once in a while I think, oh, I should read poetry. I should edify myself. Look where that got me." She gestured to her leg.

Uncas knew that at some level what she was saying should comfort him; clearly she saw the man as pathetic and wasn't haunted by the idea of what might have been. Still, Uncas found it wasn't enough. He wanted to know why his wife had kissed Philip.

"I wish you'd known him when he was a boy, Unk. He was bookish, of course"—Uncas was getting impatient. He wanted to tell her to stop dodging about, stop avoiding the truth; he wanted to shake it out of her—"and he was never without a diary or notebook. In mid-conversation, he'd write in it for several minutes even with a pretty girl across the table. Oh, he could be tedious even then—but he was also sensitive and funny, and so popular. I never quite knew what happened—whether it was the war, or drinking, or just not growing up."

"I saw you kiss him." Uncas felt his voice catch.

"Uncas Metcalfe, what on earth are you talking about?" She sounded both angry and puzzled. "Oh, my Lord, Unk. Oh, my Lord. You didn't see that. Did you?"

"I came home earlier than expected," he said.

"Oh, Unk. I'd almost forgotten it ever happened. Oh, my Lord. Why didn't you tell me before?" She was quiet for a moment. "Oh, it must have looked horrible, but he'd pestered me so and he was a friend and, and, I remember he said he'd always wanted to know what it would be like, that he'd always wondered. It seemed like a small request from a miserable man. He was leaving for good, and I just gave in when you left with Miss Mynes."

She was shaking her head. "Oh, it was awful. I loathed him for that." She looked relieved and almost angry. "Uncas, oh, you silly ass. I've been searching my mind for why you'd call him my paramour. My paramour. What a thought."

"You gave in?" Uncas said.

"In case you've forgotten, I'd just had a miscarriage. We had lost our first—" She broke off and swallowed. "Oh, Unk. What a terrible thing to think all these years. Why on earth would you bring this up now?"

He left their room without saying a word. He'd humiliated himself enough.

Two hours later, after a session on his stationary bicycle, Uncas warmed up the chicken and green beans that Hannah had left, and brought Margaret up a plate, along with some bread and a glass of water. Time and exercise had done little to calm his outrage: she'd scolded him and then retreated. She received her meal virtually silently, without looking at him, saying only a perfunctory thank-you. Uncas ate his own meal in the kitchen, while watching an old movie on television about a detective who was being set up. According to Alex and anyone else who advocated clarifying old misunderstandings, he should feel elated by his wife's clear pity for Philip; she had put to rest any notion that she might still be harboring feelings for him. While all of this was true, it was not, he realized, what he'd expected. He'd expected her to be devastated and then contrite. That all he would have to do was make reference to the incident and she would ask him for forgiveness. And he would bestow it. This last part he knew: he would have forgiven her, if she'd asked him to.

As he made his way upstairs, checking the doors and turning off lights, he considered sleeping in the guest room, but decided against it. There was no need for him to skulk around; he hadn't done anything wrong. He removed Margaret's glasses for fear that she would break them, but he climbed into bed without removing the book that lay open on her chest; he seemed unable to prevent himself from committing that pettiness. He wanted her to register the different choices he'd made when she awoke. He wanted to wake her up and tell her that it was he who should be doing the scolding; he who had been wronged. How dare she bring up the miscarriage, as though the one excused the other. They were separate. He realized, with some unease, that she must have gotten herself to and from the bathroom. He had to believe she wouldn't endanger herself, that her leg was on the mend, and not that she was too proud to ask him for assistance.

He switched off the light, and with the darkness came manufactured pictures of Margaret and Philip on outings with Ted, Myrna, and Peg, before Uncas had known any of them. Though it was always as though he were discovering it afresh, he had often, over the last thirty or so years, come to the conclusion that the person Philip had always been in love with was Margaret. Sometimes Uncas felt smug; after all he had "won" Margaret. At other times he felt furious that Philip still carried an adolescent torch for his wife because it had, until now, begged the question: was she pining for him as well? In his youth, Uncas had dated local women, who were now Margaret's friends, a fact that had always seemed to amuse, not threaten her. As he lay beside his wife, Uncas inserted himself into his manufactured scenes and deleted all the others but Margaret. He remembered their joy and surprise when she was pregnant. And when the inconceivable happened, when Margaret lost the child, only days after they'd told their families, they had wept together. He was a terribly small man, one whose virtues were far outweighed by his jealousies. And as long as he was taking full stock—his confession to Alex wasn't quite complete. He'd done nothing to reassure Margaret, even in her fragile state, that he had had no interest in Helen Mynes. What kind of man was he? He and his wife seemed to both take refuge in their marriage, as though that was the antidote to jealousy, the cure for loss. They hadn't ever asked each other for reassurance; maybe Margaret had never needed it.

EIGHT

After an early lunch, Uncas set out for his office to collect his briefcase and the seminar papers; he'd take them to Wright—he had told his students they would be able to pick them up from the department secretary anytime after three o'clock today. The final drafts were due a week after vacation ended. As he drove, he shifted uncomfortably in his seat. His backside was still sore from riding out to Poplar Creek. He unbuttoned his overcoat and loosened his tie a fraction. He had overdressed, but the report said to expect a temperature drop in the afternoon, and it was always colder on campus because of the nearness of Laconia Lake. He'd been glad to escape the chaos of the house, and the cold silence of his wife. Uncas parked the Jeep in the lot behind the Menelaus Building and removed his overcoat as he walked to the door.

Inside the small lobby, the dried leaves and dirt that ran from the elevator to the outside door puzzled him. He supposed one of the other tenants was getting rid of old plants, but it was thoughtless to leave the debris for everyone else to tromp through. It lent a disheveled air to the building. It was like seeing fast-food wrappings on park benches. Those who ate such rubbish should clean up after themselves. That's what trash receptacles were for. The sight put Uncas in an even crankier mood; more than once he'd told litterbugs to pick up their trash, and if they scorned him he picked it up himself.

There were more leaves on the landing of the fourth floor, where Uncas's office was. Uncas was flabbergasted. It looked like a bad raking job. He felt a flush grow on his face. The leaves and debris ran in a path from the elevator to his door. He was puzzled and embarrassed; he couldn't recall having any plants here in town. There were some, of course, at his office at the university, but here he had no one reliable to take care of them. Perhaps he had inadvertently let some forgotten plants die, and the janitor who cleaned the offices had disposed of them. He felt in his pocket for his key and noticed that the door was ajar. He'd probably left it open yesterday, in another bout of distractedness. Or possibly the janitor had needed to get in to tend to leaky pipes. Then he saw that the door molding was cracked near the lock and wondered why the janitor wouldn't have used his key. He pushed gently on the door but quickly encountered resistance; something was blocking its path. He then forced it inch by inch, as it slowly dawned on him that his office had been broken into. On every surface—on the windowsills, the radiator, the desk, the writing slides, the chair, and on the floor—were plastic green pots filled with dry dirt and dead plants. There were dead plants everywhere. Withered cacti, dried-up geraniums, stalks of amaryllis, brown ivy. Uncas could hear the radiator hissing. He felt the blood drain from his face. Stuck into the back of the chair with the letter opener was a large note that read LISTEN TO ME ASSHOLE!!!!! Uncas closed his eyes. It was Carl.

He went to the janitor's closet and got a broom. He swept the leaves and dirt from the hallway into his office. He didn't want his neighbors thinking this was his garbage. He cleared a path to his desk chair and pulled the letter opener from the back of the chair; he ran his finger over the gouge mark. The chair had been his father's and before that his grandfather's. He crumpled the note and jammed it angrily into his pocket; he took the plants off the seat and piled a few of the dead ones on top of one another to make room for his feet. He didn't know what to think. He couldn't imagine what he could have done to Carl that would bring on such a reaction; he must be confused. Uncas considered reporting him to the police, but something stopped him. The contents of the notes, their vulgarity, and the possible wider exposure weren't something to which he wanted to subject his family. In the end Carl would likely be fined and issued a restraining order. Unless Uncas sued him, he wouldn't even recover the cost of cleaning the office. On balance he might be better off solving this quietly himself.

He heard the floor creak, and without thinking jumped out of his chair and looked for something with which to protect himself. Whoever it was passed by Uncas's door; Uncas sat back down, his heart thumping. As he heard the door of the office next to his being unlocked, he tried to slow his breathing. It was the accountant. Uncas was relieved that he had thought to clean up the mess in the hall. He relaxed his shoulders. This was ridiculous. He had to put an end to his fear.

Uncas let himself quietly into the hall and again took the broom from the janitor's closet and also several large black garbage bags. He didn't feel comfortable just throwing the plants away. Maybe Fauna and Doug would have a use for the dirt and for the plastic pots. Uncas decided he'd clean up and then bring the Jeep around and as surreptitiously as possible bring the bags down and head out to Wright.

He filled five bags. Though he wasn't half through, he didn't want to waste more time. He needed to deliver his papers to Wright. The rest could be attended to later—the janitor wouldn't be there until Friday evening. He brushed the dirt off his desk, and off the stack of papers, but they weren't the right ones. He was puzzled. Maybe he had already put them in his briefcase, which he always stowed under his desk. It was probably at the back of the kneehole, behind the thick wall of dead plants. But it wasn't there. He looked around the sides of the desk. The case had nothing much in it. Nothing irreplaceable, except the papers—in the unlikely event that his students hadn't made copies—and the bag itself. Another relic left over from his father. It was nowhere to be found. He sat back in his chair with an air of defeat. There was nothing to do but go out to Benson's Nursery. Carl must have known that if the dead plants didn't work, then the stolen papers would. Uncas wouldn't ignore his obligations to his students. At least the nursery was on his way to Wright.

How he wished he'd never entertained the idea of talking to his wife about Philip. The mere thought of the conversation had driven him to ride his bicycle to Poplar Creek as though he were some sort of disgruntled teenager, which in turn had made him vulnerable to the likes of Carl. He sat back in his chair. When he'd finally opened his mouth, where had it gotten him? A scolding. Why didn't he say something, indeed? He'd like to know what good talking had ever done. A man was better off acting than talking. He looked around his office at the destruction Carl had wrought and thought, well, at least he had taken action. He barked out a single, unsatisfying laugh. Being threatened was hardly the most agreeable way to do business, but there was no question that he had to get his students' papers. He placed his hands on the desk and pushed against it. There was work to be done.

Uncas put the last garbage bag in the back of the Jeep and slammed the door shut. He checked to see that it caught.

"Spring cleaning, Uncas?"

He turned to see Elsie Brewster coming out of the Menelaus Café. He nodded to her. "You might say so."

"That's like you. Always wanting to get a jump on things."

Uncas smiled and looked at his watch. He'd stop off at Benson's Nursery and talk with Carl; he wasn't exactly looking forward to seeing him, but Uncas couldn't deny a curiosity; he was drawn in by Carl's seriousness.

"I wish it were so. Today, I'm running late, I'm afraid," Uncas said. After Benson's he would turn in the papers at Wright. But he couldn't tarry; he wanted to be back in plenty of time for dinner. He didn't want to give his wife or Fauna or, for that matter, Alex, any more cause for worry. "Is there somewhere I can drop you?"

"That would be lovely. Margaret's expecting me. I was going to walk to your house, but the sidewalks are awfully wet, and I'd hate to slip."

Uncas opened the front door of the Jeep. On the floor, on the passenger side, he saw Carl's first note. He was relieved to see that it was folded. He picked it up and tucked it into his jacket pocket, with the other note.

"I understand you got your bicycle back."

"Yes. I was most appreciative of your call."

"That was my pleasure, Uncas. I always enjoy doing a little favor. I chuckled when I saw it in the paper. Any idea who took it this time?"

Uncas hesitated. "I try not to worry about that too much. I'm happy to have it back."

"You're too kind a man, Uncas. And where does this bright sunny day take you? To the dump?"

Uncas was puzzled. Why would he go to the dump on a Tuesday? And then he remembered the bags in the back. "No, no, I'm off to Benson's." As soon as he said it, he wished he hadn't. Margaret was right. Elsie was something of a busybody. Still, there were plenty of reasons he might go to a nursery.

"Flowers for the party?"

"Not exactly. I'm off to Wright to drop off some papers." He hoped he could get off the subject of Benson's, but she didn't seem to hear him.

"I don't fancy Benson's myself. I know lots of people swear by them, but I think Carl— He and Floyd Junior were friends for a time before Carl's father died. The police, you probably heard those rumors same as we did, and maybe they were just rumors, about the marijuana. They say Carl was growing it and selling it at the local high school. But I suppose if your mother's an alcoholic that's what happens. That's why Floyd Junior stopped being his friend, because of the marijuana. But I hear the nursery's doing well, though I've heard rumors that he's still growing the dope."

Uncas slowed at his driveway and turned in. Doug was pushing the shovel through the slush. Uncas drove up to the garage.

"Door-to-door service. Oh, aren't you the gentleman." Elsie put her hand on Uncas's arm. "I could have walked up the drive. They don't make them like you and Floyd anymore, Uncas."

Doug opened her door and helped her out.

"Hello, Mrs. Brewster. Hi, Uncas." Doug waved to Uncas as he gave Elsie Brewster his arm.

"Why, thank you, Douglas," Elsie said. "Isn't it lucky that you can help out with the shoveling on a workday and all." She turned back to Uncas. "Thank you; my knight in shining armor. I'll see you tomorrow. I surely hope you find what you want at Benson's."

Uncas found the place easily and was surprised he hadn't taken it in before. Carl's red pickup, with BENSON'S NURSERY painted in script on the door, was in the lot next to the building marked OFFICE. Un-

cas read the motto also painted on the truck door, PLANT LIFE FOR
ALL, which had to him a vaguely seventies ring. He let himself in
and looked around. Swinging doors led to an area enclosed by thick
plastic sheeting that joined the largest of the greenhouses to the office and to the flower coolers. There were large plastic bags of peat
moss, and garden tools for sale in this makeshift foyer area. Uncas
could see Carl talking to someone in the greenhouse. Carl waved
him in, but continued to speak with a young man. There seemed to
be no one else around. He wondered where Carl's mother was.

Uncas half listened to the conversation. Either Carl's manner of
speaking had already seeped into his brain, or Sunday's visit had rea-
woken Uncas's familiarity with it. There was the formality and slow-
ness, but gone was any menacing tone. He was giving instructions
on watering and feeding the plants. The younger man was jotting
things down in a spiral notebook. He reminded Uncas of Hannah's
seriousness in taking notes for the party. Uncas wandered the aisles;
there were flats of newly planted seeds with markers to indicate what
was growing. Not much that Uncas was drawn to; the seasons
seemed off as well as the types of plants for this area. There was a
market, he supposed, for orchids, far from their natural habitat.
Their exoticism must entice some buyers. Margaret, he remembered, had brought several starter kits back from Hawaii to give as
presents.

"So the great professor pays house calls," Carl said. Uncas turned
and realized they were alone. The boy with the notebook was
nowhere to be seen.

Uncas refused today to be daunted by Carl's tone. He would be
polite, but firm. He would find out what Carl wanted and make it
right if he could. Uncas would hear him out, but he disdained the
games from Sunday's encounter.

"This is business or pleasure, Professor? I believe you received my presents, my message," Carl said.

Uncas nodded.

"Business or pleasure?" Carl asked again.

"Business, I suppose."

"I also suppose. I didn't feel we had finished, and yet I thought you would need encouragement to come and visit. And I see I was right. You needed an invitation. I have this planned."

"You will come with me," Carl continued. He led Uncas back out to the makeshift area.

"I've come for my briefcase."

"Follow me."

Uncas hesitated but followed a few steps behind Carl into what he supposed was the main office. There were two desks and several file cabinets. One desk was pristine and the other was piled high with paper and the ubiquitous green plastic of contemporary garden equipment—there was a short section of garden edging, made to re-semble a picket fence; a trowel; what looked like knee guards—helter-skelter on the desk. Carl opened a file cabinet with a key from a large ring and brought out a folder labeled in red capital letters METCALFE, UNCAS (PROF.). It chilled Uncas to see his name as though he were a patient or a client, as though they had a long-standing professional relationship. Even as the file intrigued him, it repelled him as well. It was like a child spying game gone awry. Carl thrust the file into Uncas's hands.

"Carl, I'll look at this another time." Uncas set the folder on the empty desk. "I've come for my briefcase."

"You will do me a courtesy. Please open the file."

Uncas weighed the possibility of standing his ground. He needed to get his students their papers; that was his first responsibility. It seemed that looking at the file would be the shortest route. "Dear Sir," began the carbon copy of a typewritten letter addressed to Uncas at the university. He read quickly. Carl introduced himself; apparently he had only audited Uncas's class. He had an unusual request to put to Prof. Metcalfe, one that he wished to speak to him about in person. Prof. Metcalfe would understand better through conversation, et cetera, et cetera. He tried to read quickly as he flipped through the pages. Though he had been head of the department at the time, Uncas didn't specifically remember having seen any of the letters, but he might have. He could imagine that the office secretary had known that Carl was simply an auditor; she might well have told him there was no need for a meeting. He was stretched thin with the full-time students under his care; auditors had no claim to his office hours. It was sufficient, Uncas thought, that he had let him speak so frequently in class; often enough that his speech patterns were embedded in Uncas's memory.

Each letter was increasingly specific about what Carl wanted, which was for Prof. Metcalfe and his department to look into alternative cures, through plants, for amyotrophic lateral sclerosis. According to Carl, his father had such faith in plant life that Carl figured that was where the cure lay. It was a fantastical idea.

Uncas turned to explain briefly what little he knew about how cures were researched, but Carl cut him short, saying what difference did that make now? Uncas continued reading—the final letter was more pleading. It was desperate, crazed almost, Uncas thought, and included phrases such as "certain hallucinogenic substances that ignorant government officials have seen fit to deem illegal," which in addition to sounding positively loopy made Uncas realize that Carl had wanted the botany department to oversee the growing of marijuana for therapeutic uses. Like students who wrote papers

on peyote—in order to justify reckless experimentation. He seemed
to have had the notion that the authorities wouldn't question such
experimentation at a university. He would have been quite wrong,
then as now, but Uncas wished someone had told him at the time.
He closed the folder and met Carl's gaze full on. If he had seen the
letters and then ignored them, he owed Carl an apology, which he
wouldn't shrink from. The least he could have done was answer. But
when he opened his mouth to say how sorry he was, Carl turned his
back and walked to the door. He took a large down parka off a hook
and slipped into it. Uncas followed him out. They crossed through
the plastic-sheeted foyer and out to the parking lot. Uncas was relieved to have the session over; he would ask for his briefcase and be
on his way.

"And now, please, give me your overcoat," Carl said, once they
were back in the parking lot.

Uncas instinctively pulled his coat tighter. In its desolation, the
nursery had the feel of a place where there was no warmth except for
the humid heat of the greenhouse. "Carl, those letters . . . Someone
should have answered—"

"Your coat, Professor."

He was impossible, Uncas thought. Again, he pulled his hands together; his coat bunched in front. "I've got to be getting along. If
you'll return my briefcase, I'll be on my way." The weather report had
been right; the temperature was dropping. It was already noticeably
colder than when he'd dropped Elsie off. "What is it that you want?"

Carl smiled. "Ah. Suddenly the great professor wants to know. At
the moment, I want your coat."

"Why?"

"You will be uncomfortable while I tell you this story. In junior
high, perhaps Fauna will remember this, our English teacher read to

us a story of the Alaskan wild. She stood at a window. The rest of us outside on a day like today. We jeered her. But I remember that story; I remember that feeling of cold. Give me your coat."

"There has been a misunderstanding. Please give me my brief-case and I'll be on my way. I think we'd both prefer not to get the police involved."

"You will first listen to my story. Your coat."

Uncas considered his options. If he gave him the coat, he'd be in effect handing over power, if that weren't stating it too dramatically. On the other hand it might mean that Carl would see that he was in-terested in bringing an end to this business. He had no other expedi-ent options if he wanted to return his students' papers today. Uncas slowly unbuttoned his cashmere coat—another hand-me-down from his father. Carl took it and laid it on the hood of Uncas's car.

Coatless, Uncas walked by Carl's side. He led him in silence around one lap of the nursery and the snow-covered fields.

"Your uncle," Carl began, "was my father's best friend. He left him his house."

Arthur Carver was married for a short time to Uncas's aunt, just before the Great War. Then she divorced him and moved to New York. The man had continued to trade on the Metcalfe connection, though no one in the family had kept up with him; Uncas himself had never met this Mr. Carver, the man who billed himself as his un-cle. Uncas had heard that he had died with no family; he had often wondered if the man had had any Metcalfe heirlooms.

"I had thought there would be family feeling," Carl continued.

There was no blood tie, Uncas wanted to say, to underscore, but decided it was best to let Carl talk. It seemed he had been waiting a long time to tell his story. The least Uncas could do was to listen in silence. He thought, with not a little bitterness, that the "least" he could do was growing every minute.

"I had such pride in myself for my idea of writing to you. My father would never have done such a thing. Nevertheless, I tried to do it in his style and to adhere to a business tone. I was certain that you would see your role and the necessity of my plan."

Despite an undercurrent of fear, Uncas felt pulled in by Carl's solemnity: he must know that if Uncas were to call the police, it would be easy to trace the debris in his office and the two notes back to Carl. Surely any published news would be bad for business; yet Carl was willing to take this risk.

"Even when you said no immediately, no to my using minutes of your precious office hours, I persisted. I knew I would prevail. No one, I thought, who could, would not help a dying man. But no answer came. I waited for you, for the doctors, until I could wait no more."

As they rounded the nursery's far field for the third time, Uncas made to walk to his Jeep to get his coat. The metal rims of his glasses exacerbated the cold and had given him a headache. Carl, who was dressed in a large down parka and ski cap, took hold of Uncas's arm above his elbow and pulled him back. "Each time you think you can no longer bear the cold, I want you to think of my father and the skin tightening around him. The creeping paralysis. And you will see what you can bear."

Carl's tone of voice began a slow evolution from superiority and bitterness to a swallowed grief. He detailed each step of his father's illness—evoking scenes of gagging and retching as Carl tried to massage his throat. He described the fear that each cough was his last breath, while Uncas, his hands deep in his pockets, fingering Carl's two notes, trying to fight off the bitter cold—he could no longer feel his feet—contemplated the part this boy supposed Uncas had played in not saving his father from death or pain.

"I wanted to kill him, O Great Professor. How is that for a confession? I wanted to kill my own father, put him down like a horse with a broken leg, put him out of his miserable pain."

Uncas felt sick. "He had," he said, finally remembering the name, "Lou Gehrig's disease?"

"Lou Gehrig's," Carl said, snapping with bitterness again. "Such reduction. A nickname for a fatal disease."

He was silent again and then continued. "Finally, my own research pointed me in the right direction. I thought if there is no cure, there must at least be ways to ease the horrible pain, the gagging, the shaking, without making him sick to his stomach. I thought of marijuana. Yes. I had already been warned by the police for earlier childish infractions. I could not buy it without risk, and my mother wouldn't, and so I turned back to the great university. I'm surprised you didn't turn me in. But I see I fell outside your limited vision. When, again, there was no answer, no acknowledgment of my communications, I grew it myself and convinced my mother to let him use it."

Uncas felt himself on the verge of tears, but it was as though the cold had created a kind of temporary Lou Gehrig's disease—he felt paralyzed. Tears wouldn't come and God knows how Carl would have reacted to them. It was fully dark by now; Uncas was glad Carl couldn't see him.

"You will be interested, O Great Professor, to learn of a collateral benefit: for the next few months, my mother's displeasure at me for growing the marijuana and her fear of the police took her mind away from my father dying. He accepted the joints I rolled. And then I failed him again. Out of loneliness I trusted the maggot Floyd Brewster, and in turn the police doused my supply with gas, and that was the end of my father's comfort. A few weeks' solace was all I was able to offer him. A chain of events begun by your refusal." They walked in silence; as they approached the parking lot, Uncas tried to tamp down his hope that he might get in his Jeep and turn on the heat.

Carl didn't slow and they began another lap. "For a long time I felt I had failed him, and then I realized it was you who failed him, but that I cannot say now. You were not big enough to fail him. You were not big enough to save him, or even to help him."

Carl began, in a low voice, to describe the actual death; Uncas was thankful he could barely hear him. And then suddenly Carl stopped talking. He was silent, as he led Uncas back to the nursery buildings. It was as though he wanted to disappear back into his own world.

Uncas waited outside the office for his briefcase and coat. He had managed to get the two notes Carl had written him out of his jacket pocket. He wanted to offer them to him; to show him he was willing to forget Carl's threats; to make some gesture of conciliation. His arms were huddled in front of him, his body shaking violently.

Carl returned with Uncas's briefcase, which he dropped at Uncas's feet. He seemed to have regained some energy. "You are nothing, great professor. You don't deserve what you are so lucky to have," Carl said. Then he saw the notes and snatched them from Uncas's frozen fist. He reached into his pocket and took out a lighter and set the notes on fire, waving the flames in front of Uncas. They lit up Carl's angry face and hand. "Worried that someone might read that I called you an 'asshole'?" Carl dropped the notes and ground the burning sheets into the asphalt.

Another slap. Uncas felt sorely misunderstood. He shook his head. "Carl, what is it that you want?"

Carl was silent. Uncas tried to work his hand to open the Jeep's front door. When he finally managed to pull it open, Carl kicked it shut.

"Even on students' papers you are afraid," he said, toeing Uncas's briefcase with his boot. "You prescribe. You decree. You mandate. You are nothing. You are more willing to strike out a complicated passage than to sort through less than logical writing to discover the buried gem. I dreamed of studying the plants full-time with you. I would learn more from tending weeds in the desert."

Uncas didn't respond to the insults. "What is it that you thought I could do? There was no cure for your father."

"Help my father not to die in pain. But for you he didn't exist." Carl crossed to his truck, climbed in and drove off, leaving Uncas in the parking lot, with his briefcase at his feet.

Uncas managed finally to get the key in the ignition and set the heat on high. Even the cold air that initially came in through the blowers felt warmer than he did. He climbed out and retrieved his coat from the hood of his car and managed with difficulty to get his arms in the sleeves; he climbed back in the car without buttoning it. His glasses fogged over. He was almost thawed—his hands had begun to burn and itch as the blood found its way to his fingertips—almost ready to drive to Wright, when he heard a knocking at the window and turned to see his daughter. With effort, he rolled it down.

"You okay, Dad?" she asked. "I feel like that's my refrain lately." She looked at him suspiciously. "The university called looking for you. Doug said he thought Mrs. Brewster had mentioned that you were coming out here. I came as soon as he told me. I can't believe you're here. It's almost six. Where's Carl?"

Uncas said he was fine. He felt a swelling in his chest; the extremes of temperature had dazed him.

She looked at him, wanting, he supposed, more answers, but he didn't know what to say and so was silent. He glanced at the car clock. It was late. The papers. It was too late to drop them off.

"Dad, what is going on? What are you doing here? You look pale." She choked and swallowed, and then continued. "I can't believe that you're out here after what happened. I can't believe we're still giving this lunatic business. Why don't you do something?"

Uncas had no idea how to answer his daughter, how to explain what had gone on. "I'm driving home now," he said. He didn't know what else to do; he was too late to turn in the papers. He'd have to run them over first thing in the morning.

Fauna had followed him to the driveway and then continued on. Uncas felt utterly drained and was relieved that the house was empty except for Margaret. Though it was early, her eyes were closed. He wanted to will them open, to have her, with a squeeze of her hand or a sympathetic look, reassure him of their connection. Words or iciness might crush him. He opened the hot water tap fully and opened the cold tap partway. He was enervated. He climbed into the steaming bathtub, laid his head back on the rim, and allowed the exhaustion to seep in; he let the tears that brimmed in his eyes run into his ears; he felt no need to stop them. Pure exhaustion. A scene took shape in his thoughts; the power to suppress was overtaxed, and so, as though emerging from smudged charcoal, Uncas saw Carl feeding his father by "working his throat for him." It brought on a wave of nausea. Please, God, Uncas said to himself, when my time comes, let it be quick and painless.

NINE

Uncas was eating his breakfast when he heard Fauna's voice behind him.

"Dad, I'd like to talk to you."

He looked at her, surprised. She circled around the table until she was facing him. He continued with his breakfast. It was early. He had hoped to get out the door to Wright before everyone descended on the house to prepare it for the evening's festivities.

"I wasn't sure you'd be awake yet." Fauna looked at him expectantly, as though he were supposed to know why she was here. He put down his cereal spoon. He couldn't have forgotten another promise to help her.

"Dad, this is hard for me to say, but I've been up all night, and I can't . . ."

Uncas felt uneasy. Still, he could be patient; it was best not to say anything.

"What's going on with Carl?" she asked.

He studied her, and he wondered what she knew. He wanted to tell her everything. He wanted to share the weight of yesterday, of Carl's father's death, but there was a risk that instead of relieving it, she would only add to the burden—by exploding in anger, by urging on him a course of action that felt inappropriate. He would be giving in to weakness. Muddying what he'd finally cleared up. She hadn't seen anything yesterday to suggest that Carl had done anything. All she knew was that Uncas had paid a call at the nursery. She didn't know about the dead plants; she didn't know about the walk in the cold; she didn't know about the letters. Based on the information she had, which was what she'd seen in the kitchen at Poplar Creek, it was an exaggeration to say that anything was "going on." The long and short of it was that the business with Carl didn't concern her. He didn't know how to say that without appearing rude. Fauna stared at him for several seconds and shook her head.

"Why didn't you tell me?"

"Fauna, I'm not sure—"

"Why did Doug have to hear from Sparta's biggest gossip that you went by yourself to see Carl? You can't do that, Dad. You can't tell Mrs. Brewster and not tell me, especially after— Look, I don't think Carl's going to hurt you, he's not that type of guy, but he's no Boy Scout either. You should have told me you were going to visit him. Why didn't you tell me?"

Uncas looked at her. It hadn't even occurred to him. She had appeared in time to give him a ride home from the lake, and he had been grateful and—now that he thought of it—pleased by her practicality in arranging things once they got back to the house, but there was no need to involve her further. And of course he hadn't meant to share his whereabouts with Elsie Brewster.

"Dad, look— I— I wish— I don't think—" She sounded as though she were about to cry. She stopped talking for a moment. He could hear her swallow; she wiped tears from her cheeks with the back of her hand. He could imagine her trying not to cry. He wanted to tell her it was okay; he was fine. He hated to see people cry; it made him feel helpless. At that moment the phone rang. Uncas rose to answer it and then sat down when it stopped mid-ring. As much as he would have liked to interrupt Fauna, it was probably just as well that he hadn't. He looked at her expectantly, and was surprised by how composed she suddenly seemed.

"Dad, you haven't been yourself recently. After that whole thing with the boiler, I was telling Doug how annoyed I was, and he reminded me that it's the first time you'd ever done something like that. And then you ride your bike to Poplar Creek like you're twelve years old or something."

"I'm fine. There's nothing to worry about."

"That's very thoughtful of you, Dad, I'm sure. It's like you think you're some kind of goddamn oak tree. I'd like to help, but it doesn't seem like you want it. It must be hard with Mom in bed. But it seems like you always make it harder, and you always have. You're so, so— removed. You never say you're sorry. You never, ever say thank you. For anything." Fauna started crying again. Uncas pulled out his handkerchief and offered it to her. She waved it off and instead pulled a paper towel off the roll and loudly blew her nose and dried her tears. She crumpled up the paper towel and threw it in the garbage. It affected him to see her so upset, but he honestly didn't know what she was talking about. He had been raised in politeness and had, he hoped, passed that on to his children. He looked at his cereal; the grains were bloated with milk.

"You can do what you want, obviously, and pretend nothing is wrong. But I can't. On two separate days you've ended up looking like a total wreck after you see Carl, and then you're so goddamn, excuse me—gosh darn—mysterious. Maybe it's none of my business, but I'm not going to pretend nothing is wrong. I'm not raising my kids that way either. If you want anything, I hope you'll ask."

She stood there as though she were waiting for an answer. He felt tired; it was as if he remembered a death, or bad news, that he'd momentarily forgotten. There was an ache, a void beneath the surface. He wished that there was something he could ask her to do. He didn't know what. Something to lessen the sorrow he felt. He didn't seem to be able to help anyone anymore. Fauna had always been sensitive, quick to tears and anger as a child. He supposed things hadn't changed much.

"Honey," he said.

Fauna's face quickened with an expectant look. Uncas couldn't think of what to say.

"I, have you been up to see your mother?"

"No, Dad. I came to see you." She looked at him in a way that he imagined mirrored his own sadness. "I don't know why I expect you to say something," she said. "You never do." And then Fauna said goodbye; she'd see him at the party.

As Uncas was dumping the last of his soggy cereal down the drain, Margaret's voice floated out of the baby intercom. She sounded tentative, unsure whether or not she was speaking to an empty kitchen, wondering if he were there. They hadn't exchanged more than a few words since their conversation, if one could call it that, about Philip. But Margaret, he contemplated, had been chilly instead of angry. She could move in seconds from genial to frosty, whereas Fauna mostly smoldered and then exploded. Yet both seemed eventually to find room temperature, which was where Uncas hoped he resided most days.

He climbed the stairs aware that he was nervous, unsettled by the thought that she might continue their conversation.

"Unk, is that you?"

He detected no iciness. "It is I," he answered.

"You're up with the birds."

"Tweet tweet." Uncas flapped his forearms. "Migrating south."

"South?"

He meant only the few miles to Wright, but he couldn't deny that Florida or some warm beach where he could fulfill a lifelong fantasy of being a layabout was a temptation. "To Wright," he said.

"But I thought you'd taken care of Wright yesterday. What happened?"

"The best laid plans," he said, gesturing with his little forearm wings. "I need to drop off papers."

"Oh, Lord. I was counting on you and your car. Fauna's taken mine again. Would you mind awfully running Alexandra around for errands? For rock salt and place cards? And a trip out to Benson's. That was Carl who called. He can't—"

"Carl Benson? Why would he? You *know* Carl Benson?" Uncas asked Margaret.

"I do indeed!"

Uncas felt sick to his stomach. Of course she knew him—this was a part of the picture that he'd willed out of his mind. Fauna had said Margaret did business at Benson's. *That* was how Carl had known about their party. Still, Uncas knew that wasn't where she typically did business, that nursery bore a man's name. One syllable. He decided to start at the beginning. "What do you know about his father?"

Margaret closed her eyes. "Oh, it was awful." She opened her eyes and looked at Uncas. "He died of Lou Gehrig's disease. The same thing Peg died of. Oh, it was simply awful. When it got bad, Carl left school to help out at the nursery." She stopped. "You don't remember any of this? Oh, Lord, they had special sales to raise money. I must have bought a dozen geraniums, some of which still bloom. They were without any sort of insurance. They finally sold that house they'd been given by—"

Uncas nodded.

"Oh, I can't think," Margaret said. "What was his name?"

"Arthur Carver."

"That's right. They had planned eventually to live in it, but instead watched it razed to make room for those storage units."

Uncas nodded. The units were next to the nursery's far field. He'd walked by the flimsy structures several times yesterday afternoon.

"And now poor Leila's in the hospital again. Carl's had his trials," Margaret said.

"Leila?"

"Leila Benson. Carl's mother."

Elsie had mentioned her. "Yes. Elsie said she drinks."

"Pure nonsense. The woman's a teetotaler. Always has been. Anyhow, once they sold the house and the land there was more money. Oh, it was just awful. I remember when I visited Peg toward the end. She couldn't talk, but, thank God, she wasn't having trouble eating. Oh, Cy Benson died even more slowly than she did. Poor thing. His poor wife. And poor Carl. And then the sheriff found the marijuana plants. That's where Floyd Junior made himself so helpful."

"Yes," Uncas said.

Carl had bitterly spit out Floyd Junior's name as the boy who'd brought the law in. Uncas couldn't understand why his wife always sounded so repelled when she mentioned him. He knew she didn't care for Elsie's coy efforts at gossip, but she was essentially a harmless sort, and surely Floyd Brewster Sr. made up for what was wanting in Elsie. With a man like that as your father, there was little chance, it seemed to Uncas, of not inheriting character. As Elsie pointed out yesterday, Carl's involvement with marijuana had made Floyd Junior uncomfortable. Maybe Carl had raised marijuana for medicinal purposes, but conveniently he'd also smoked it himself now and again. If he admitted to that, most likely his use was more frequent. Enough to make Carl a user and a pusher, if what Elsie Brewster said was accurate.

And if Carl was growing marijuana, Floyd Junior should have reported him. That took a kind of rectitude. Margaret must see that. He hadn't even landed Carl in jail. On the contrary, the sheriff had been curiously lenient. According to Carl, he had destroyed the plants and had let Carl and his parents off with a warning.

"It turned out Floyd Junior, and you'll never get Elsie to admit to this, was selling marijuana that he stole from Carl. Once the sheriff caught him, he made a deal and told him where he was getting it. Now, I'm not an advocate of marijuana, but I think that what Floyd did was just rotten. Cyrus Benson was certainly no addict, and the stuff helped."

"Is that true?"

"Oh, Unk, that's not news. I'm awfully fond of Floyd, but Floyd Junior? I wouldn't trust him to look after a can of garbage. He's no Carl Benson."

Uncas looked at his wife as if from a distance. How little she knew of Carl. Carl's efforts to help his father were admirable (and at the same time he supposed he'd have to reevaluate Floyd Junior), but even Margaret, he suspected, would find Carl's more recent behavior difficult to support. His father had died years ago. Why had calling Uncas to account suddenly become imperative?

"Why the interest in the Bensons—you haven't been to see Carl, have you? He always asks after you, for years now. I've told you that. I've tried to get you out to the nursery. Did you finally go? I think he admires your work at Wright. Luckily he's never asked what you think of nurseries."

Uncas shook his head. "He's invited me out there?"

Margaret laughed. "Countless times. Unk, I persisted beyond what I normally would only because Carl was so persistent. But you made it pretty clear that it was something that simply didn't interest you."

The boy's name didn't even stir a memory beyond the last few days. He recalled nothing of Carl's phone calls to Fauna; and it was "Si" that he had thought ran the nursery his wife got her flowers and plants from, who he now realized was Cy Benson. It was difficult to believe that he didn't remember his wife's entreaties and that the boy's story was as familiar to her as it was unfamiliar to him. It was as though he'd been in some remote wilderness without access to a phone or television or newspapers and was trying to play catch-up. It was disturbing.

"Why don't you call Alex and tell her I'm on the way." Likely, it was churlish of him to imagine that Fauna could run the errands, and it seemed easier to go along; his wife wouldn't be laid up forever. Alex was better company than most; that was a consolation. Still, he couldn't help but feel some trepidation. He didn't relish the combination of Alex and Carl—both courted extremes of emotion.

"You really don't remember, do you?" Margaret asked, as he was leaving. She looked wistful. "I've always wondered if you don't listen to begin with, or if you listen and then forget because whatever it is doesn't interest you. I suppose it amounts to the same thing. You know your mind." She said this without the chill Uncas might have expected. There was a kind of resigned wonder. As though she were used to it, but it still puzzled her after all these years.

*　*　*

"Are you okay, Mr. Metcalfe?" Alex and Uncas had been riding silently for a block or so. There were two stops they needed to make, in addition to Benson's. Uncas wished, not for the first time, that Alex had a driver's license. But even that wouldn't have solved the matter—he wouldn't have let her go there alone. Uncas was taken aback when he realized how Carl's behavior worried him. While Carl had done nothing but menace and posture, he couldn't be trusted; it was too late to stop things in time for the party, but afterward he'd speak to Margaret; they'd take their business elsewhere. In any case it was impossible that Alex go there alone. He couldn't drop her off. The waste of his time was infuriating; the preying on his mind was unforgivable. The more he thought about it, the more he wanted to throttle Carl—dead father or no.

"I'm fine."

"I'm really sorry you have to do this. I know I should have gotten a license, but I haven't got a car, and in New York, well, neither of my parents even have a car."

Uncas said nothing. He was trying to map out the morning; he could bring Alex to Wright if necessary. That shouldn't take too long.

"My dad's really, really impressed that you still ride your bike. I sent him a copy of the newspaper picture of your bike and the snow and everything."

"Does he?"

"Does he what?"

"Does he bicycle?"

"My dad? No way. He thinks taking the stairs two flights is exercise. That and golfing. He walks, but mostly he takes cabs and the subway. I can't even picture him on a bike. I don't even know if he knows how to ride one."

"I rode a bicycle in New York once. All the way down Fifth Avenue."

"From where to where?"

"Let's see. From Eighty-eighth to Twelfth Street and over to Sixth Avenue." It had been the night of the party in Greenwich Village. His roommate had found a bike, and soon enough there was a challenge, and Uncas rode to the party. At first, he'd felt invincible. And then he'd been caught between two buses for a block, and had feared for his life. He'd met his friends in the Village, where he'd carried the bike up three flights. Uncas had no recollection of how he had gotten it back up to Eighty-eighth Street. He'd almost forgotten the incident altogether.

"That's close to four miles. Not bad."

"Here we are." Uncas pulled up to Parties Plus. Margaret had requested place cards to use to identify the various sauces and dressings and other dishes that would make up the buffet dinner. Alex got out and walked to the door. Uncas watched her pull on the handle and then peer in the window. Patience, he thought. He looked at his watch. Nine forty-five. Probably not open until ten. They'd move along to Fife's for salt for the sidewalk.

"Not open for another fifteen minutes." Alex stood outside looking up and down the street. "Mind if I go to Bagel Falls and say hello to Hannah? I can get you a cup of cof— I mean Sanka."

Uncas exhaled slowly through pursed lips.

"Mr. Metcalfe?"

"Sure. Why don't you? I'll wait here."

"No sugar, but milk, right?"

"Sanka. With low-fat milk. No sugar. That's it." He reached into his jacket pocket and drew a five-dollar bill out of his wallet. "And why don't you get yourself something too?"

Alex looked at the bill. "I don't need any money. They let us take all the coffee we want. But thanks."

Uncas watched as Alex crossed the street. She stopped at the window of Bagel Falls and squished her face against the glass. Seconds later Hannah opened the door. Both of them were laughing, as if they'd discovered that trick. He found, in his Carl Benson–induced irritation, that their obvious closeness made him nostalgic somehow. He thought about Margaret's reaction to his saying "tweet, tweet." There had been a time when a gesture like that would have them calling each other silly bird names; oh, they could still joke and, of course, did, but Uncas recognized a distance too. It was nonsensical to compare their long, rich marriage to the friendship of two teenaged girls. Maybe so, but it made Uncas yearn for the early days with Margaret, before Cambridge but after they'd gotten engaged. Their engagement—that was a bit of derring-do. After a picnic along the river behind her parents' house, he'd plucked a daisy and fashioned a ring out of it; all the while he'd had a diamond ring, flanked by her favorite rubies, in his pocket. He'd even sung "Daisy, daisy, give me your answer, do," as impossible as that seemed now. She'd said yes, but gaily refused to replace the daisy until they told her father. Now it was dried and pressed between the pages of her mother's prayer book, marking the blessing of the ring. He had known what he'd wanted to say, and he'd said it. And Margaret had returned his affection, his love, which he'd known she would, while it also had seemed out of the realm of possibility. They were less reckless now.

Alex knocked on his window with her elbow. She had coffee cups in both hands. "This one's yours," she said, once he had the window down. She raised her right hand. He took his cup from her. She handed in the other cup, which he set gingerly on her seat. "Forgot to mark which is which. Oh, here comes the Parties Plus lady. Be right back."

He rolled up his window, and then watched her as she stood next to the clerk from Parties Plus; Alex had her hands deep in her now familiar camouflage pants. Facing out to the street, as though she were a lookout trying to mask the opening of the door, she seemed focused on Bagel Falls.

After a quick stop at Fife's for rock salt, they were on their way to Benson's. Alex was talking about her father. "What I meant to say"— she was laughing—"is that . . ." And then Uncas stopped listening. He barely heard her, much less registered her words. He was unnerved by the dread that he felt being back at Benson's, at the anticipation of seeing Carl again.

"What's wrong, Mr. Metcalfe?" Alex had read him quickly.

"Here we are, then."

"You look horrible. Maybe we should go back to your house."

He turned to Alex as he shut the car off. "Let's make this quick."

"Sure, but—"

"I'm fine. Just running behind schedule."

A sign on the door said CLOSED/SORRY FOR ANY INCONVENEINCE. Naturally, the word was misspelled. Uncas looked at his watch. He couldn't fathom why a business wouldn't be open by ten-fifteen. Where the hell was Carl? He turned from the door.

"We can go in," Alex said, her eyes searching his face. "Mrs. Metcalfe said he'd expect us. We're supposed to ignore the sign and walk in. At least that's what she said." She sounded subdued.

Uncas pushed the door open. He could feel his anger build. As always with Carl, he felt at a disadvantage. Now, as a customer, he felt that same frustration. Today, he would take no nonsense.

Uncas strode back toward the office, pushing aside the plastic curtains, telling himself as his anger built to calm down. Carl would likely be a different man around Alex; he had seemed like a model, patient boss with his employee.

"Slow down, Mr. Professor," Carl said. He was behind them in the foyer near the greenhouse. Uncas turned sharply and Alex ran into him.

"Sorry," she said. "I wasn't watching."

Carl had a smile on his face, as though he were a typical businessman welcoming typical customers. "You're here for Mrs. Metcalfe's boughs, I am assuming."

Uncas was flummoxed for a moment. He didn't know what they were there to pick up. Margaret hadn't said.

Alex looked back at Uncas and then ahead to Carl. "That's what Mrs. M. said." She turned back to Uncas. "That's what she said we should pick up."

"I am in a hurry," Carl said. "I expected you earlier. They are around back. I'll show you where and then, I'm afraid, leave you."

Afraid? thought Uncas. *Afraid?* He clenched his jaw and followed Carl and Alex around the outside to a temporary shed, where there were neatly bundled piles of pine boughs. This was the height of absurdity: he would be shelling out money for something he could pick up for free in the woods behind Poplar Creek. Uncas had half a mind to walk away.

He turned to Alex. "How many did Mrs. Metcalfe say we should get?"

Alex shrugged. "She said he would have everything ready." She turned to Carl. "Do you know how many—"

Carl looked at Uncas. "These four bundles are for Mrs. Metcalfe's party. And the wreath is a present from the nursery. We make them for our best customers. I hope you will also please take that to her."

"Very good," Uncas said. "Alex, I'll pull the car back."

"If that is all, I'll be leaving," Carl said.

"Bye," Alex said. "Thanks."

"You are welcome, young lady."

Uncas tensed his shoulders but didn't break his stride when he heard Carl come up behind him. And yet, in ignoring him, he felt childish, and impolite. So automatic were his manners, he couldn't stop himself from turning around to say goodbye. But Carl was already stepping back inside the nursery door.

Uncas felt like a sap—patronized and dismissed. He backed the car alongside the shed next to which the boughs were placed. Alex opened the tailgate. "Should we pile them on top of this stuff?" Uncas had forgotten the several bags of detritus that Carl had left in his office.

"No, no," he said. "These are a present for Mr. Benson."

"Garbage?"

"No. They're dried-up plants and such. I thought he might find a use for the dirt." Uncas was pleased with his hasty plan: to give the trash back to its rightful owner. Alex looked doubtful, but pulled a bag out of the car. Uncas felt a kind of petty satisfaction as they unloaded the bags. Then he heard an engine start, and he found himself trying to hide the bags from view. He looked up to see Carl backing his truck directly toward Uncas's station wagon. Uncas moved quickly to shield Alex. Carl then braked hard, shifted, and drove out of the nursery, taking the left onto the main road so quickly the wheels squealed.

"Oh, my God," Alex said, "you scared me."

"Forgive me. The sudden— I thought— I guess he was in a hurry."

"Yeah. He's kind of a weirdo."

Uncas wanted to chase Carl down and ask him what gave him the right to terrify others. He wanted to shake the man until he cried. Uncas inwardly writhed with helplessness—the most he could do was leave five bags of trash. Probably Carl wouldn't even notice them, and if he did, he'd merely get his employee to dump them on the compost. Uncas considered retrieving his file from Carl's office and burning it—the way Carl had his filthy notes. He'd leave a little heap of ashes on Carl's desk chair. Uncas could then find the originals at Wright, if they kept such things, and burn them. He could erase all trace of any connection with Carl. He imagined Carl merely sweeping the ashes into a wastebasket and dumping those also onto his compost pile. There would be no satisfying revenge.

TEN

Uncas could hear the trio tuning up. As he fitted his studs into the buttonholes, he felt himself perk up, he could feel a buoyancy, as though he had checked off the last item on a long list of onerous tasks. He knotted his bow tie and adjusted it in the mirror. He liked wearing a tuxedo—it took away any guesswork. It was all of a piece—no need to worry about the color of his shirt or the pattern on his tie; his burgundy velvet cummerbund was a perfect seasonal addition. He slipped into his patent leather dancing pumps; shoes he well knew no other man would be sporting—they had bows after all, but they were the shoes one wore to dance. Though his tuxedo from college still fitted, a few years ago when he'd received some idiotic award for "service" to Wright, Margaret had insisted he buy a new one. Malc had pointed him to a man in New York City who made suits to order, and Uncas had to admit that it felt different from his grandfather's hand-me-down. There was no unnecessary bunching; it was a suit that made one relax; he felt he was in the arms of someone confident when he put on the jacket—the fit was that good. Almost worth the price of the extravagance.

He hummed "Ridin' High"—he smiled when he realized it was because of the *Gazette* caption for the picture of his bicycle—and felt years younger. He'd have to mention it to Steve Weckstein; he'd seen the editor's hand in the title to the caption. Uncas tried to contemplate what his toast would be, but the nightmare of his walk around Carl's nursery kept insinuating itself—obviously inappropriate, but difficult to shake nonetheless—along with Fauna's speech this morning. He hadn't known what to make of her anger and upset, and the bit about not saying "thank you" troubled him. No doubt she was exaggerating. The move back had obviously been a strain on her. He wondered if Doug had gotten the job out at the mini steel mill. He liked to make his annual toast brief and humorous. He'd thought about it in the tub the evening before, but visions of Cyrus Benson kept presenting themselves then too. There was a man who had barely been able to move during his last three years, much less dance. It sounded as though he had been in dreadful pain.

Uncas walked into the bedroom. Margaret was nowhere to be seen. He felt aimless. Their argument about Philip would be shelved, and possibly even forgotten, in the excitement of the party and the to-do around Christmas. He hadn't yet gotten her Christmas present; he'd have time to see to that in the next few days. He was done with Wright duties until after New Year's. He could look forward to the party. He was looking forward to catching up with old friends; he was even looking forward to meeting Alex's father. He and Margaret couldn't dance, but there had been lots of parties where they might have and hadn't. That wouldn't interfere with his having a good time. Or with hers, he supposed. He looked out the bedroom window and watched a light snow falling past the streetlight. Picturesque, yes, but it was also the kind of snow that could make driving treacherous. He hoped it would stop in time for the party.

After he and Alex had come back from Benson's, Uncas had spent

most of the day undoing more of Carl's damage. Infuriatingly, he
had written comments in the margins of the seminar papers, comments on the papers themselves, and comments on Uncas's comments. Uncas had had the students bring in their photocopies. Of
course one student had neglected to make a copy; in the event Uncas had whited out any of Carl's comments that were in the body of
the paper and he had folded over the margins and then photocopied
it; he then rewrote his own comments onto all of the fresh copies.
Carl's marginalia had ranged from puerile to astute. There was one
instance where he'd been able to unravel a few clumsy sentences to
reveal a direction in which it was wise to push the student. Uncas
had considered including the comment on the fresh copy, but
couldn't bring himself to. He wondered if it were a big mistake not
to report Carl. The visit out to Poplar Creek was one thing, but the
plants and the walk in the cold were another. In the end, though,
nothing had happened. Nothing. Here Uncas was, ready to dance.
He pictured himself finally getting the door of the Jeep open and
Carl kicking it shut—a move from a B movie. The next move would
have been to step on Uncas's hand as he reached for a gun that had
been kicked next to the tire.

Uncas turned quickly around before he had time to think—was
someone in the room?—and held up his hands in front of him as
though to ward off a blow.

"Oh, Unk, I'm sorry. Did I startle you?" It was Margaret in her
wheelchair. She smiled. "I guess these tires don't make enough
noise." She was wearing what his mother had referred to as "the
headlight," a large aquamarine stone set in a sunburst of diamonds.
It had come down through his mother's family, something leftover
from their time in the diplomatic service between the wars. There
wasn't much occasion for it in Sparta.

Uncas's heart was pounding. Carl was hardly going to sneak up on him in his own house, much less his own bedroom. The bags of dead plants he'd returned left him feeling a tad ashamed of himself; at the same time, they seemed a small payback for the scare Carl had given Uncas when he'd backed toward him and Alex so quickly. Carl had been here early this afternoon. As Uncas arrived back from Wright, the now familiar red pickup was pulling out of the driveway. Uncas had nodded at him, but Carl hadn't recognized Uncas's car, or hadn't seen him, or, most likely, was ignoring him. Uncas had been sweating and his heart pounding as he drove up the driveway, until he realized Carl had been there to deliver the flower arrangements.

"Shall we dance, Mr. Metcalfe?" With one fluid motion, as though she were changing direction in a rowboat, Margaret pivoted herself around to face the door. He looked at the back of her head; her long hair was gathered higher on her head than usual. She looked elegant, the wheelchair notwithstanding. "Little Charley tells me my tennis is going to come in handy. Forearms are very important in maneuvering these chairs."

"Would it count as dancing?" Uncas asked, following his wife out the door to the landing above the stairs. Her dress was draped over her leg, which was straight out in front of her. He couldn't imagine how he'd even spin her around in the simplest of moves.

Margaret hoisted herself out of the chair. "Now, if you carry that, I'll get myself down."

Uncas was doubtful. "How, Mags? Will you slide down the banister?" He'd assumed that she would lean on his arm and use the banister for support.

She looked at him quickly and directly, and then looked away, as though she had decided not to chastise him. "The same way I've been getting to the john recently. My hindquarters." She sat down and brought herself down step by step. Uncas watched from the top of the stairs; he might have known she'd find a way to do it on her own.

The guests weren't due for an hour, but Margaret wanted to inspect the downstairs and supervise the finishing touches. Uncas pushed her into the living room, where the trio was warming up. The singer had on a long sleeveless black dress that left, as his father would say, nothing to the imagination. Uncas was startled to see that the bass and piano players were also women. There was no drummer, but a large drum with "Broad-Way" written in script across the front, set to the side of the piano. Malc and Libby had said that show tunes were their specialty. Uncas was dubious. He'd never seen a woman bass player, but he was ready to reserve judgment. His only requirement was that they play the old tunes, Porter and Gershwin, and none of the newer junk.

At the other end of the room was the tree—as decked out as they were. Margaret gasped when she saw it. "Oh, Unk, you outdid yourself. The tree is wonderful. And it's a blue spruce." Uncas looked at it appreciatively. It fitted the room exactly. Hannah and Alex had hung the white lights and silver icicles and sprayed touches of fake snow, just as his father used to do. The boughs had been artfully arranged on the mantelpieces and on the dining room table and on the windowsills and on the curtain rods. Through the windows on either side of the tree he could see the snow-covered front lawn in the moonlight. He had to admit it was spectacular.

"What's that?" He pointed to the angel on top of the tree. "Where's the star?"

"They couldn't find it, so I told them to go ahead and put the angel on," Margaret said.

Uncas felt a prickle of irritation; he was sure it was with the rest of the decorations; they'd always had a star on the top, but it was hardly worth getting the ladder now.

Margaret was studying the large floral arrangement on the mantelpiece. "Oh, my. Carl has outdone himself. I'm glad you finally met him, Unk, though I wish I'd been the one to introduce you. It's one of the many reasons I was looking forward to tonight. Oh, he must have been thrilled to finally meet you. I would love to have been there. He's a lamb."

"Tonight?"

"Yes. Remember, Unk? We're having a little soirée."

"You invited Carl Benson?" Uncas worked to keep the fear out of his voice. He ran his finger between his neck and his collar, which had less give than those to which he was accustomed.

"Yes. Oh, Unk, you saw the list. With his mother in the hospital, I thought he could use a break. But come to think of it, she was operated on today. I'm not even sure he'll make it. He's a little older than the girls, but I thought it might be more fun for them, with someone close to their age besides Floyd Junior." Margaret gave a disdainful look. "Oh, I don't care for that boy. But Carl and Fauna and Doug, oh, and Floyd too, I guess, were all at Sparta High together. Until Carl had to leave. Don't worry, Unk. You won't have to do a thing."

Uncas reached for his handkerchief. There would be plenty of people here. Carl wouldn't dare try anything.

"Oh, my," he heard Margaret say, "don't you look smashing?"

"Thanks, Mrs. M." It was Alex. "Hi, Mr. Metcalfe. You okay? You look hot." Uncas forced himself to look at her.

"Fine. I'm fine." He mopped his face, and then studied her more closely. "What are you wearing?"

"It's my brother's old tuxedo. Cool, huh?"

At least she had taken out the earring from her nose for the occasion.

"I think she looks really cool," Hannah said.

What Uncas thought was, It's a good thing my father's dead. Because if he weren't, a young woman wearing a tuxedo might just send him to his grave. There were limits to girls wearing boys' clothes. Hannah at least was in a dress, a full-length sleeveless black dress, similar to what the singer was wearing, but more elegant. He was impressed — it was what a formal evening required, but there would be plenty of women, Fauna for one, he was sure, who wouldn't be wearing one.

"Wow, are those all tie tacks?" Alex asked, pointing to Uncas's shirt studs. "I just used a regular shirt with buttons."

Uncas laughed. "These are shirt studs. My grandfather wore them to welcome the king of Denmark to the Norwegian embassy." The world really was topsy-turvy: he was instructing the help, a young girl with a bleached-blond crew cut no less, about men's accessories.

"Any royalty coming tonight?" Alex asked.

Only Lord Reticent Taciturn. And, Uncas thought, Baron Carl the Bad. Unless Uncas stopped him. He could telephone and tell him not to come. Unfortunately, that introduced the possibility of setting him off again. And maybe he wouldn't come anyhow. It was hard to imagine that he'd have the nerve to show up, but Carl didn't lack impudence. Uncas put his hand on his wife's shoulder and felt her hand on top of his. It calmed him. Whatever had happened with Philip could be forgiven.

"My parents said to say sorry again that they couldn't come; I mean, they said to send their regrets," Hannah said. "My dad's just getting over the flu, and now my mom has it. She's really disappointed not to be here."

"Oh, I'm sorry, dear," Margaret said. "Do tell them I was so looking forward to seeing them. At least they were able to see you all
gussied up. They must have fainted dead away!"

"No. Alex and I got dressed at Mrs. Delafield's house. Her father
and Betty are staying at the Riverrun Inn."

"Well, you girls spend every minute you have together, don't you?
My girlfriends and I were like that. Even after I got married. We lived
in Cambridge for a year, and it was as if we had two extra room-
mates. Peg and Myrna were there all the time. There's nothing like
old friends."

Alex and Hannah giggled. Uncas felt a flash of embarrassment
and irritation. He wondered if they were laughing at him. Alex had
probably told Hannah his version of their year in Cambridge. But he
glanced at Alex, and he realized he needn't have worried: she was in
her own world, which at this moment seemed to consist of Hannah
and herself. They giggled as though Margaret had said the funniest
thing imaginable. Girls were just different creatures.

"I'm pleased as punch that Betty and your father are coming,
Alex. I think it's neat that he wanted to attend all the way from New
York. I bet Betty is glad to see him. She's had her hands full with
Lizzie."

Alex rolled her eyes. "He'll be here. And you'll know it when he
arrives. He loves Sparta. He's already corrected Betty about some historical fact about the underground-slave movement here."

"Now I need you girls to show me what you've done in the dining
room."

Alex took control of Margaret's chair and wheeled her off with
Hannah at her side. Everywhere Uncas looked there were flower
arrangements. Small vases with buds and large baskets that were
beds of color. They struck the right note, Uncas was reluctant to ad-

mit. Impressive without being too formal. Carl knew his business, as far as that went.

"Mr. Metcalfe." The singer of the band was at his arm. "I hate to disturb you. I'm Lucky Ferguson of Broad-Way, and I—"

"Yes. Yes. Hello." Uncas turned to her. "Let's go over the play lists."

"You must get this all the time, but I wanted to tell you I loved your Intro to Botany. I was a special student from Mott about ten years ago, and I heard you were good, but I just loved the class. My friends thought I was crazy. They kept asking me why I'd take such a weird course from such a hard professor."

Uncas forced himself to smile. He never knew exactly what to say. Another professor might remember this girl's face, but it didn't mean a thing to Uncas. He would like to ask what was so "weird" about botany.

"Well, this is what we'll be singing, if it's okay with you," she said, handing him a piece of paper. "Mostly stuff from the thirties and forties and, and I hope you won't mind, but we've thrown in a couple of originals too."

Uncas frowned. This was what local talent brought, aspirations beyond the greats. On the other hand, a couple of originals might not be so awful. Nothing said everyone had to dance to every number. Maybe Fauna and Doug would enjoy a contemporary tune. Beyond feeling troubled about Carl, he was feeling magnanimous about the rest of the evening.

"If you keep it to a couple, we'd be happy to hear them. I'd like you to open with 'Let's Misbehave.' We need to set the tone for the evening." He perused the list. They had all the standards as well as a few unusual selections. "Downtown" was hardly from the forties and he didn't think much of it, but he knew from past parties it was one that got people out on the floor, because everyone knew the refrain. Margaret often hummed it. "This looks fine." He handed the list back, and looked across the room to the bar. Edgar was already there in his red jacket and black bow tie. Bless him. He was the best Sparta had to offer. An excellent bartender. He'd done Uncas's father's parties and knew what the word "professional" meant. Uncas went over to shake his hand. They had known each other for over fifty years. He had served Uncas his first Scotch and soda.

"Edgar."

"Uncas. How are you? It's going to be quite a party, as usual."

"Looks that way. Finding everything you need?"

"Can't see a thing missing. May I get you a beer?"

"Nonalcoholic."

"Of course." Edgar pulled a cold bottle from an ice chest.

Fauna came through the kitchen door over to the bar. She looked positively glamorous; exactly the opposite of what he had expected. She had on a long velvet dress and a single strand of pearls. Her hair was pulled up on top of her head. The looseness of the dress masked her pregnancy. "Edgar Findley! How are you?" Fauna stretched out her arms and hugged Edgar. "It's been so long," she said. "And I can't even ask you to make me one of your excellent martinis." She pointed to her stomach.

"For you, my dear, I'll issue an official rain check. As soon as the little one is born, leave the kids with Doug, and come by the house. Fran would love to see you. Dry with three large olives."

Fauna smiled and said she'd do that. Uncas felt a moment's discomfort; he had never been invited to Edgar's house; he found himself surprised by their familiarity. He hadn't realized that Fauna would even remember Edgar. She turned to Uncas. Her high heels made her taller. She craned her neck and kissed him hello on the cheek. She met his glance and then looked away.

"Save me a dance, Dad. Those bows"—she pointed to his dance pumps—"always kill me." Doug came up behind her and with each of his hands encircled her biceps. "Something slow. I'm not quite used to these heels yet."

"Don't you look fetching," Uncas said.

"Doesn't she just?" Margaret wheeled up beside him.

"Well, thanks," Fauna said. "Wait till you get the bill." Fauna spread the skirt of the dress with her hands. "You did say to buy a pretty little frock."

Uncas looked around the room. The guests would start arriving soon. He and Margaret would station themselves by the door.

"And thanks for the babysitter, too, Mrs. M.," Doug said. "This is our first free night in a month."

"Somehow a black-tie party didn't seem to me the children's cup of tea," Margaret said.

"Janey was dying to come. We left her in tears. I promised a dinner dance for them tomorrow. I don't know how we're going to pull that off," Doug said.

"Dad," Fauna said, "you seem distracted."

Uncas pulled out his pocket watch, which said one minute to seven. The clock in the library started to chime. He reset his watch and placed it back in its pocket. "Duty calls," he said, taking the handles of the wheelchair. "All men to their stations." He looked at Fauna. "That includes women too."

"Whatever you say, Dad. Whatever you say."

※　※　※

The doorbell rang again, and Uncas pulled the front door open. It was the only time it was used from year to year, except for the occasional errant visitor. They had a system set for the first thirty minutes or so. Uncas and Margaret would greet the guests, and Uncas would help the ladies take off their coats, which would then be handed off, along with the men's coats, to Hannah or Alex, who would run them upstairs and park them on Uncas and Margaret's bed. Later on, Uncas and Margaret would mingle and leave one of the girls stationed to greet and run coats. About thirty or so people had arrived. The Brewsters, including Floyd Junior, who had stared openly and lasciviously at Hannah until his father had said come along; Dave and Dorothy; Emily and Kirk, who was now, sadly, her fiancé; and Malc and Libby among them. No sign of Carl. Uncas hoped that if he came, he would be late. Alex periodically asked if her father and Betty had arrived, as though they might slip by while she was gone for thirty seconds dropping off coats. She seemed to have forgotten her petulance from the other day when Clarence Granger had mistaken her for a boy, which he might well do again were he to see her in her tuxedo. Alex and Hannah were standing next to each other on the stairs, waiting for the next batch of coats. In addition to her long dress Hannah had elegant kidskin gloves that buttoned three-quarters of the way up her arms. At a glance the two of them made a dashing couple.

Uncas shook hands with Steve Weckstein and was introduced to his date for the evening. Uncas asked briefly after the *Gazette*, but decided he'd save longer conversations for later. The idea was to get the guests to the bar and circulating, not to have them clog up the hall. His wife's wheelchair and the increasing number of galoshes by the radiator didn't leave much room. "Bar's open," he'd hear Margaret say to slow-moving guests. Uncas reached into his inside pocket

for his billfold—he wanted to remind himself to request "Ridin'
High"—but of course he'd left it upstairs. He would simply have to
remember on his own. The stream of guests was coming to a lull just
as Betty Delafield and Alex's father came in the door. Peter Miller
was an enormous man; he dwarfed his wife. Not fat at all, just huge.
He was a little shorter than Uncas but twice as wide; one of the few
types of men who could make Uncas feel small. As he said hello,
Uncas could feel his loudness. He shook hands with Uncas and then
grasped the armrests of Margaret's wheelchair, and squatted to say
hello to her. She offered her hand and said, "Welcome to Sparta, Dr.
Miller," and he said, "Aw, cut it out with the doctor stuff. Call me Peter." Alex came down the stairs and leaned into her father's outstretched arms. He enveloped her.

"You're a knockout, doll! I would have brought you studs and cuff
links if I'd known. And I presume this is the famous Hannah," he
said, looking up at Hannah, and studying her as though she were a
piece of art. "Another knockout! Hi, doll. Am I happy to meet you."
Everything he said seemed to be followed by an exclamation point.
He climbed up a few steps and gave Hannah a bear hug too. "Hope
you don't mind, doll! I feel like we met a long time ago."

Uncas was warm. He opened the front door to see if anyone else
was on his way up the walk. It was empty. No Carl. Through the center of the wreath, he saw the tape on the door leftover from the
PLEASE USE SIDE DOOR sign, which they had taken down for the evening. Carl's two notes and the dead plants and the walk in the snowy
fields seemed to him hallucinations from a previous life. So far removed from the party and the warmth. He couldn't let himself be
frightened; even Fauna had said the boy was harmless. One of her
quieter appraisals to be sure. Quite the opposite of this morning. *You
never, ever say thank you.* Surely he'd expressed his appreciation to

Edgar, for example. It made sense all the way around to speak only when one had something to say. He turned back to his wife. A circle had closed around Alex's father, who was telling a story about checking in at the Riverrun. Uncas heard the cadence of Margaret's laugh and knew that she approved of Peter Miller. Uncas nudged his way past. He'd check on the band and get himself another nonalcoholic beer.

"This next one is for anyone who's ever loved"—there was a screech from the amplifier in the middle of the singer's introduction— "somebody so much you thought you'd explode, and then they just do something that makes you feel tiny. We're Broad-Way."

> My heart's as big as a puffball
> When you're around.
> My love mushrooms, baby,
> It's profound.
> But you slice me and you dice me
> And you shrink me down to size.
> You'd think after once, I'd get wise.
> But to you I'm just a fungus
> Athlete's foot
> Mold in the shower
> Our love's kaput.

Uncas listened to the lyrics. It was a song he'd never heard before.
"That was an original. 'My Heart's as Big as a Puffball.' Hope yours is too."

That explained it. But the song was clever; and he could imagine humming it in years to come. He stood at the buffet table and speared a stuffed mushroom.

"Uncas. What a party! I haven't been to anything like this in ages. Not even in New York. Thanks for having me." It was Alex's father, standing at one end of the dining room table, which had been extended to its full length. Trays of delicate sandwiches, a large roasted ham, thin slices of roast beef, hors d'oeuvres, wedges of cheese, strawberries and grapes, had been placed around the centerpiece, two glass swan vases that held birds-of-paradise.

"Our pleasure," Uncas replied. "Every year I wonder if we're going to pull it off. And this year with Margaret's leg . . . Well, we both felt very lucky to have your daughter's and Hannah's help. I don't think we could have—"

"They're a sweet pair." Peter motioned his head toward the other end of the table, where Uncas was surprised to see Alex feeding Hannah a piece of cake, as though they were newlyweds. Then he remembered Hannah's gloves; perhaps she couldn't feed herself. They were both giggling, which seemed to be their favorite activity. Funny for two such hardworking girls. But they *were* girls, after all.

"I didn't think they'd make it," Peter said. "But the course of love never did run smooth. Not for us, or me, anyhow. Don't know why it should for them."

Uncas couldn't follow his conversation, but he nodded all the same. Didn't think they'd make it where? The good Dr. Miller sounded confused; maybe he was a little drunk. Then he worried that Alex might have said something to him about Margaret and Philip. He felt his jaw tense.

Peter nodded fondly toward the girls, who were leaned against the wall talking. "She said you were a real help." Peter clapped him on the back. "I don't mind telling you I was surprised they'd find such tolerance here. I know it's not true across the board, but then it's not true across the board in New York City, probably not even in Greenwich Village, but somehow I think it means more in a place like this to have the support of people like yourself and Margaret. You were quicker to accept things than her old man. And it's my job to accept things like that. But it's different when it's your own kid." Peter drained the last of the champagne in his glass. "When she first told me she was that way, I'm afraid I blew up. I thought she'd gotten it out of her system in high school, but I could tell she was serious, and it forced me to do some research, and well, they're in love, God bless them." Uncas nodded, but he knew there had been some kind of mistake. He felt as though he had been caught in a lie, being given credit for tolerance that hadn't been tested.

"Her mother and I didn't make such an ideal couple, and we were supposedly the right sexes. But you don't need to hear this. I got it right this time, and it looks like Alexandra did too. Neither of us was as lucky as you the first time around. Margaret's a gem. But I don't need to tell you that." He raised his empty glass. "Cheers, Uncas. And thanks for taking care of my little girl. I'm going to go find my wife."

Uncas half-raised his beer glass and watched as Peter walked off. He looked down at the end of the table. Alex and Hannah were gone. Then he saw they were walking toward him. He felt a little distaste and embarrassment, but he supposed none of it was his business. They weren't asking anything of him.

"So that's my dad, Mr. Metcalfe," Alex said. "Did he say anything embarrassing? He really likes you and Mrs. M."

Uncas could see she was a little tipsy.

"I don't know, Alex." Uncas knew he sounded cold. It made him uncomfortable that it must have been Hannah whom she'd seen kissing someone; her problems with a girl had been the impetus for Uncas to jabber on about his marital troubles. He tried to think of what Margaret would say in this situation. She'd smooth things over with enthusiasm or a compliment of some sort. "Is it embarrassing that's he's proud of you?"

"Oh, Mr. Metcalfe. That's nice."

"Alexandra, Alexandra. Hurry. I can't find Betty and I need to dance." Peter Miller had come back into the room at a half-run, holding out his hand, waiting for his daughter to grasp it. "They're playing one of my favorites."

Uncas could hear the singer rise to the refrain of "Blame It on My Youth." He wanted to tell Peter Miller that his daughter preferred to be called Alex.

He watched as Alex turned toward Hannah, with a big smile on her face. "Sorry, Han. I'll be back."

Uncas looked at Hannah for a moment. He knew it would be polite to ask her to dance, but at the same time it didn't feel right. The news about her and Alex was too fresh, and while she was Joe Stephenson's daughter, she'd also been working for Uncas and Margaret for the past three weeks. Probably she didn't like dancing with men. Nothing was clearly delineated anymore, thought Uncas. The things he thought he could count on, he simply couldn't. "Blame It on My Youth" segued into a much faster number that Uncas couldn't place. As he watched Peter Miller and Alex dance together, both beaming at each other, he sensed other people watching them as well. It wasn't just their height, or Alex's hair, it was the idea of two people in tuxedos—as they spun quickly around the floor they looked like two men. It made Uncas uncomfortable, but others watching them seemed to be smiling. Uncas himself had yet to dance; he thought about partners. With Margaret unable, there were only a few people with whom he felt it would be appropriate; though Margaret probably would have encouraged him to dance with Hannah. He scanned the crowd for Libby, but she was already out there with Malc. Fauna was another possibility—maybe she'd come find him for her dance—and then he saw her on the floor with his brother Dave. Dorothy was dancing with Kirk, and Emily was talking to Margaret.

The song—it had been "In the Mood"—ended, and Peter Miller stood in front of Uncas, holding Alex toward him, with his other hand outstretched. Uncas was confused and embarrassed—was Peter delivering Alex to him to dance with?—she had one hand outstretched too. He tensed with sudden horror at the thought that Peter was asking him to dance. Then he saw Betty take Peter's hand and Hannah take Alex's hand. Alex turned toward Uncas and said, "Thanks. I really appreciate everything." And the two couples, Peter and Betty and Alex and Hannah, began to dance to "String of Pearls." Uncas couldn't figure out how the whole misunderstanding had happened. What had he said that made Alex feel she had anything about which to be grateful to him on that score? Part of him wished he had unraveled the speeches behind her "theys" and "thems"; he should have known she wouldn't make such obvious, continual grammatical errors; at the same time, he wished Fauna could have heard her thank him. He looked across the room, and on the other side of the dance floor was Margaret, turning away from the dance floor; she seemed irritated but trying not to show it. He felt enormously relieved by the thread that connected them; that he could read her thoughts by looking at her face. He longed to hear her say "Good night, Mrs. Calabash," but she was too far away. He watched her turn to Malc and then to Libby, who were leaning on either side of her chair. They made a cozy circle. Uncas made his way over to join them.

"Cool, isn't it?"

Uncas turned to see his daughter at his arm. He smiled. "It feels warm to me."

Fauna rolled her eyes, and pointed her chin toward Alex and Hannah, then pushed him lightly with her hand. "This is pretty wild for Sparta, Dad. The whole town's going to be talking tomorrow. Mom's having a cow."

Uncas turned to see Margaret's tight-lipped disapproval. "Try not to add fat to the fire," he said.

"Dad, I just . . ." Fauna shook her head. "Okay, I'll try."

Uncas glanced back out at the dance floor and continued toward his wife. He and Fauna reached Margaret at the same moment.

"There you are," she said, looking up. "Those two look like they've danced together for years." Peter Miller and Betty Delafield were about four feet away, dancing cozily; Margaret was concentrating on them and studiously avoiding, it seemed to Uncas, Alex and Hannah, who were dancing on the far side of the room. He didn't see why they found it necessary to dance together.

"I never realized how much Betty looks like her brother," Fauna said.

"Doesn't she just?" Margaret said. "Oh, that sweet boy."

"Mom, forty isn't a boy."

"In the choir he was. What a voice."

Uncas looked around. Where was Betty's brother? Surely they'd invited him. He lived next door to the Stephensons. Uncas bent between Margaret and Fauna. "I don't see him," he said. "He *was* in—" Uncas stopped when he saw their faces.

"Uh, Dad, you wouldn't see him unless you've got a séance planned."

"Fauna, what a terrible thing to say," Margaret said. "Unk, you were at the funeral."

"Sorry, Mom. It's just that Dad's selective memory sometimes amazes me."

Margaret had teared up. "Oh, Lord, what a wretched event."

Uncas froze for a minute. But he was practically a child, he thought, he couldn't be dead. "But when?"

"Two years ago, Dad. I remember Mom saying it was so big you almost didn't get a seat."

"Unk, you didn't ask Betty where he was, did you?" Margaret looked pained.

"In the cold, cold ground," Fauna said.

"Fauna!"

"Sorry, Mom."

The band segued into another number, and Uncas heard Dorothy ask him to dance. "You don't mind my being bold, do you, Unk?" She smiled up at him. "I need to take a spin with someone my own age."

"Happy to oblige," Uncas said, and gestured her out to the floor. As he danced, he tried to conjure a memory of Bob Delafield's funeral. But he couldn't.

Several numbers later, Alex appeared at his side and asked him to dance. He was pleased and then reluctant; it wasn't just an aversion to homosexuality, which he could see also made some of his guests—Floyd and Elsie, and his brother Dave—uncomfortable, or that they would look like two men dancing together, but he wondered if it were appropriate. But as often seemed to happen with Alex, Uncas bent rules; the band struck up "I Got Plenty o' Nuttin'," and she made it easy to say yes and allowed him to lead. She was rather light on her feet, which for the first time weren't ensconced in combat boots. She had on black loafers and was dubious about Uncas's pumps, though she said she'd look for a pair for herself in a secondhand store she knew in New York. Once again, he felt in her presence bonhomie, a camaraderie which elated him, even as it also seemed faintly ridiculous and mistaken.

"What do you think of the song, Mr. Metcalfe?" Alex laughed.

"A fine Gershwin hit," he said.

"I requested it for us. It's our song. Get it?"

"*Our* song?"

"C'mon, Mr. Metcalfe. We both made something of nothing and now we're dancing to plenty of nothing. Ironic, don't you think?"

Uncas smiled. There was no getting this girl down. He saw Fauna approach. She tapped him on the shoulder, indicating that she wanted to cut in. Uncas found himself reluctant to be parted from Alex; but he was relieved too that Fauna had wanted to dance with him. But Fauna placed her hand on Alex's shoulder, and after a few missteps ("You lead," Fauna said) they danced off. Another way of tweaking Uncas, no doubt. He stepped back into the onlookers and had a brief conversation with Hannah, who seemed beside herself with delight. A glance around the room revealed a similar glow— Malc dancing with Betty Delafield, Peter Miller with Libby, Dorothy with Doug, Little Charley with his mother.

"Unk, do you have a minute?" Uncas's brother Dave slowed next to him.

"What can I do for you, Dave?" Everything was going smoothly; Carl hadn't shown up, and everyone seemed to be having a good time. The band wound up "I Got Plenty o' Nuttin'" and went on break. Before they started up again, Uncas would propose his toast. He surveyed the room while Dave spoke about clearing some trees below the tennis court at Poplar Creek.

There were empty champagne glasses on the mantelpiece and a sprig of mistletoe hanging in the doorway between the living room and the hall. As he watched, he saw Doug point up to it and give Fauna a peck on the lips. He'd forgotten about that superstition. He hoped he wouldn't have to watch Alex kiss Hannah. Bonhomie or no, there were limits.

Uncas had asked the singer to come get him at the end of the break. As he saw her approach, he went over his toast. He wanted to welcome visitors from near and far (a nod to Peter Miller); he wanted to tell a story his father had told him about one of the earliest parties when the singer in the band never showed up and people took turns at the mike; and he wanted to say how grateful he was to live in a town like Sparta. His eye caught the tree: the angel was tilted; it had been a poor substitute for the star to begin with, and now it looked inebriated.

"Hello, Professor." It was Carl; Uncas heard his voice, and a wave of fear came over him. He told the singer to go ahead; he'd make the toast next time around. He wanted to deal with Carl and be done with him. He looked like a madman. He hadn't shaved and was in dungarees and an ill-fitting tweed jacket over a plaid flannel shirt—just what he'd been wearing that morning at the nursery. His eyes were rimmed red, as though he'd recently been crying. Uncas looked around the room for help; someone he could notify that Carl was here and couldn't be trusted. He considered Fauna, who shared his distrust, but when he located her across the floor in the doorway of the dining room, he felt he'd be overreacting, responding to her upset earlier in the day, and not to any actual threat.

"Professor?" Carl's tone had changed. There was no challenge; it was almost collegial. "You were able to arrange the boughs, I see. I'm sorry I wasn't able to assist you. I had an early appointment." At that moment, the band started up again.

"Sorry?" Uncas cupped his ear and leaned closer to Carl.

"Is Margaret nearby? I have some news for her."

Uncas felt a fresh surge of irritation. Of course Margaret was nearby. This was their party, after all. Minutes ago Uncas had watched her wheel herself into the library, followed by Libby. Since when did Carl call his wife by her first name?

He nodded to his left. Then thought better of it. "Let me bring you to her." He was going to keep an eye on this unstable ruffian, especially in regard to Margaret. Uncas led him to the library. There was no one there.

"She was here a minute ago," he said.

"A difficult woman to keep track of," Carl said.

Uncas started to say, wanted to say, "Stop talking about my wife," but knew it would sound foolish.

"I see you returned my plants, Mr. Professor," Carl said.

Uncas felt his face flush. He had stooped to Carl's level.

"That was a thing that surprised me," Carl continued. "A response from the great professor."

Uncas half-wished his wife and daughter could hear Carl. *Listen to him*, he wanted to say. *I do respond*. More absurdity. The last person he wanted to respond to was Carl; he owed him nothing.

"Did you really think I would take the time to run you over? Did you imagine I wanted to kill you? Or maim you? No. I wanted—"

"Carl, that's enough." Uncas spoke in a lower voice than he normally did. "For your own good, that's enough."

"I wanted to scare you. Which gave me less pleasure than I had fleetingly thought it might. I so hoped the girl would see your true colors. I admit that you surprised me, Professor. I was surprised to see you step in front of her. Yes, that was another surprise."

It infuriated Uncas to hear Carl talk as though Uncas's instinct to protect Alex was a complete aberration of his normal actions. As though he knew what Uncas was really like, as though Uncas didn't protect his family every day. That merely because he hadn't dropped everything and grown marijuana illegally for a man he didn't know, he must not help anyone. It was an appalling judgment handed down by a sneering bully.

"Good for you, Professor. You are learning."

"There you are." It was Margaret. "Shop talk, I bet. Oh, I am thrilled to see you, Carl Benson. Your flowers look wonderful. Now, tell me about your mother. How's she managing?"

Carl kneeled down next to Margaret and said with a shaky voice that the operation had been a success. "Please forgive these, Mrs. M.," he said, indicating tears that were now running down his face. "It's just that I couldn't imagine what I'd do if— I can't even say it. They said they got it all. We have every reason to think that she will be fine, is what they told me."

"Oh, what splendid news. Oh, Carl, you must be relieved."

"I went to the hospital straight from your house this afternoon, and came straight back here. As you can see. The roads are covered with snow, but not yet icy. With the truck there was no danger, but it was slow. I am sorry for my dress. I didn't want to risk the time to go home."

Margaret said, "You look just fine. Considering the circumstances, I'd say you look very handsome indeed."

"You're a very kind woman. Thank you."

Carl stood up and dried his eyes on the cuff of his shirt. Uncas wondered what had been wrong with his mother, but he wasn't going to suddenly befriend him and pretend that nothing had gone on. Still, he felt some kind of wariness melt.

"Everything okay in here?" Uncas and Carl and Margaret all looked up at Fauna, who stood in the doorway with her hands at shoulder height, pressed against the frame.

"Fauna, you remember Carl," Margaret said.

Fauna looked at Carl, and then at Uncas.

"We're all fine," Uncas said. "Carl was just—"

"Glad to hear it, Dad. Just wanted to make sure everything was okay." She turned and left quickly.

Uncas closed his eyes briefly, contemplating his daughter's ability to raise the tension in a room several degrees. When he opened them he saw Carl kneeling by Margaret once again. They were talking in low voices. Uncas was startled by their familiarity, by the embrace in her voice. He suddenly felt outraged that this boy expected that he could walk in as though he were just another local friend. As though having a sick mother was enough to absolve him of his attempts to intimidate Uncas. Lots of people had sick mothers and didn't use it as an excuse to terrorize innocent bystanders. Uncas watched Carl wheel Margaret out toward the living room. ("May I?" he'd said, and Uncas could scarcely object; he found the very correctness of his question maddening.) He clenched his jaw and tried to slow his breathing; by rights, Uncas should be pushing the wheelchair. He wished that Fauna had made a scene. She might have been his ally.

He wished he hadn't given Carl the two notes so he would have proof of the boy's true nature. The memory of Carl waving the flames in his face made him tense and angry. He wanted to push him aside. He felt overwhelmed by a desire to be physically close to his wife; he wished she were up on her feet so they could dance. She was a joy to dance with; it took no conversation: she responded to the slightest pressure of his fingertips.

Uncas closed the door of the library as the grandfather clock began to chime, signaling ten P.M. He counted the strokes without thinking and listened for the other clocks as well. He could dimly hear the living room clock as it picked up where the library clock left off. Uncas counted nineteen when the front hall clock began to chime; its first stroke overlapped with the last of the living room's. He retrieved a bottle from the liquor cabinet. By the thirtieth chime, he was settled into a club chair staring into the fireplace. He was drinking cognac, in which he occasionally indulged. He had also thrown a small log onto the fire's coals. The bark had caught, and the log sat in a U-shaped cradle of flames. No doubt at all that the evening was a success.

Uncas swirled the liquor in his snifter. He felt unsettled sitting alone, while his guests danced and ate and drank. Though he wanted to pace the room, to rid himself of the terrible tension he'd been encased in since Carl had first said hello, he made himself stay seated. The party was going well; nevertheless, Uncas wasn't able to erase the fury he felt at Carl, at his brazenness. The disquiet he had injected into the evening pervaded Uncas's thoughts the way mold could take over the heartiest plant—there was little else he could think about.

Carl had shown up, Uncas suspected, merely to taunt "the great professor." But the tears when he'd spoken to Margaret—surely he was no actor. Uncas recalled Margaret saying something about Leila Benson being checked into the hospital. Though Elsie had said she was there for her drinking, what Carl had described sounded like cancer. And Margaret had been adamant that she was a teetotaler. But Margaret had also called Carl "a lamb." Carl had ruined his evening. His drive-by visit in his dungarees and flannel shirt, his sweaty, teary face, and how Margaret had lit up when she'd seen him. All of these played on Uncas's mind.

His shoulders were locked, ossified, as he stewed. Carl had stepped out of line. Not so very long ago, his behavior would have warranted a duel. Instead of laughing at the absurdity, Uncas glowered. He wanted to set the record straight. He wanted to recount the story of Carl, and of Philip, and he'd throw in a description of his own petty foibles. He knew he wasn't perfect. His brother Tom would understand; in their youth he'd helped Uncas with occasional decisions; he'd encouraged his marriage to Margaret—not in so many words, but in his appreciation of her. Uncas glanced at the clock—five minutes after ten, which made it seven in California. It was a ridiculous thought, completely absurd that he'd call and whine to his eldest brother. Even if he knew exactly what he'd say to Tom, or to anyone for that matter; even if he had the script written out in front of him, he doubted that he'd be able to get through it.

Fauna would understand; she had seen the dark side of Carl—his cool bullying out at Poplar Creek—but she couldn't see Uncas. Alex's understanding would include a fairer portrait of Uncas, and she'd seen Carl careening toward them, trying to run them down (no matter that he denied it), and knew Uncas had stepped in; she'd seen the first bilious note as well, and she knew about Philip; she'd seen Uncas get choked up. He had been a fool to let that happen. It was astonishing that he would think of turning for an accurate character assessment to a nineteen-year-old he'd met a month ago, who was probably at that very moment entwined with another girl. That was an image he didn't want to linger over, any more than he wanted to replay Carl's whispering to Margaret. Under Uncas's gaze, with his seeming benediction. Was there anyone who saw Uncas for who he was? Margaret, he hoped. But she had called Carl "a lamb."

Plenty of nothing. Uncas had found himself dismayed that Alex equated their situations. But he could now see the possibility of Philip's kiss being nothing. Of it meaning nothing anymore. The indiscretion with Philip wasn't a burden he'd carried throughout their marriage, or at least it hadn't pestered Uncas. *Why on earth,* he heard Margaret's voice, *would you bring this up now?* It was spending the night without Margaret that had brought up the memory from so long ago. After sleeping at his desk at the museum, he had gone back to their apartment the next morning for breakfast. He'd spent much of the night fuming, but also much of it trying to write Margaret to let her know that he still loved her, that whatever she'd thought was going on with Helen Mynes, it was a friendship—she was one of the boys. He'd never given his wife the letter. He could hear Margaret's recent words: *We had lost our first— I had just had a miscarriage.* That event had been buried. And then there was another miscarriage. And then, thank God, Marcia had been born. Was the third between Marcia and Fauna? No, Fauna had already been born. Margaret's final miscarriage was somehow more dispiriting than the earlier two. It had happened on the night of the Christmas party. They had been at Uncas's parents' house, and Mags had decided she shouldn't—couldn't—go home. Uncas had tried to convince her to leave, but she was adamant. *What am I supposed to do?* she'd asked. *Go home and weep?* It had righted itself. The following year she was six months pregnant with Hank, well on her way to rounding out their family.

Rounding out. Margaret had gotten enormous with each pregnancy. Her face would fill out; her feet would get swollen. For the last three months of her pregnancy with Marcia, Uncas remembered preparing a dishpan of Epsom salts so she could soak her feet. There was no time for soaks once there was a child around—too much to do, Margaret would say, too much work to slow down. Her pregnancies seemed to weigh her down; they made her seem shorter than her five feet seven inches. Fauna, on the other hand, looked merely as though she were carrying around a basketball—she didn't slow down; her features didn't change. One could forget she was with child at all. She'd looked striking tonight; Uncas was surprised at the alteration. He'd expected her, he realized, to look shabby, dowdy. For her dress to be short instead of long and to be not in the least becoming. Most often she wore a T-shirt, stained with food from feeding Nik, though there were likely stains left over from Janey and Tommy as well. Tonight she'd looked like a youthful Margaret from her debutante days. Uncas hadn't known Margaret then, but she had albums of photographs, and some framed too. Uncas pushed off the arms of his chair to look at them, to see if his memory served him correctly. He studied the two crowded on the shelf among other family pictures. There she was. Eighteen years old, standing between her parents, in front of their hall fireplace. There were tiny buds in her hair. She was stunning. She'd talked at times of having the girls make their debuts, but Marcia would never have agreed to such a dog-and-pony show. Fauna would have showed up in a swirly-colored T-shirt and torn dungarees. Carl might have been invited to Fauna's debutante ball. Uncas pictured him at a New York cotillion, in work clothes, unshaven. The idea seemed impossible when Uncas looked at the picture of Margaret and the gardenia that encircled her wrist. And yet Carl had been in this house, to a black-tie affair, in this room whispering to that very woman; and Margaret had welcomed him. The world's idea of what was acceptable had changed too quickly for Uncas's taste. Next to the picture of Margaret with her parents was Margaret with Peg and Myrna—of course, they'd come out together. And of course Philip's name, Uncas was certain, was on his wife's dance card that was glued to a page in an album on the lower shelves. But Margaret's dance cards had always been full; she had been a popular girl, the same way she was a popular woman—curious, with a quick sense of humor.

There was only one picture of Uncas—taken maybe ten years ago—of him and Margaret in the airport on Kauai. They had leis on and were exhausted. They were visiting Myrna, who had taken the picture after thrusting a drink with a little umbrella poking out of it into his hand as they'd stepped off the little puddle jumper. For all that, he and Margaret both looked pleased; happy, he thought, with each other, and to be visiting old friends in slightly absurd circumstances. The flora in Hawaii had been stunning—so lush and garish. Uncas had spent much of that vacation updating his basic botany book. It had been disconcerting to become absorbed in the rewrite and then to look out the window, expecting to see conifers where palm trees swayed. Margaret and Myrna, and Myrna's husband, would come back from some excursion—to the beach or shopping or to an art gallery—in time for a nap and then dinner, in or out, when Uncas would join them.

He put another log on the fire and sank back in the leather chair. Oh, how he longed for Margaret to come to the door and join him in a cognac. All their guests would be gone. They would compare notes on the party. It was one of the rare times they still drank together, Uncas having given up their evening cocktails and wine with dinner. He refilled his snifter—too large by a long shot, for his taste, but he'd been unable to find the Bohemian glass from which he normally drank. His wife would ask what he made of Carl and would tease the details of the last week out of him; she would be horrified, and he would calm her. Her distress at how he'd been mistreated would bring them closer. I had no idea, she would say. Oh, Unk, how did you stand it? Why didn't you say something?

He tightened his throat as he took another sip of cognac. *Lord Reticent Taciturn.* That's not in the least how a review of the evening would go. Were it to unfold, he would be circumspect about Carl, and Margaret would fill him in on Carl's mother's illness or about Elsie Brewster's latest transgression, or possibly they'd talk in a most general way about Hannah and Alex. Uncas had seen that Margaret had been taken aback by their dancing and lack of discretion. In truth, he had been offended himself, but he'd also been flattered by Peter Miller's assumption that they'd been supportive. He liked Alex Miller—he liked that she joked with him. His instinct had been to protect her. What was it she'd said when they'd been unraveling Carl's first note? "Sorry to be blunt, Mr. Metcalfe, but that's something anybody could ask: 'Why don't you say something?'" Her bluntness didn't seem to mean anything—she didn't try to tell him things the way Fauna did. With Fauna he felt a perpetual rolling of her eyes—the sarcastic reference to the séance because he'd forgotten that Betty's brother was dead. It was a lapse, but Fauna didn't miss a chance. He could picture himself at St. John's, and he could picture a funeral service that he thought must have been Bob Delafield's, but Margaret wasn't there. He must be imagining someone else's—Margaret wouldn't have missed his. Then he remembered:

he had been in the pew alone. Margaret had sung, not a solo, but Bob had requested the full choir. His shoulders relaxed perceptibly; he wished he could explain to Fauna and Margaret why he hadn't immediately remembered. He wasn't one to wallow in self-pity, but they could have given him the benefit of the doubt. Perhaps there were other deaths he'd forgotten.

During a lull in the music Uncas heard the clocks strike ten-fifteen—tripping after one another. He brought the snifter up for another swallow, but found himself taking a large gulp. He braced himself as he felt the sudden heat and then the warmth of the cognac. He stood up and with thumps of the poker—hitting a little harder than he intended—he broke up the charred pieces of wood in the fire, and then laid two logs onto the bed of glowing cubes. He wanted to menace Carl; to make him afraid; to hurt him. He wanted to sweep the figurines off the mantel, and using the poker like an ax, smash the smallest of the three glass-topped nesting tables on which he'd been resting his drink. His eyes darted around: he'd knock the pictures off the wall and then go after the grandfather clock. He'd crack the glass and splinter the wood and expose the inner workings. He'd silence its ticking and whirring and chiming and still the painted face that revealed itself as time passed. Gripping the metal shaft in the middle, he brought the poker handle close to the glass and then tapped. Once, then twice. On the third tap, which was only modestly harder than the earlier two, though his rage was mounting, Uncas cracked the handblown glass, and watched as a line, more delicate than a strand of hair, spread an inch on either side and then stopped. Uncas's clenched jaw released slowly as the ticks of the clock made their way back to his hearing. He hadn't, of course, stopped time; he hadn't even slowed it.

He moved toward the fireplace to put the poker back next to the tongs and bellows. He breathed deeply, shocked. It was a crack so fine it would likely be seen as inevitable in two-hundred-year-old glass, but Uncas would know how deliberate it had been. He sat for several long minutes, breathing in and out deeply, feeling the chill of the room behind him even as the fire before him threw out heat.

Uncas stood up slowly. He felt faint. He needed to clear his head, to see his wife. As he pulled the library door open, he heard the first strains of "Ridin' High." He walked across the hall to the living room. Leaning against the doorjamb, he tried to relax back into the party. The song moved to full swell. He felt his foot lift involuntarily as he tapped his dance pump to the beat. He thought of Margaret's note under the caption of the picture of his bicycle—*Hiya, swinger, Going my way?* Something in it touched him.

She was across the floor in a thicket of intimates—someone's hand rested on her shoulder, her head tipped toward someone else, a third person was crouched alongside her chair. Uncas was drawn to her; he wanted to bring her something. Laughter rose and receded; the singer's voice embraced *Gloating, because I'm feeling so hap-hap-happy, I'm slap-happy.* He was pulled off course by the sound of applause. On the dance floor, in front of Margaret, was Carl, offering his hand. Uncas slowed. He let the crowd close around him. He watched Margaret's face light up as Carl took the arm of her wheelchair and gently pulled her around the room. Willing him out of the picture, Uncas focused only on his wife, who disappeared and reappeared as she spun around the floor. He could barely hear the music. Small sobs were building within him that he worked to control. He couldn't let them break. He longed to curl up, to be pulled by gravitational force back to a familiar burrow or to be catapulted ahead to a time beyond the present, where he and his wife would relive the giddy details of their engagement, or thumb through photo albums, or admire the blue spruce felled with Margaret at his side for what would be their final Christmas, only neither of them would know it. Uncas felt his dread give way to the sorrow roiling beneath, a vast, uncharted sadness. This was of his own making.

Oh, God, how he wished he had asked her to dance.

ACKNOWLEDGMENTS

For steadfast help along the way, I would like to thank Liz Muir, Scott Ferguson, Peter Ginna, Rosemary Mahoney, Nichole Argyres, the incomparable Svetlana Katz, and, especially, Madeleine Stein. Friends and professionals all.